Praise for *In Sleepi*

"Making their way into the spotlight again, classic fairy tale characters like Rapunzel, Little Red Riding Hood, Cinderella, and Sleeping Beauty, just to name a few, are brought back to life in Mitzi Szereto's delightful collection of erotic fairy tales. Mitzi takes these stories back to their roots and re-creates them with an intriguing mixture of humor, satire, and wit. I particularly like the way she preserved the tale's original disposition, giving a mysterious, Eastern flair to stories like 'The Goblin of Adachigahara' and 'The Magic Muntr.' Deserving a write up all their own, the bonus introductions written for each story were a brilliant touch. Mitzi relates the history of her fairy tales in fascinating detail. As with her stories, this background information is delivered in Mitzi's clever and humorous, tongue-in-cheek manner, which is a real pleasure to experience. In her romp through the classics, Mitzi Szereto breathes life into even the most ancient tales dating back to a time before recorded history. Fairy tale lovers will definitely want to add her rousingly fun and entertaining book to their collection.

—Nancy Madore, author of *Enchanted:*
Erotic Bedtime Stories for Women

"Opens whole new perspectives into the lands and lusts of fairy tales. After reading this enchanting book, you might wish to read bedside tales to adults, rather than mere children..."
—Maxim Jakubowski, editor of *The Mammoth Book of New Erotica*

"Szereto explains that the sexual content of most fairy tales was deleted by the likes of the Brothers Grimm to make them more family-friendly. Instead of researching and restoring the original erotic elements of each tale, however, the author chose to work from the clean versions and eroticize them as she saw fit, making the stories her own. The writing is sometimes uneven, as she attempts to maintain an antiquated fairy-tale narration but includes some modern phrases. While some of her rewrites take the obvious route (the above-mentioned shoe fetishism of 'Cinderella'), each story contains some surprising new aspects, and none seems clichéd or unoriginal. The results, in fact, are sexy and often quite humorous. Rapunzel, for example, becomes a 'rapstress,' enticing a horseman with her rhymes. The tales chosen by Szereto, who has published four volumes of erotica under the pen name M.S. Valentine, are quite diverse, and she includes an introduction explaining the origin and history of each. Enthusiastically recommended."

— *Library Journal*

In Sleeping Beauty's Bed

Erotic Fairy Tales

In Sleeping Beauty's Bed

Erotic Fairy Tales

By Mitzi Szereto

Preface By Tobsha Learner

CLEIS PRESS

Published in the United States by Cleis Press Inc., P.O. Box 14697, San Francisco, California 94114.
Printed in the United States.
Cover design: Scott Idleman
Text design: Karen Quigg
Cleis Press logo art: Juana Alicia
10 9 8 7 6 5 4 3 2 1

CONTENTS

Preface

Tobsha Learner

If you were one of those children who always suspected there was something else lurking beneath the bedcovers of Red Riding Hood's grandmother's bed after the Wolf had eaten her, or that Sleeping Beauty's kiss might be just a little bit naughtier than mom described, or that Cinderella's shoe isn't simply a shoe or that it isn't just a magic wand extends when rubbed — this is the book for you.

Mitzi Szereto has put together a wonderfully salacious and extremely well-researched collection of fairy tales we will all recognize — however, her scintillating interpretations we will find far more exciting than the censored Grimm's versions.

Szereto's introductions to each fairy tale are not only very well researched but also trace both the cultural and literary evolutions of these stories which have now taken their places as Jungian archetypes in the global zeitgeist. Because of this I would also be audacious enough to argue that the book has its place on academic shelves as well as the drawer in the bedside table (and would make very entertaining reading for the bored research student!).

Who would have guessed that Cinderella was originally based on a Chinese fable dating from the ninth century and is as much an ode to small foot fetishists as a warning about abusive stepmothers? Or that Sleeping Beauty was a medieval metaphor about sexual awakening? I particularly liked the way Szereto has mixed very well known fairy tales with lesser known ones — some of which have more exotic heritages like "The Goblin of Adachigahara," a Japanese morality tale about the misadventures of a traveling preacher who encounters a kind of female Bluebeard with a penchant for S/M and beautiful, young religiously earnest men. Or the very naughty "Ebony Horse," which is a version of one of the stories from *The Arabian Nights* that puts a whole new spin on the veil.

There are tantalizing literary echoes for the book reader as well as the seeker of pleasure, such as the echoes of Chaucer in the story entitled "The Twelve Months." (In "The Merchant's Tale" from *The Canterbury Tales*, Chaucer has a particular reference to a marriage between the old blind knight January and his young wife May, who eventually cuckolds him in the branches of a pear tree with a young squire until Pluto, God of the underworld, takes pity and blesses the old man with sight — just as the infidelity is reaching a climax). Szereto's use of the months and their appendages is somewhat perverted by comparison! And for the lovers of large vegetables we have "The Turnip" — a fable in which a humble man is both blessed and cursed by an ever-growing member; Jack and his beanstalk never had it so good. And how can one resist the echoes of Voltaire's *Candide* in the hapless but highly eroticized debauchery of the simple, orphaned youth in "Michel Michelkleiner's Good Luck" — a fairy tale based on an obscure folktale from Luxembourg?

As for the prose itself, Szereto manages to balance an innocent bawdiness with an erotic implicitness. She has also created a kind of delightful sexual naivety for her protagonists that allows the reader to suspend disbelief and for the protagonists themselves to fall unwittingly into all sorts of sexual misadventures — both magical and literal.

Overall, *In Sleeping Beauty's Bed* there is a particular attraction for the reader inclined towards any "disciplinary" action and for those whose propensities include oral gratification. Yet the range and voice for each story changes according to the narrative's cultural context with a wicked understanding of the sexual play of status — those who brandish the whip and those who don't.

Tobsha Learner

Introduction

The fairy tale has no landlord...or so say the Greeks. One has only to initiate a cursory investigation into the origins of any common fairy tale to discover the truth of this. Fairy tales that at first glance appear easily identifiable to the reader may in actuality have roots reaching back to the Middle Ages and even into antiquity. Such tales are believed to have originated in oral form (the word *tale* deriving from the Anglo-Saxon *talu*, meaning *speech*) as folktales of the common people, taking on the character and imagination of the storyteller in accordance with the culture in which they were told—only to undergo further development and refinement as they came to be written down. Indeed, traces of what we consider the "classic" fairy tale have been discovered in written form in Egyptian records dating from 1600 B.C. as well as in Indian, Persian, Greek, and Hebrew writings and inscriptions more than two thousand years old.

Of these known and lesser-known tales, variants exist throughout the world. In fact, it would seem that there is rarely a story for which a parallel cannot be found in the folklore of another people. Scholars remain convinced that these folktales originated in Asia and were brought west by the Crusaders, the Gypsies, the Judaic peoples, and Mongol missionaries. In the nineteenth century, Sanskrit scholar Theodor Benfey provided evidence that a significant portion of what has been widely considered traditional European folklore came from India via Arabic, Hebrew, and Latin translations. However, many anthropologists are likewise adamant that this folklore has its true grounding in the "savage superstition" of the primitive cultures. Regardless of where they began, all folktales deal with the basic motifs of human existence: good and evil, life and death, weakness and innocence, temptation and intrigue. Such themes know no boundaries of culture or time.

By the tenth century, much of the material attributed to the Late Classical period would be imported from the Mediterranean by traveling entertainers and missionaries following pilgrim routes. During the time of the Crusades, folktales from places as widely dispersed as Ireland and India managed to make their way onto the fields of Europe and, hence, into the ears of those who tilled them. (Around this same period the Hindu *Panchatantra* would for the first time be translated into a major European language, offering readers a glimpse into the exotic East—a glimpse that would later turn into a grand passion.) As the Crusades reached an end, the lusty prose of the late medieval towns came into popularity. This signified the first major flourishing of a literature of the common people in Europe, and perhaps the first appearance of material of a sexual nature. Since these stories were relayed at adult gatherings after the children had been tucked safely into bed, their peasant narrators could take considerable liberties, thus indulging their natural penchant for sexual innuendo. It would not be long before such erotically charged folktales insinuated themselves into the literary works of the late Middle Ages, the Reformation, and the Renaissance.

Only in the late seventeenth century did a conscious literary interest in the folktale begin in earnest. Around this time it had become the fashion for the upper classes of France to seek out their entertainment from the ways and amusements of the common people, whose folktales were often markedly unpretentious in manner. Up until the late 1600s, the oral folktale was not even deemed worthy of being transcribed, let alone transformed into literature. The aristocracy and intelligentsia of Europe had banished it to the realm of the peasant, associating such material with pagan beliefs and superstitions no longer relevant in a Christian Europe. If acknowledged at all, the stories were at best considered a crude form of entertainment, anecdote, or homily passed on by peasants, merchants, clergy, and servants—and, as such, something to be chuckled at or clucked over by the upper classes.

From the late Middle Ages up through the Renaissance, the oral tradition of telling tales proved popular with many groups. Nonliterate peasants told them among themselves at hearthside or in the fields. Nevertheless, these folk narratives were not relegated exclusively to the illiterate. Priests quickly discovered their value, utilizing them in sermons in an attempt to reach out to the peasantry. The tales eventually received an even wider hearing by the members of all classes, as literate merchants and travelers relayed them at taverns and inns, while in the nursery wet nurses and governesses told them to the children in their charge. As the stories of the common folk spread from place to place and from person to person in their many variants, they grew to be more cultivated, eventually entering the French salon by the middle of the seventeenth century — and, in the process, losing much of the unpretentious quality that made them so appealing and entertaining in the first place.

In what can be seen as the rise of the literary fairy tale such as those attributed to Charles Perrault in his *Histoires ou Contes du Temps Passé* (*Tales of Past Times*), one must look to the Paris salons formed in the 1600s by women of the French aristocracy. Because they lacked access to institutions of higher learning, these ladies of the boudoir organized gatherings in their homes, inviting other women and eventually even a few men to discuss art and literature. Narratives based on oral folktales would be introduced and continually improved on, thereby setting the standard for the *conte de fée*, or literary fairy tale. As a consequence, the peasant settings and content of the tales would be restructured to appeal to a more aristocratic and bourgeois audience, including that of King Louis XIV himself.

By the close of the seventeenth century, the salon fairy tale had become so acceptable that women as well as some men (including Monsieur Perrault) wrote down their tales. Eventually these tales made their way into the public arena in the form of publication. Yet such elegant reworkings of what had once been the folktale of the peasant were not always intended as an innocent form of entertainment. A crisis was brewing in France; living conditions had deteriorated at every level of society, leaving neither aristocrat nor peasant immune. With Louis XIV waging costly wars and annexing more and more land, it had become a time of high taxes and poor crops, not to mention a time of rigidity caused by the king's ever-increasing piousness. Ergo, these salon tales eventually began to be utilized as a means of criticism, prompting many writers to fall into the king's disfavor.

By the 1700s, the lure of the exotic rather than the common had captured the fancy of the French, with *The Arabian Nights* and the Hindu *Panchatantra*. The diminishing grandeur of the court of Versailles and the continuing decline of France further fueled this intense interest in the Orient, and by 1720 the once-irresistible appeal of the literary fairy tale had all but diminished, resulting in a conventionalized form suited more for pedagogical purposes than the sophisticated entertainment of the aristocracy. *Colporteurs* (peddlers) took these tales into the villages in the form of the *Bibliothéque Bleue,* which contained abbreviated versions of literary tales adapted for use in oral presentations. With this continuing institutionalization of the literary fairy tale, people of all ages and classes could have access to them, thereby creating still more diffusion of the tales throughout the Western world.

In the Germany of the early 1800s, former law students Jacob and Wilhelm Grimm collected more than two hundred tales in their *Kinder- und Hausmärchen* (*Nursery and Household Tales*), of which seven editions were published during their lifetimes. The project initially began as a scholarly enterprise, their goal being to capture the German folk tradition in print before it died out. Since the brothers believed that the idiom in which a story was told had as much value as the content, they were extremely devoted to the oral folk tradition. Indeed, early-nineteenth-century Europe was possessed with a romantic admiration for the simple folk—an admiration that encompassed a decidedly nationalistic concern with local traditions. Although it has generally been assumed that the Grimms collected their folktales directly from the peasants who heard and retold them in the oral tradition, in fact they took them from nonpeasants (often the brothers' own relatives) on whose memories the Grimms had come to rely.

Up until the Franco-Prussian War, the art of composing the narrative folktale remained popular with adults in many parts of Germany. As the Industrial Age took hold, the necessity for the types of collective household and harvesting activities that had once provided a perfect forum for the oral narrative began to be eliminated, thereby bringing an end to the folktale as a form of public entertainment for adults. Fairy tales soon fell out of favor worldwide as more and more young people became educated.

The household arts would all but vanish, as would local dialects, which were usurped by the use of a widespread language. With the arrival of the newspaper, the reading of serious material had supplanted the more frivolous entertainments of the past. Wars and issues related to government captured the attention of the reader, not the romantic awakening of a beautiful princess.

By the twentieth century, adults had turned away from fairy tales altogether, leaving them to the domain of the nursery. Because so many of these tales had been written down in literary earnest during the time of the Grimms, it had become the norm to expurgate fiction, especially with regard to sexual matters, thus further relegating the fairy tale to the only audience apparently remaining to enjoy them: *children*. Nevertheless, it is interesting to note that despite the brothers' efforts to sanitize elements of the tales they found objectionable—or believed their audience would find objectionable—the Grimms appeared to have no qualms about perpetuating the unwholesome themes of cannibalism, murder, mutilation, and incest.

Although expunged in more modern times by various authors and collectors, eroticism was alive and well and, indeed, flourishing in the oral tales of the peasant and in the literary works of such authors as Boccaccio, Chaucer, and Straparola. Yet no matter how cleanly excised from the stories of our childhood, elements of sexuality still remain even today—if only in subtle form. Perhaps our normal human interest in matters of the flesh inspires the fairy tale to live on and on. For whether curious child or curious adult, we all have the desire to know The Forbidden.

No matter where they came from or who has had a hand in their retelling, fairy tales have captured the imagination of the world and the imaginations of writers such as Charles Dickens, C. S. Lewis, and George Bernard Shaw. It is in this very same creative spirit that I continue the age-old tale-telling tradition by offering my own variations on these fairy tales, choosing to rely not on the unexpurgated versions of the past, but rather on those considered suitable for *all* eyes—including the eyes of children. By working in this way, I can remove myself from all previous erotic influences and make these tales my own.

Mitzi Szereto

Cinderella

Scholars and lovers of fairy tales will no doubt agree that "Cinderella" is one of the most popular and widely known stories of all time. Nearly a thousand versions from Europe and Asia have been collected—a number that indicates that "Cinderella" has probably undergone more versions than any tale known to us today. For whether appearing during times of famine or in the elegant salons of Paris, the lowly hearth dweller who has lost her shoe can always be recognized.

"Cinderella" has witnessed a long and varied history, hence its present form as known to the Western world is simply a variation on an already existing folktale dating back to antiquity. Although its earliest written form has been traced to a Chinese book from the ninth century, even before the arrival of the Ch'in dynasty "Cinderella" lived in the story of Yeh-hsien—a poor wretch of a girl ill-treated by her stepmother, but aided by a mysterious man from the sky. In fleeing her family at a festival, Yeh-hsien loses a shoe, which eventually falls into the hands of a king, who orders every woman in his kingdom to try it on. Finding the shoe's rightful owner, the king marries Yeh-hsien.

Despite the great age of this Chinese "Cinderella," many scholars believe that the tale actually originated in the Middle East. In the story of Rhodope, collected around the time of Christ, an eagle absconds with the sandal of a beautiful courtesan, only to drop it onto a pharaoh—who finds himself so taken by it that all of Egypt is searched for the sandal's owner so that he can marry her. However, some elements in the tale may be far more ancient than even those found in the stories about Yeh-hsien or Rhodope. In the primitive hunting and grazing societies appearing at the end of the Ice Age, the female was placed at the center of society and, as such, would often be sacrificed so that she could return as an animal or tree—as did Cinderella's mother, who after death returns in some versions of the tale in the form of a calf.

Although Charles Perrault and the Brothers Grimm (with whom we equate "Cinderella") are household names, less familiar to nonscholars is Giambattista Basile, a Neapolitan of seventeenth-century Italy. In his collection of tales derived from the Neapolitan oral tradition entitled *Il Pentamerone* (The five days), a less ancient precursor to "Cinderella" can be found in the tale "La Gatta Cenerentola" (The hearth cat). Interested in manipulating circumstances to suit herself, Basile's protagonist, Zezolla, conspires with her governess to murder her stepmother. But matters do not turn out as expected, for Zezolla's new stepmother (the governess) has several daughters, all of whom are placed above her in importance. Hence a life of drudgery of even worse proportions is bestowed on Zezolla. Indeed, this prevalence of stepmothers in folktales and fairy tales resulted not merely from creative license, but from the reality of the times. Many women died young from frequent childbearing and unsanitary conditions, only to be replaced by the husband's new spouse, which usually left the remaining offspring at the mercy of the not-always-kindly stepmother.

A literary critic, poet, and court attendant during the reign of Louis XIV, Charles Perrault created the version of "Cinderella" that seems to be the most preferred. Since he intended his tale to suit the refined tastes of the court of Versailles, anything considered vulgar was removed. Published in 1697 in his *Histoires ou Contes du Temps Passé*, Perrault's "Cendrillon" is a cleaned-up version of its Neapolitan predecessor. Unlike Basile's murderous Zezolla, Cendrillon sits passively by while those around her act with the utmost cruelty. Changes in social attitudes would contribute much to the folktale's evolution into literary tale, for it was in Perrault's day that the motif of the passive female appeared—a motif that served to reinforce the patriarchal values of the times.

In the versions collected during the nineteenth century by Jacob and Wilhelm Grimm in their *Kinder- und Hausmärchen*, the protagonist is as passive as her ash-bespattered counterpart in Perrault. Aside from being a reflection of contemporary standards, this indicates a possible diffusion of the Frenchman's literary tale into German oral tradition. The brothers' "Aschenputtel" restores much of the violence and gore of earlier non-Perrault versions by including the stepsisters' mutilation of their feet. Of course, this particular element demonstrates that still more diffusion may have tainted the supposedly German versions of the Grimms via the Scottish tale "Rashin Coatie"—in which the stepsisters compete for the slipper (and the prince), resulting in the mutilation of Rashin Coatie's stepsister's foot. A story in *The Complaynt of Scotland* dating to 1540 is considered the basis for the tale, which makes it predate not only the versions of the Grimms, but Basile as well.

Perhaps not as erotically infused as other fairy tales with so lengthy a history, "Cinderella" is not altogether lacking in matters pertaining to the sexual. Clearly, the presence of the slipper is the most important element in the story and, as such, can be construed as an object of eroticism. Indeed, in a variety of Chinese folklore, the slipper serves as a symbol of the vagina, with further evidence of Cinderella's link to Asian cultures being assumed from the ancient practice of binding a woman's feet. A small foot was considered sexually appealing—and much mention is made of the petite nature of Cinderella's feet. With this in mind, how could any self-respecting prince possibly resist worshipping the slipper into which so dainty a foot could fit? ❧

Cinderella

THERE ONCE LIVED A WIDOWED GENTLE-man of minor distinction and much loneliness. Although he had a daughter of his own, it was the companionship of a mate he desired most. The daisies had not even begun to spring up from the freshly turned earth beneath which his poor late wife had been buried before he took for himself another wife — the proudest, vainest, and haughtiest woman to be found in the entire kingdom. It so happened that she had a pair of daughters herself, both of whom possessed even greater pride, vanity, and hauteur than the mother who had given birth to them. The three came to live with the unsuspecting widower, whose own daughter had the sweetest, most temperate nature imaginable and was the complete opposite of her father's new wife and stepdaughters. Hence the trouble begins.

For no sooner had the ink dried on the parchment of the couple's wedding decree than the new bride made the true wickedness of her character known. Unable to bear the goodly virtues of her pretty young stepdaughter — for they served to make her own flesh and blood all the more abominable — the

4

woman took it upon herself to foist on the girl the dirt-iest and most disagreeable of household chores: chores that only a common char would have per-formed. Each day from sunup to sundown the stepdaughter washed dishes and scrubbed floors; she polished silver and emptied chamber pots. When she had finished, she swept out the cellar and gathered up cobwebs from every corner of the house—and all while being at her stepmother's constant beck and call. For the grand lady had a good many garments to be laundered and much dust to be cleared from her bedchamber.

As did her two spoiled daughters, both of whom had been given rooms of their very own with fine parquet floors for their oversized feet to walk upon and tall gilt mirrors to reflect their lumpen forms from top to toe. At night they slept on the softest and most luxurious of beds, their heads resting comfort-ably against fluffy pillows stuffed with goose feathers, the costliest of lace-trimmed duvets tucked cozily up beneath their disdainful chins. Meanwhile, the girl in whose father's house they dwelled had for her soli-tary quarters a cramped space in the corner of the dark and musty attic, with only a small oil lamp to see by and the squealing of mice for conversation. Since she owned no bed of her own, she slept on the stone hearth among cinders remaining from the coal fires that provided heat for the rest of the house, cinders that she purloined when no one was looking and took to her room. Although terribly uncomfortable, at least they were warm.

As a consequence of this sleeping arrangement, the girl became known in the household as *Cinderwench*. However, the youngest of the stepsisters, who was not quite so cruel in temperament as her mother and elder sibling, would instead bestow upon her new sister the more melodic appellation of *Cinderella*. Even in her ragged old garments and clumsy wooden clogs, the girl possessed a far prettier face and figure than either of her two stepsisters with their grand dresses and glittering jewels. Despite her dismal situation, Cinderella dared not complain to her father, since he would have scolded her most severely and taken his wife's side. For ever since the wedding day, the woman had made it her mission to control her husband's every breath, especially those drawn in the household.

With the impending arrival of spring, the King ordained a festival of food and dance at which his young son and sole heir to the throne would choose a bride from among the many guests. He invited all persons of social standing, and, being well known in society, Cinderella's two stepsisters received an invitation, thereby creating still more work for the poor girl. There was linen to be ironed and ruffles to flute, along with a myriad of other personal tasks in need of attending to. In the preceding weeks the sisters talked of nothing but the nightly dances and what they planned to wear to them; not even the most minute of details would be overlooked. They ordered special headdresses stitched from the finest silk with rows of pearl trimming, and they selected beauty patches from the best maker in the town, their pride not allowing them to accept otherwise. The sisters next summoned Cinderella to solicit her opinion, for, irrespective of her lowly appearance, she had been endowed with an innate sense of taste of which the two desired to avail themselves. Being dutiful and kind at heart, this unwanted female relation provided as much assistance as she could, even offering to personally dress her stepsisters' hair — an offer that both enthusiastically seized. The King's son was very handsome and stood to inherit great riches, not to mention the wealth of the entire kingdom. Why should it not be one of *them* whom he takes for his princess?

While pressing yet another perfect ringlet into place above her older stepsister's temple, Cinderella was asked with an unmistakable mocking of tone whether she might like to accompany them to the royal ball. Naturally, she realized that she was being teased, since who would desire *her* unworthy presence at such a grand event? "Oh, sisters, whatever would I be doing at the Prince's ball?" she said with a laugh, trying to cover the bitter sting of tears.

"Indeed," snorted the eldest, "whatever *would* a miserable Cinderwench be doing at the Prince's dance? How people would laugh!"

One might imagine that the humbled girl would have used this opportunity to sabotage her stepsister's hair after having been made the victim of so heartless a joke, but Cinderella had such a sweet and loving nature it would not have been in her mind to do so. Instead she continued pressing the ornate ringlets of hair into place, refusing to cease from her labors until both sisters were ready to have their expensive headdresses placed atop their stylishly coifed heads. For luck, Cinderella tucked a tiny gray mouse beneath each headdress, her sisters having told her that mice brought very good fortune and that she should be grateful to have so many of them living with her in her attic quarters.

So excited were the two siblings as the hour of the Prince's dance approached that they refused to eat a morsel all day, desiring only to spend their time preening and primping before their mirrors and ordering their exhausted step-relation to lace their waists tighter and tighter till they could scarcely draw a breath. Cinderella found herself being dispensed time and again to the cellar to fetch rags so that the wilted growths on her stepsisters' chests might be granted an opportunity to project more conspicuously outward from the tops of their corsets. (Unbeknownst to Cinderella, the proud swellings atop her own chest had provided her stepsisters with yet another reason for their hatred of her.) Fortunately, there would be rags aplenty for the task,

Cinderella having just that morning used them for cleaning the chamber pots.

That evening, Cinderella watched her stepsisters' elaborate departure with melancholy eyes. No sooner did their elegant coach disappear from view than she hurled herself among the cinders in the hearth and wept. Although she occupied an inferior position in the household, she was still a young woman with a young woman's dreams and desires — dreams and desires that did not preclude meeting the handsome son of the King. As the torrent from her eyes formed salty puddles on the cold flagstones beneath her, she sensed another presence in the shadowy attic. Suddenly through the sheen of her tears she saw a wispy, winged figure hovering in the air. It lit up the room, radiating a quality like sunshine on a summer's afternoon. "Do not weep, dear one," came a voice as pleasant and musical as tiny bells. "I am your fairy godmother, and anything you wish for, it shall be my duty to fulfill." As her visitor drew nearer, Cinderella noticed something curious that seemed to jar with the creature's tinkling tones and diminutive dimensions — a something that took the form of a prickly black stubble on the face and a proliferation of curly black hair on the forearms. Having never before met a true-to-life fairy, she thought no more about it.

In a mad rush of words, Cinderella began to tell of her heart's desire, her plaintive pleas mingling with her hopeless sobs. Needless to say, the gist of her plight would be easily understood. "Of *course* you shall go to the Prince's ball!" trilled the fairy. "But first you must fetch me a pumpkin from yonder garden."

Although puzzled by this demand, Cinderella did as she was told. While on her quest, she came to find herself momentarily distracted by a patch of parsnips. She had oftentimes observed her two step-sisters stealing out in the dark of night to collect the stout white root, which they took back to their rooms for use in a special ritual. Cinderella knew this, because she would steal up to their doors, only to hear a tremendous commotion coming from the other side consisting of a whining and whinnying that reminded her of her father's favorite horse. The following morning when she went in to clean, she discovered a heap of wilted parsnips on the floor by their bedsides. Taking a cue from her older and wiser stepsisters, Cinderella thought she should collect some parsnips as well, so she uprooted several from the soil and placed them inside the frayed pocket of her apron, deciding not to mention this extra acquisition to her stubble-faced fairy godmother.

With the biggest and orangest pumpkin Cinderella could locate cradled in one hairy arm, the little fairy scooped out its pulpy flesh until all that remained was the shell. Satisfied with her handiwork, she touched to it her tiny wand and lo! The pumpkin was no longer a pumpkin, but a fine golden coach.

"Now fetch me that mousetrap," she instructed, pointing to a corner where six gray mice squeaked and complained inside a wire cage. Another stroke of the magical wand, and three pairs of horses rose up in their place, each a lovely dappled gray. Cinderella pinched herself to bleeding, unable to believe her eyes. Nevertheless, she did not hesitate an instant when charged with the disagreeable task of checking the rat-trap for new arrivals. Three large and very black rats glowered indignantly up at her. The fairy considered them carefully, selecting the one with the most imposing set of whiskers. As her tiny wand glanced its spiny head, up sprang a coachman dressed in shiny black livery, his mustache as grand a specimen as could ever be seen and covering nearly half his face. The snug hide of his uniform rippled with the sheer bulk of him, and when he turned away to take his place alongside the golden coach, Cinderella flushed with embarrassment, for the seat of his pantaloons had been cut completely away, revealing twin globes of pale flesh. Never having seen such costuming on a servant, she looked to her fairy godmother for confirmation that this was, indeed, proper attire for a coachman, only to find the fluttery-winged sprite fixing the exposed flesh with a wicked eye. Alas, Cinderella's discreet clearing of the throat resulted in the wearisome requisitioning of six squiggly green lizards, which instantly sprang to attention as an equal number of green-liveried footmen. "You may now go to the royal ball," announced the fairy with a hint of irritation, the girl having returned with the lizards far more swiftly than expected. Even the coachman appeared put out as he plucked at the seat of his uniform, as if it required adjustment.

Cinderella danced happily about, her mind filling with glamorous images of herself and the handsome Prince. Then, just as suddenly as she had started, she stopped, glancing down at herself in dismay. "How ever can I go to the royal ball in these old rags?" she lamented, indicating her soiled and tattered garments. Why, she could not even recall the last time she had been allowed to wash them. Her mean-spirited stepmother scolded her endlessly about wasting soap—unless, of course, it was intended for washing the lady's garments or those of her two spoiled daughters. In response, the magical wand came down on Cinderella's head and the dirty rags covering her body dissolved into a magnificent gown woven from threads of silver and gold and encrusted with precious gemstones.

All at once Cinderella felt herself in danger of toppling over, and she flailed her arms about in an effort to regain her balance. Upon discovering the reason for this sudden unsteadiness, she cried out in astonishment, for the chipped wooden clogs that swam about on her tiny feet had been replaced by a pair of delicate glass slippers. Indeed, the heel was as tall as the slipper was long, tapering down to a piercing spike. "Oh, Fairy Godmother, how ever shall I walk in these?"

"Some people are never satisfied," grumbled the fairy, her hairy forearms crisscrossing one another in annoyance.

Feeling like a real-life princess, Cinderella wobbled regally up into the waiting coach, its golden door held open for her by the mustachioed and scantily seated coachman. "Remember, you must return by the stroke of midnight and not a moment later," cautioned the fairy godmother with undue sternness, "or everything will be as before." By now the little fairy had become all too accustomed to these flighty young things paying her no mind, and she sometimes wondered why she bothered any more, particularly when so many others in the profession had long since retired. Promising to be home at the appointed hour, Cinderella rode off to the royal ball, too delirious with joy to have taken any notice of the meaningful looks being exchanged between her fairy godmother and the muscular coachman.

As it happened, Cinderella's glass-encased feet had not even teetered across the threshold of the King's palace before the Prince received word about the arrival of a beautiful Princess. Although no one claimed to know the identity of this Princess, her appearance garnered considerable attention from those in attendance, including the two sisters, whose envious eyes almost sprang from their sockets when they saw the eligible young Prince putting forth a velvet-clad arm to escort the unidentified Princess into the ballroom. They scratched their heads with apparent curiosity, although perhaps this scratching had been brought on by the tiny mouse placed beneath their headdresses by their lowly relation.

At the couple's grand entrance, a hush fell over the crowd and the instruments stopped playing and the dancers stopped dancing. Never had any of the King's guests set eyes upon such an exquisite creature, let alone such extraordinary footwear. The ladies made a careful note of the elegant style of Cinderella's hair and gown and the dagger-like sharpness of her heels, while the gentlemen willed the turmoil taking place within their tightening breeches to cease lest they make public spectacles of themselves. The ornate bodice of Cinderella's garment had been cut immodestly low in the front, placing on view two graceful and luxurious mounds of milky-white flesh that formed a neat and most eye-catching crease down the center. As for the glass slippers, the height of the heels directed the wearer's carriage into that of an *S* shape, forcing Cinderella to walk with an exaggerated out-thrusting of the posterior and thereby inspiring desires of a not altogether chivalrous nature to ferment in the minds of the gentlemen in attendance.

During the entire evening the King's son refused to stand up with anyone but the mysterious Princess, and hence when the hour came for the magnificent supper to be served, he insisted that Cinderella be seated in the place of honor at his side. Alas, the Prince would be incapable of swallowing even the tiniest bite of the fine fare that was displayed. Despite the many attempts made to engage him in conversation or draw his gaze toward a succulent cut of meat, his attention could not be swayed from the ever-more succulent presence of his female table partner. Be that as it may, the Prince would not go hungry on this eve, for his bewitched eyes gorged themselves on the heavenly movement of his companion's primrose lips as she chewed and on the gentle rise and fall of her chest as she breathed and on the delightful wriggling of her tiny feet in the spiked slippers as they sought to create for themselves a restful position beneath her chair. Later, the Prince's chosen companion wobbled purposefully past her stepsisters, who even close up failed to recognize their Cinderwench. As she was about to identify herself, Cinderella heard the portentous striking of the clock. With a hurried curtsy to all, she dashed outside to the golden coach, arriving at her father's home mere moments before it and everything else returned to their original humble states.

As Cinderella replayed in her mind every magical detail of the glamorous ball and the King's handsome son—who had extended an invitation to her for the following evening—a presumptuous knock sounded at the attic door. Without waiting for a reply, the two sisters barged into the little attic room and proceeded to regale their step-relation with tales of the royal events and the enchanting Princess who had turned everyone's head with her beauty and her extraordinary glass slippers. "It is unfortunate you did not choose to accompany us," replied the elder sister with intentional cruelty. "For she was the loveliest of princesses and paid us a good many compliments on our dress and hair."

"Indeed," interjected the youngest, whose fingers scratched and poked persistently beneath her headdress. "She has promised that I may have personal use of her slippers whenever I wish."

Swallowing a powerful urge to take them both to task about these bald-faced lies, Cinderella instead inquired as to the identity of this Princess, only to be answered by a matching pair of shrugs. Yet one thing the sisters *did* know—the King's beloved son had withdrawn to his rooms in great despair, telling anyone who cared to listen that he would be willing to forfeit half his father's kingdom to discover the identity of the lady who had stolen his heart. "Dearest sister, might I borrow your old yellow frock so that I, too, may catch a glimpse of this beautiful Princess?" asked Cinderella, eager for some evidence that deep down her stepsisters possessed kind hearts. She was well aware that the garment in question had not been worn in many years and now hung like a discarded rag on a hook in the rear of its owner's wardrobe.

The elder sister snorted. "Lend my dress to a miserable Cinderwench? Why, I should be frothing mad to do such a thing!" Apparently finished with their torment of her, Cinderella's stepsisters fled the musty attic room, their scornful laughter echoing through the house and piercing the heart of the one who had inspired it. A moment later, they could be spied in the moonlit garden, where they set about pulling up the largest and meatiest of parsnips from the earth to take back with them to their rooms. For the remainder of the night, a cornucopia of whinnying and neighing could be heard coming from behind their doors till dawn finally broke over the horizon, at which time Cinderella would be required to undertake the monotonous task of clearing up after her stepsisters, each of whom had left a mound of broken and wilted parsnips alongside their beds.

The following evening at twilight, the two sisters set jubilantly off for the King's palace in their stepfather's horse-drawn coach, leaving behind a disheartened Cinderella, who watched their boisterous departure through the soot-covered panes of the dormer window. The *clickity-clack* of hooves had not even faded before she fell weeping to the hearth, receiving no solace from the cold flagstones. As all hope of ever again seeing the handsome Prince seemed forever lost, Cinderella heard a familiar fluttering of wings, followed by the diminutive sight of her fairy godmother, whose facial stubble had grown noticeably denser since their last meeting.

Moments later, yet another from the household was riding happily off to the Prince's ball, albeit with an entirely new coachman, the previous one having been recruited to remain behind with the little fairy. On this occasion Cinderella would be attired more magnificently than before in a gown stitched with rubies, its snugly fitted bodice propelling the fleshy swellings on her chest outward like offerings of fruit. The very same glass slippers encased her tiny feet, but by now she had become more accustomed to walking and dancing in their steeple-like heels and did not in the least mind the attention that both her footwear and her out-thrust posterior garnered. Having been for so long an object of neglect, Cinderella enjoyed the appraising looks and suggestive comments directed her way by the gentlemen guests, and for some inexplicable reason she found herself thinking of parsnips.

Once again the Prince refused to be parted from Cinderella's side, even to the detriment of neglecting his other guests, many of whom were titled young ladies most eager for his company and whose families were still more eager to experience a commingling of fortunes. Of course, no one thought the least bit ill of him for his unintended rudeness, for the charm and the beauteous attributes of the glass-slippered Princess were far too great for any humble mortal to resist. The King's son lavished so many compliments upon Cinderella that she forgot the warning issued by her fairy godmother. For who could worry about pumpkins and mice, with the fire of the Prince's breath in her ear and the scorch of his fingertips on her arm? Nevertheless, the clock's first strike of midnight reminded Cinderella that she must take heed, and, without a word of farewell, she fled into the night, her impassioned suitor dashing after her in frenzied pursuit. Try though he might, the Prince could not keep pace with the spike-heeled apparition who had captured his heart. He stumbled and fell to the dew-dampened ground in an unroyal sprawl. He had been tripped by a tiny glass slipper. Its distinctive heel glittered provocatively in the moonlight, bringing a cry of longing into his throat.

Cinderella arrived home breathless and shaken and minus the pomp and glory of her coach and footmen, her garments once more the tattered rags that designated her subservient position in her father's household. All that remained of her former splendor was a glass slipper, its delicate spike-tipped mate having apparently gotten lost somewhere along the way. To look at her now, one would never have guessed that Cinderella was the mystery Princess who had twitched her hips so invitingly on the dance floor or who had willfully encouraged her royal suitor to press his foot to hers beneath the supper table for a time far longer than one might have deemed prudent. For when the Prince quizzed the palace guards as to the direction in which this Princess had fled, he was informed that they had seen only a poor peasant girl hurrying toward the road.

A short while later, Cinderella's two stepsisters charged into the dusty mice-ridden attic to entertain their miserable drudge of a relative with still more tales of the glamorous proceedings and the unnamed Princess whose behavior on the dance floor they deemed highly scandalous...though neither sister would be above claiming that *she* had been personally singled out by the glass-slipped Princess as an arbiter of beauty of fashion. This time Cinderella was prepared for them and their outrageous falsehoods. "Dearest sisters, I have collected for you some very fine parsnips from the garden, since you must be greatly fatigued from the Prince's ball." She gestured toward a basket of straw filled to overflowing with parsnips, each one fatter than the next. Having returned home well in advance of her sisters, Cinderella had rubbed them with the crushed seeds of chili peppers — her stepmother's favorite condiment and one that undoubtedly accounted for the woman's perpetually pinched expression.

The two sisters flushed to a dark purple, only to reclaim their usual braggadocio when pressed by Cinderella for further details of the royal festivities. The eldest spoke in excited tones of the rather hasty exit of the lady in question and the glass slipper that had fallen from her dainty foot. It appeared that for the remainder of the evening the King's son had gone moping about the palace grounds, clutching the spike-heeled little slipper to his chest and gazing forlornly at it as if it held his heart imprisoned inside. "Imagine that a prince should fancy himself in love with a shoe!" snickered the older sister, whose crude cackles were immediately joined by those of her younger sibling.

Had Cinderella's stepsisters but known the truth of their words, they would have flushed yet again. For the good Prince swore a solemn oath that he would locate the owner of the glass slipper, no matter if it took him till the end of his days. On that night he would be granted no sleep. The last of the guests had not even been escorted out through the palace gates before the King's son bolted himself inside his rooms, his unfulfilled passions making him dizzier than all the mead he had drunk during the evening's merriment. "Oh, my lovely one, where art thou?" he wept, pressing the still-warm hollow of the fragile slipper to his nose and breathing in the faint scent of the tiny foot that had occupied it. With trembling fingertips, he caressed the heel, savoring the smooth perfection of the glass as it tapered down to a sharp point. While doing so, the embarrassing affliction that had disturbed so many of the gentlemen guests when confronted with the charming presence of the slipper's wearer began to make itself known inside the Prince's breeches. Indeed, it afforded a constriction that proved extremely distressing, and he nearly collapsed to the floor in a faint. "I must seek relief from this wretched suffering!" he gasped, reaching down to loosen the straining laces that kept the front of the garment closed and his manly modesty intact.

No sooner had the Prince succeeded in doing so than an object of substantial length and girth sprang forth from the escape his fumbling fingers provided. The weeping purple crown at its apex jumped wildly about in his palm, growing so fat that his fingers could no longer contain it. The aggrieved heir to the throne stuffed as much of it as could be gotten inside the diminutive slipper, the fleshy mass bursting out from the jumble of unfastened laces and swelling even larger within the narrow glass confines. Had he not been in such desperate straits, the Prince might have thought better of his actions. The bloated entity promptly became stuck and commenced to throb most painfully, matching the wild throbbing of his love-stricken heart.

Taking great care not to shatter the translucent contours, the Prince twisted and joggled the little slipper about until he had regained some freedom of movement. Satisfied that matters were at last under control, he cleared all thought from his head in readiness for the task before him. Allowing his instincts to rule, he urged his hips forward and back, thereby encouraging the bulbous protuberance to slide across the slipper's slender instep. By this time the surface had become suitably moist and slippery, and the

Prince discovered that he could slip along it quite easily and with considerable enjoyment to himself. And indeed, the impassioned young royal spent several luxurious moments doing so until, in a sudden flash of memory, the image of the slipper's lovely owner materialized in his mind's eye. Ergo, both hands would be grasping onto the heel with such desperation that its gleaming point cut the flesh of his palms to ribbons. A garbled groan caught in the Prince's constricting throat, and he shuddered as the glass filled to overflowing with an endlessly spurting stream of hot, frothy fluid.

The very next day, the King's son sent forth several teams of trumpeters with a proclamation that he would marry the lady whose foot fit the glass slipper. Not surprisingly, every young woman in the kingdom, and even those no longer young, offered up a hopeful foot for the royal equerry, praying that it could be squeezed into the impossibly tiny shoe. At first all the princesses tried, followed by the duchesses, each grouping of toes being greeted by a marshy warmth. For when the avid aspirant removed her too-large foot from the dainty vessel of glass, her bruised and battered toes would be sticky with cream.

As the search for the slipper's owner expanded, it eventually came to the house of Cinderella's two stepsisters. They tried every trick they could think of to force the slipper to fit, curling and contorting their proffered extremities until they scarcely resembled feet. Determined to see a match take place between one of her daughters and the handsome young heir to the throne, their mother brought forth a carving knife so that they might slice off their toes—a tactic that was summarily thwarted by the horrified equerry. All the while, Cinderella had been quietly observing these activities from a shadowy corner, having immediately recognized the distinctively heeled slipper as the mate of the one she had kept with her since the night the chiming of the clock had forced her to flee the Prince's ball. "Please allow me to try," she pleaded, stepping boldly forward.

The two sisters squealed and guffawed, jabbing their fingers mockingly toward Cinderella's cobweb-covered form. The Prince's equerry, who had been endeavoring in vain to wedge their clumsy feet into the narrow slipper, looked closely at the raggedly dressed servant girl and, taking note of her natural comeliness, agreed to give her a chance. His instructions had been to try the slipper on every woman in the kingdom—and he dared not disobey an order from the palace, if he placed any value on his head. Gesturing for the pretty wench to be seated, he knelt low to slip the delicate spike-tipped slipper of glass onto her dirt-smudged foot, availing himself of this convenient opportunity to steal a glance up her skirts. Concerned that her foot had become swollen from performing chores all day in her wooden clogs, Cinderella parted her knees just enough to afford the walleyed equerry a better view, thus ensuring that this imperial deputy would do his utmost to make certain that the slipper met up with its rightful owner. And to everyone's astonishment, it was a perfect fit.

Turning her glass-slippered foot every which way to admire it, Cinderella removed from the frayed pocket of her apron a slipper identical to the one the equerry had placed on her. All at once a fluttering could be heard, and from out of the air materialized the Lilliputian form of the fairy. Seeing Cinderella wobbling unsteadily on the impossibly tall heels, the stubble-faced sprite broke into a mischievous grin. A hairy arm clutching a tiny wand shot forward from beneath one iridescent wing to tap the girl's tattered garments, changing them to a gown woven from threads of gold and trimmed with diamonds.

Recognizing the beautiful Princess they had seen at the Prince's ball, the two stepsisters threw themselves at Cinderella's glass-encased feet, begging for forgiveness and lavishing her with honeyed flattery. They even went so far as to bequeath to their previously unwanted relation the next harvest of parsnips in the garden—which, under the circumstances, was no great sacrifice, for their nether parts had been suffering a terrible burning of late. Indeed, the sisters' woeful braying would keep the entire household tossing in their beds till the wee hours, inspiring many a black look and cross word at the breakfast table.

A magnanimous Cinderella placed a regal kiss upon the tops of their falsely bowed heads, bidding her stepsisters only the kindest of wishes, the words tasting bitter on her tongue. Although vengeance might have sweetened them (as might the act of driving the deadly heels of her slippers through their imploring hands!), surely the best revenge of all would be her becoming the bride and therefore the Princess of the King's handsome son. Besides, she could always issue a decree for a sisterly beheading at a later date.

Attired in all the magical finery her fairy godmother had bestowed upon her, Cinderella was escorted to the palace for her wedding to the Prince, who found her even lovelier than she had been in memory. Upon seeing *both* of the exquisitely heeled glass slippers on her dainty feet, he gathered her teetering form into his arms and carried her up the stairs to their matrimonial bedchamber, which had been thoughtfully prepared for this special moment with candles and perfumed sheets and a lute player strumming and singing in an antechamber. Making haste to draw the bolt on the door securely behind them, the Prince placed his beautiful bride with marked gentleness upon the satin-covered bed, where she lay flushed and trembling. Thanks to the parsnips procured from her father's garden, Cinderella had some small knowledge of the matters that transpired between a man and a woman. Furthermore, she frequently overheard her parsnip-collecting stepsisters discussing the subject with a markedly unwholesome relish, and she closed her eyes in happy anticipation of the loving lips that would soon be covering her own.

Rather than presenting his Princess with a tender kiss, however, the bridegroom, who had by now grown quite feverish with desire, plucked the glass slippers from Cinderella's tiny feet, chafing the flesh of her heels in his impatience to remove them. Ripping the laces from the perilously straining front of his specially embroidered wedding breeches, the Prince plunged the bulky protuberance he had released into the right slipper, babbling incoherent words of love as he drove it back and forth across the foot-heated instep. Paying no mind to the damage inflicted upon his hands from the dagger-sharp heel, he performed the same ceremony with the left, his hips charging faster and faster, as did the purple-crowned object jutting out from his unfastened breeches. By the time he finished, frothing lakes of equal depth and stickiness filled the glass of each slipper.

And the Prince and Princess lived happily ever after. Especially the Prince, who had at long last located the missing mate for the dainty little spike-heeled slipper that had fallen from a dainty little foot. For now that he was in possession of both, he vowed to fill them with his love each and every day.

As for the Princess, she would seek her own marital bliss by paying frequent visits to the palace gardens in search of parsnips, as well as by visiting the home of her father and step-relatives, in whose kitchen she collected the crushed seeds of chili peppers to store inside her glass slippers expressly for her beloved husband, the handsome Prince. ❧

THE MAGIC MUNTR

"The Magic Muntr" comes to us from *The Three Princes of Serendip*, or *The Serendipity Tales* — a collection of stories from the fifth century and earlier, considered to have their roots in Persia. Although originally the ancient name for Ceylon, the word *Serendip* evolved into *serendipity*, which in its more modern context would be used to mean the gift of making fortunate and unexpected discoveries by accident. It is a theme that can be found throughout "The Magic Muntr" and its accompanying tales.

Contained in *The Serendipity Tales* are the seven stories heard in the seven palaces of the Emperor Beramo — stories told to him on the advice of three brothers, who suggest them as a means to cure the illness brought on by the emperor's love of a slave girl he believes he has sent to her death. According to the frame story, in the Far Eastern country of Serendippo there lived a king and his three sons. So that the young princes could experience knowledge, their father sent them out into the world. During the course of their travels, they come upon the kingdom of Emperor Beramo. When the emperor falls ill, the brothers advise him to build seven palaces and place within each one seven virgins and seven of the kingdom's best storytellers. Hence the tale telling begins.

Translated from Persian into Italian, *The Serendipity Tales* originally underwent publication in Venice in 1557 as *Peregrinaggio di Tre Giovani, Figliuoli del Re di Serendippo* (Peregrination of the three sons of the king of Serendip). However, the stories were already known in Venice at least a century before their publication, being told in oral form and performed before an audience. And they might well have also been known elsewhere, for despite the ascription in the title to its translation, uncertainty exists as to whether the stories are, in fact, Persian. The *Peregrinaggio* contains tales that may have their origins in the Indian *Panchatantra* and the *Jakata*. A further connection to India can be seen by the character of the parrot, which appears quite prominently in Indian folk literature. So, too, does the theme of humans being transformed into animals (as is demonstrated by the characters in "The Magic Muntr"), the concept of one's soul entering the corpse of an animal being a commonly held Indian belief.

Although the arguments for India may be convincing, the evidence supporting Persia as the *Peregrinaggio*'s true place of origin still cannot be denied. The adventures of the three princes who supply the narrative framework for the seven stories appear in strikingly similar form in the Persian epic poem *The Seven Beauties,* attributed to Nizami. Like the Emperor Beramo, the ailing and lovesick Behram (who regrets his decision to expel from his empire his favorite slave/mistress) is told seven stories by seven princesses in seven different palaces in the hope that he will become well again.

As the Italian *Peregrinaggio* came to be translated into other languages, much of its content would likewise undergo change—including content of a sexual nature, since many of the tales were considered quite ribald in character. Indeed, "The Magic Muntr" does not lack its share of sexually oriented material. The original story concerns an emperor with four wives and an insatiable interest in the wonders of nature—an interest that leads him into being deceived by his chief counselor, who fools the emperor into exchanging spirits. In his new form, the counselor decides to indulge in intimate relations with each of the emperor's wives, finding the youngest so desirable that he returns to her a second time. Noticing that the caresses of her "husband" are not like those of the emperor, the young empress claims to have experienced a terrible vision and must henceforth remain chaste, therefore he cannot approach her bed again. Meanwhile, the real emperor — who has exchanged spirits with a parrot — experiences adventures of his own as he adjudicates an argument over the financial negotiations between a prostitute and the man to whom she wishes to ply her wares. Eventually the emperor-parrot returns home and plots with the young empress to trick the impostor by having her agree to sleep with him if he can change himself into an animal, thus offering proof of being the true emperor. Finally able to resume his original human form, the real emperor dismisses his other wives, keeping only the youngest.

Such frank and, indeed, highly adult content as that seen in "The Magic Muntr" appears regularly in folktales from the Middle East and India, demonstrating that, despite their strong ties to religion, these cultures possessed far less sanctimonious-ness in sexual matters than their more modern Christian counterparts in post-seventeenth-century Europe. Therefore, it is with this very same sense of frankness that I have turned my lit-erary attention toward "The Magic Muntr" and its serendipitous protagonist, whose gift of finding the valuable may well prove to be his undoing. ❧

†HE ᛗAGIC ᛗVᚾ†R

I N A FARAWAY LAND RICH WITH THE SCENTS
of tamarind and jasmine and shaded by the
branches of the banyan tree, there lived an
inquisitive young ruler named Vicram. Known to his
people as the Maharajah, he felt undeserving of so
grand a title. He also felt unworthy of so beautiful a
Ranee. For Anarkali possessed the exquisite beauty of
a flower — a beauty that frequently left her husband
wondering whether she might have been dazzled into
becoming his wife because of his place on the throne
rather than by his average countenance.

Indeed, Vicram's curiosity about matters both
great and small extended far beyond the domain of
his household, as did his reputation. So powerful was
his desire for knowledge that he undertook to erect a
temple dedicated to Saraswathi, the goddess of learning. The eager ruler spent many an hour in the jungle,
organizing every detail of its construction, convinced
that the temple's completion would augur well in his
ceaseless pursuit of intellectual fulfillment.

One day as the jasmine exploded into fragrant
bloom, a pair of travelers claiming to be philoso-
phers arrived at the gates of the Maharajah's palace.

Although one was in truth a very old and learned seer, the other was but a demon rakshas in disguise. Hearing that such men of erudition had condescended to grace his doorstep, Vicram ordered them to be made welcome. Each was given comfortable robes to wear, woven from golden thread, and a tasty meal to eat of curried rice with slivered almonds and sweet figs plucked from the trees growing in abundance on the palace grounds. After a good night's rest in the finest guest quarters the household had to offer, the two were brought before the Maharajah, who had much of interest to discuss with his guests.

Sensing opportunity in the air, the wicked rakshas wasted no time. Instead of involving himself in a lengthy and arduous discussion of philosophy and politics, he bowed his head low to the floor and tendered his services for the post of prime minister, which by some coincidence just so happened to be vacant. Of course Vicram felt extremely flattered; his government would be most fortunate to secure such a learned individual within its humble ranks. After putting forth a series of difficult questions and receiving the answers he desired, the Maharajah appointed the rakshas to the office with the title of Prudhan. As for the new prime minister's aged companion, he lowered his head in sincere homage, asking only to be granted the supreme privilege of sharing wisdom with the young Maharajah. Vicram could not have been more delighted, for he now had at his constant beck and call two men of great learning. Surely no other ruler could lay claim to such intellectual prosperity.

As the rakshas used his newly acquired authority as Prudhan to plot mischief, the Maharajah and the old philosopher met together daily so that the younger could learn from the elder's tremendous store of wisdom. This ancient savant had come to witness many remarkable events in his travels. Yet perhaps the most wondrous had taken place while he was out walking along a dusty road where he encountered a boy and his dog, the latter of which lay fast asleep in the cooling shade of a banyan tree. The youth had placed his hand over the animal's heart and mumbled a strange and eerie muntr the likes of which had never before been heard by its venerable listener. And there before his rheumy eyes the young master's spirit had slipped into the slumbering form of the hound, whereupon the animal had hopped up onto its four paws and proceeded to sing and dance as its human companion fell lifeless to the ground, his once-robust body an empty husk.

Such a tale sounded amazing, if not impossible, to the Maharajah, yet many more amazing things were to come. After some hours had passed, the dog returned to its master and, placing its front paw over his heart, let loose with a series of barks and whines strikingly similar to the muntr recited earlier. The boy's spirit instantly returned to his body and all became exactly as before, with the hound sleeping peacefully beneath the banyan tree and the master resuming his activities of collecting twigs for the night's bedding.

At this point the philosopher grew uncharacteristically reticent, for he thought it unwise to elaborate further on what had transpired that day. When prodded by the Maharajah — whose curiosity to learn more of these astounding goings-on had lodged itself like a dagger in his chest — the aged seer finally admitted that he had pursued the youth and begged from him the secret of the muntr. "I journeyed with him for many moons so that I might prove myself worthy of owning so dangerous a piece of magic," he explained. "I can now make my spirit pass into that of another living creature at will."

"Oh, Great Sahib, I beseech you to teach me the secret words!" cried the Maharajah, certain he could not live another moment without possession of this valuable knowledge. "For, with all due respect, I must see for myself that this is true."

Although he held grave doubts as to the wisdom of sharing such witchery with the earnest young ruler, the philosopher felt it was not his place to refuse. During their exchange, a sparrow had alighted upon the windowsill and he caught it gently in his hand. With a finger placed over the creature's tiny heart and the utterance of a few mystical words, the savant's ancient body crumpled into itself, dropping to the silken carpet in a withered heap. Shaking off the cage of fingers imprisoning it, the little bird flew up onto Vicram's shoulder and began to sing in the croaking voice of the old man. Yet before its final note had even been released from its warbling throat, it flew back down to settle upon the seer's unmoving chest, with each spirit once more residing within its proper home.

In this way the Maharajah came to learn the secret of the magic muntr. Being of an inquiring nature, he could not wait to try it for himself. That evening as dusk blurred the viridescent landscape, he sallied forth into the jungle, vowing to experiment by changing places with the first creature he encoun-tered—an owl that had made the mistake of perching upon too low a branch. Vicram flew far and wide over bucolic farmland and village rooftop, stopping fre-quently to rest and to listen to the conversations of his people. As he grew more daring, he ventured into the cities, his feathered ears aprickle for the words that might help him to better understand those over whom he ruled. And indeed, the more he learned, the more he desired to learn. Hence the Maharajah would often be gone from the court for long periods of time, leav-ing government matters in the wicked hands of his new prime minister, who could not have been more pleased about this recent and unexpected turn of events. For perhaps, he thought, the vacancy in the lovely Ranee's bed might be in need of filling as well.

Wishing to ascertain the cause of these mysteri-ous and frequent absences, the Prudhan decided to follow Vicram into the jungle, where he witnessed an amazing sight—that of the Maharajah exchanging spirits with a bright-green parrot. Now here was a piece of magic of which the demon rakshas could make use! He immediately committed the strange words of the muntr to memory, since one never knew when the opportunity to apply them might present itself. For no sooner did the parrot spread its multicolored wings and fly out of sight than the scheming Prudhan would be kneeling over Vicram's inanimate body, repeating what he had heard and placing his hand over the heart as he had seen demonstrated.

Wearing his new armor of youth and power and with a sprightly spring in his step, the evil rakshas left behind the tired husk he had formerly occupied, returning to the palace to serve in the Maharajah's stead. However, he would not do so without first issuing a fateful curse: that Vicram's inquisitiveness should never be satisfied and that his most primal urges would henceforth be his guiding spirit.

Unaware of the mischief that had just transpired in the jungle, the curious young ruler soared far and wide in his flamboyant form, savoring the sensation of the cool wind against his opened wings. Indeed, the body of a parrot proved far superior to that of a stodgy old owl, and Vicram found himself riding the currents with mellifluous ease, allowing them to take him to places exotic and unknown. He even joined up with a flock of geese heading south, delighted to discover that he could understand their unique language. From them the Maharajah learned many new things and would, in fact, have learned still more had not the sight of an uncurtained window and the shadowy form beyond beckoned him toward it.

Drawn by a force beyond his control, the Vicram-parrot landed atop the sun-warmed sill, his talons softly raking the stone surface. He cocked his tufted head sidewise so that he could peer inside the room, which revealed itself to be a private place for bathing. Almost every piece of furniture, including even the walls themselves, had been covered in silk damask. Had the Maharajah been his normal human self, he might have wished to study the weave of the cloth to better understand the intricacies of its warp and weft. But a curse of great evil had been laid upon him, so instead he found his curiosity ensnared by the stone bathing vessel occupying the center of the room and, in particular, by the provocatively posed figure balancing in a half-crouch within its flinty contours.

A young woman of exceptional beauty appeared to be in the process of washing herself. Hair as black as the blackest of raven's wings draped itself in long, spirally ringlets over a pearly back and shoulders as she stood aggressively lathering a thatch of equally black ringlets growing like a jungle from between her parted thighs. Vicram observed with his left eye (for he could not see in the same direction with both) while this enchanting maiden heightened her cleansing ministrations, her head lolling about to the soapy music being played by her nimble fingers as they blissfully lost themselves within these sudsy nether-curls, their movements accelerating to an impassioned crescendo. By the time they finished their work, she was bucking and grinding against her palm and crying out in the voice of a sick lamb, her dark-fringed eyes raised toward the heavens.

Curious to learn whether others utilized the same bathing technique, the bewinged Maharajah flew from window ledge to window ledge, hoping that he might further his education through a course of stealthy observation. As luck would have it, he located many a shapely female engaged in this fascinating ritual, albeit with slight variations. Some preferred to concentrate their efforts upon the deep crevice located below the graceful arches of their backs, their industrious fingers digging deeply and with unabashed joy into the apparent treasures to be found there until it looked as if their entire arm had vanished in their enthusiasm. Vicram could only marvel at the infinite variety of washing methods employed and the frequency with which they were applied, since many bathers deemed it necessary to repeat their ablutions twice, if not thrice, before finally sinking into the watery depths of their bathing vessels with a ragged sigh, their foam-flecked hands dangling limply over the sides.

Although each individual approach proved highly entertaining as well as educational, the Maharajah's favorite were those seekers of abstersion who, in their feminine cleverness, succeeded in simultaneously cleansing themselves both fore and aft. Indeed, it would be they who bucked and grinded the most, bleating like hysterical ewes as their knees went every which way, their bellies billowing with all the sinuosity of a kohl-eyed desert temptress. Whenever this occurred, Vicram—momentarily forgetting that he had donned the guise of a parrot—hitched up his feathered shoulders and strutted about with masculine pride back and forth along the windowsill, his talons clicking and clacking as he endeavored to gain these lovely young maidens' attentions. Yet rather than having the effect he had hoped for, all it did was result in his being repeatedly shooed away from the window by these bathing beauties, who considered the bird's brightly feathered presence a minor annoyance in the performance of their daily lavations. For their eyes saw not the great Maharajah who ruled over their vast land, but instead a silly green parrot waddling to and fro on its spindly little feet and flapping its red- and yellow-tipped wings. During his travels, poor Vicram felt the threatening breath of many a broom, narrowly escaping with the loss of a feather or two.

In his quest for knowledge, the Maharajah journeyed across the length and breadth of the territory over which his human self reigned. He soared from steppe to sea in his insatiable need to learn more of the mysteries that had so recently consumed him, all the while continuing to be swatted at with brooms or the swishing silk of undergarments still warm and fragrant from their wearers. One evening Vicram became so exhausted from the coarse words and gestures directed his way that he was forced to seek rest upon the branch of a sicakai tree. He felt most unwell. Out of hunger he had eaten the seeds of the tamarind, some of which had gotten lodged inside his tiny throat. Soon a fowler happened by and, seeing the colorful bird fast asleep on the branch, snared it inside a cage. Because of his misfortune with the seed, the Vicram-parrot was powerless to call out his true identity; the only sound to emerge from his throat was a choking croak. The following morning he discovered himself being offered for sale at the bazaar, his brilliant green plumage being remarked upon and haggled over by all. It appeared that in his never-ending search for intellectual enlightenment, the young Maharajah had unintentionally traded his palace for a cage.

While Vicram endured the chaotic clamor of the marketplace, his wife, Anarkali, was made to endure something of an entirely different nature. The beautiful Ranee was becoming increasingly puzzled about the changes that had recently come over her usually predictable husband. Suddenly the man known to his wife and his people as the Maharajah no longer concerned himself with the acquisition of wisdom, but rather with the acquisition of gold and the pleasure derived from merriment. Not even the construction of the temple for the goddess Saraswathi held any interest for him. Instead he ordered the workers to dig a pool so that he might cool himself on a hot afternoon, in the interim converting the half-completed temple into a distillery. He refused to partake of his favorite foods, insisting upon being served dishes of a highly unsavory nature most unlike the flavorful curries and honeyed fruits the palace cooks had always prepared for him. Yet strangest of all was the Maharajah's abrupt dismissal of the old philosopher, whose scholarly presence he had cultivated with a near-religious devotion. Indeed, the only knowledge for which this once-inquisitive ruler now demonstrated any desire was that of the lovely Ranee's physical self.

For whether morning, noon, or night, his hands were roaming busily about her person, poking and prodding in the rudest and crudest of fashions. "Open your sweet lips to me, my lovely queen," the Maharajah-rakshas would order in a rasping voice most unlike the gentle timbre to which Anarkali had grown accustomed from her mild-mannered husband. "Unlock your thighs so that I may gaze with rapture upon your juicy pomegranate!" commanded this wicked impostor, only to trespass with far more than merely his eyes.

Confused and frightened—and, above all, made increasingly sore by her unremitting ravishment at the hands of the man she believed was her husband—Anarkali sequestered herself inside her private apartments, where she hoped to gain some peace. However, there could be no deterring the determined Maharajah, who took tremendous delight in breaking through the series of iron bolts his wife drew across the door. It seemed the Ranee had no choice except to relinquish herself to these perverse claims upon her person. And she did so with gritted teeth, wondering how her unassuming spouse had gotten such peculiar ideas into his head. For no more was the good Maharajah heard to speak of music and poetry and the plight of the poor, but only of matters pertaining to the pleasures of the flesh.

When not busy accommodating the Maharajah's fleshly demands, Anarkali would take to her bed in exhaustion. Sorry for her mistress, a faithful attendant who had gone shopping in the marketplace happened upon a cage containing a brilliant green parrot. Although it required the entirety of her month's wages, she purchased the bird from the fowler and brought it back with her to the palace, hoping it might bring cheer to the Ranee, who had come on rather wan and poorly of late.

Anarkali accepted the gift with sincere thanks, placing the cage and its feathered occupant alongside her bed. She spent many solitary hours talking to the parrot, which had apparently taken a liking to her, for it would raise its tufted head and splay its wings to show their spectacular reds and yellows, winking an eye in suggestion of something the Ranee could only have guessed at. Despite its outwardly healthful appearance, something seemed to be wrong with the bird. Every time it opened its beak, out came a terrible choking squawk. And it grew even worse whenever the Maharajah called upon his wife in her bed, which would often be several times within a single day. No sooner did the masquerading Prudhan order the trembling Ranee to offer up for his meticulous inspection her juicy pomegranate than the parrot staged a fit. It thrashed about in its cage and beat its red- and yellow-tipped wings, emitting a screeching and squawking the likes of which could not be heard in the wildest jungle. It came to be such a nuisance that the Maharajah-rakshas threatened to have the bird served up for that evening's supper with a sauce of cherries and figs and a topping of shredded coconut. Obviously it never occurred to him that this vexing entity of feathers and mites was the very man he had taken it upon himself to impersonate. Had the demon rakshas known, matters would have turned out very differently, indeed.

To placate the agitated parrot and thereby gain for it a temporary reprieve from the supper table, the Ranee began feeding it by hand pieces of dried fruit and nuts and even some bits of peeled cucumber.

Perhaps it might have been the latter that finally inspired the lodged seed of the tamarind tree to go sliding down the bird's slender gullet. For one morning when they were alone, the parrot suddenly announced to the Ranee that he was her husband, the Maharajah. At first Anarkali refused to believe such a fanciful claim. But after hearing Vicram's astonishing adventures as a winged creature of flight and all that he had seen and learned in his travels, she accepted his claim as fact. It would have been exactly like her inquisitive husband to venture forth on such an incredible mission in the guise of a parrot. Nevertheless, one mystery still remained unsolved: that of the true identity of the villainous impostor who now occupied the Maharajah's throne and his wife's bed. When queried by the bird as to whether anyone had gone missing of late, the Ranee replied without hesitation that the new Prudhan had done so—and, indeed, done so on the very day her husband, Vicram, had come to her so greatly changed. The pair then proceeded to hatch a plot that would soon set all to rights.

That evening the rakshas appeared as was his usual custom in Anarkali's bed in the guise of her husband, his gait unsteady, his breath stinking of distilled spirits. He fell heavily onto the mattress alongside the frightened figure of the Ranee, unperturbed by her violent trembles or the expression of revulsion in her kohl-rimmed eyes. "I demand that you once again give up to me your pomegranate, for this afternoon I did not find it nearly so sweet and juicy as usual. In fact, I'd say it was extremely bitter," he replied with a scowl, his hand scrabbling up Anarkali's thigh.

At this the parrot flew out from its cage, the door of which had been left intentionally ajar by the Ranee, and landed atop the traitorous Prudhan's chest. "You jackal! Give back to me my body!" screeched the bird, whose voice sounded oddly familiar to the drunken rakshas. Yet before he could identify it, the Vicram-parrot uttered the words of the magic muntr.

The demon rakshas, who had abandoned his body in the jungle without a thought toward ever making use of it again, found himself imprisoned within the bright green body of the parrot and, for that evening's supper, was served up on a golden platter with a sauce of figs and sweet cherries and covered from beak to talon with tender shreds of coconut. And not a single feather would go to waste, for even his carefully plucked plumage later served as excellent writing quills.

However, the wicked curse that had been placed upon the Maharajah by the rakshas had not been lifted and, with that evil one's death, never would be. Although Vicram once again wore the comfortable body of his old human self, he was greatly altered in mind. While he would be as inquisitive as ever before, his was an inquisitiveness that manifested itself in ways most dissimilar to the learning gained through lengthy philosophical discussions or solitary rumination. Surprisingly, the Maharajah no longer cared for such matters, but only for matters concerning that of his short-lived parrot self. Henceforth he spent his days peering into windows at the bathing figures of lovely young maidens, who, upon recognizing the flushed and ecstatic face of their ruler, dared not shoo him away with a broom as they might once have done.

As for Vicram's nights…well, there was always the Ranee's juicy pomegranate to consider. ❧

THE GOBLIN OF ADACHIGAHARA

Japan is believed to have more folktales than any of the countries of the Western world. Yet its folk literature, although quite varied, gives the impression of being conspicuously sparse when placed alongside its tale-telling counterparts in the West. This is due to the fact that the scholarly collecting of Japanese folktales would not even get under way until a century later than that of Europe. Indeed, only in 1910 did someone finally take on the task of recording the tales of the people, thereby providing proof of Japan's long storytelling tradition.

An inspector for the Japanese Ministry of Agriculture, Kunio Yanagita started the movement to collect his country's folktales by setting down some oral stories he heard from a farmer. However, this is not to say that no written form of the traditional folktale existed prior to this time, for folktales appeared in print as far back as the eighth century. In contrast with the West, the oral tradition remained popular in Japan long after it had diminished in Europe, with the *hanashika* (public storyteller) practicing into the early twentieth century.

Japanese tales consist of *mukashi-banashi* (fairy tales) and *densetsu* (legendary tales). While the former have always been considered fiction, many of these *mukashi-banashi* evolved over the years into *densetsu*, which belong to the living folk culture that even now continues to be supported by the cultural institutions of the people. In an environment consisting of little social change over long periods of time, these local legends were allowed to flourish, experiencing repeated tellings over many generations and taking on ever more fantastical elements as they went along—only to undergo further evolution via the various travelers, peddlers, performers, and itinerant monks who visited the villages, bringing with them their own tales and traditions. The three centuries of isolation imposed on Japan by imperial decree, together with an absence of colonialism, kept its stories uninfluenced by the outside world and therefore purely Japanese.

Because of its shortness of length and sketchiness of detail, "The Goblin of Adachigahara" may actually be a legend instead of a fairy tale. It contains the three important elements that comprise *densetsu:* an extraordinary event involving the presence of a supernatural being (the goblin), a reference to a particular locality (Adachigahara), and an attachment to a particular place (the ever-popular derelict dwelling). Yet unlike Western fairy tales and legends that tend to be relegated to the category of fictional and—thanks to the Brothers Grimm—pedagogical entertainment, the line between fact and fantasy is less pronounced in Japan. Even today *densetsu* are alive and thriving in the villages and cities, for the people believe them to be true.

Of the many Japanese folktales passed on down through the centuries, a substantial number of them have always been considered unsuitable for children. These stories tend to be filled with much lampooning of bodily functions, featuring copious references to scatology, flatulency, and sexual humor—particularly with regard to human genitalia. Happily coexisting alongside such bawdy subject matter are tales involving suicide, cannibalism, and the supernatural. Indeed, themes of demonology and spiritualism occur quite regularly in Japanese village tales. Like the religious pilgrim in "The Goblin of Adachigahara," villagers fear a variety of demons, which are thought to be the degenerate corruptions of ancient divinities.

The most popular demon is the *kappa*—a water monster that appears in boyish form. As one of the busier categories of demons, the *kappa* spends his time raping women and dragging his victims into the river so that he can pluck out their livers through their anuses. Another renowned demon known as the *tengu* haunts mountains and inhabits trees and can be identified by its wings and beaked nose. Demons such as these are still seen and talked about in Japanese villages today.

Although the type of demon featured in "The Goblin of Adachigahara" has not been clearly identified, it would appear that this goblin (especially in my version) possesses the characteristics one might expect to see in the *kappa*. For surely a more randy demon cannot be found. ᑐ

THE GOBLIN OF
ADACHIGAHARA

THE SPRAWLING, WIND-SWEPT PLAIN OF
Adachigahara was a place spoken of with
great fear. All who knew of it believed it to be
haunted by an evil goblin that donned the disguise of
a feeble old granny. The locals told terrible tales of
how unsuspecting folk had been lured into the hob-
goblin's derelict abode, where they found themselves
being devoured from top to toe, with only a bloodied
sandal left to indicate they had ever existed. Not surprisingly, no one dared venture anywhere near this
ramshackle residence after dark, with those of a wiser
nature avoiding it altogether, no matter how brightly
the wholesome rays of the sun shone upon its decay-
ing exterior. Yet every so often a traveler might pass
through having no knowledge of the dwelling or its
fiendish inhabitant—a traveler whose sudden disap-
pearance further fueled the grisly stories circulating
around the countryside.

One young man on a pilgrimage to spread his
message of faith to the people had been walking for
many days with his religious pamphlets and his cup
of coins when his footsteps led him to Adachigahara.

He had been told by the last person whose door he had knocked upon before it got slammed in his face that many generous benefactors lived in the area, therefore this was where he should go if he expected to collect donations. Not one to be easily discouraged, the pilgrim's persistence had resulted in little to fill his cup other than foul words and tobacco spittle. With a renewed sense of purpose, he counted the number of pamphlets he had remaining in his rucksack, hoping he would have enough to meet the demand. Indeed, he was most appreciative for the advice given him and intended to rattle his cup beneath the noses of all those he met until they sent him on his way with a coin or two.

Unfamiliar with the local lore, the religious traveler roamed the endless terrain without concern of mishap. As night moved in to cloak the land in its thick black curtain, he realized that he had lost his way. Having been on his sandaled feet since the rising of the sun, the pilgrim was weary and hungry, not to mention quite chilled. The air had grown cold, and a hint of snow threatened to spill from the darkening sky. If he could only locate some shelter, all would be well. However, this prospect looked less and less likely as the worn reed soles of his sandals tramped the dusty ground, for not so much as a friendly curl of wood smoke could be glimpsed along the monotonous plain. Just when the exhausted fellow began to lose heart, he spied a cluster of barren trees in the gloom-tinged distance — and through their sickly branches a welcoming glimmer of light.

Alas, the pilgrim's relief would prove very short-lived. Despite a battered sign proclaiming "Inn for Travelers," this light came from a dwelling so wretched and ill-kept that it gave him cause to wonder whether anyone lived beneath the rat-chewed straw of its roof. A worm-eaten front door stood wide open. Rather than having been positioned so in invitation, it accomplished the less-lofty function of allowing the fresh air from outside to flush out the insalubrious smells coming from within. Beyond this gaping threshold an old woman could be seen sitting on a mat as she sorted strips of hide into bowls filled with a yellowish-brown liquid, her bent figure illuminated by the jaundiced light of a lantern.

Swinging open the splintered bamboo of the gate, the pilgrim called out to her a tired greeting, barely managing to paste on the beatific smile he always kept ready when approaching strangers for donations. "Forgive the intrusion, Madam, only I have lost my way and am in need of shelter for the night." Contrary to his usual practice, he stuffed the religious pamphlet he was holding back inside his rucksack, since it did not appear particularly promising that any donations would be forthcoming from the inn's owner.

The ancient figure raised her grizzled head and focused on her visitor with crinkled eyes that, beneath their milkiness, were as sharp and watchful as a hawk's. "I am sorry for your plight, but as you can see, my establishment is small and I am fully booked for the night."

Although this could have provided him with a graceful out, the pilgrim found himself in circumstances of some desperation and would have been happy for any accommodations—even those as disagreeable as what he now saw before him. With the temperature outside steadily dropping, he could ill afford to put his nose in the air. "I ask merely for a square of floor on which to make my bed," he implored, "or I shall be forced to sleep out in the cold."

The wizened granny nodded thoughtfully, at last indicating that she had relented by building a fire in the hearth. Once the flames had caught, she invited the weary pilgrim to warm himself before it, furthering his sense of sanctuary by bringing him a tray of supper, which consisted of a bowl of possum stew and some wilted greens. Her guest ate of it gratefully, all the while chattering blissfully away about his theological convictions with the aged woman, who—first impressions aside—had shown herself to possess much kindness and hospitality. How extremely fortunate he was to have happened upon her! Perhaps in the morning he might ask if she cared to make a modest donation in return for one of his inspirational pamphlets.

As the fire burned down to a smoldering ash, the old woman announced that she planned to gather up some additional sticks of wood before her guest got cold. Although deliciously lazy from the warmth and the contents of his belly, the pilgrim reluctantly volunteered to perform the task himself, reckoning that this would ingratiate him for later when he put forth his pitifully empty cup for her consideration. For despite the wretchedness of her establishment, its proprietress apparently augmented her income from the tanning of hide. Refusing his offer, the kindly woman proposed instead that her guest remain behind, since he would be of far greater use if he kept watch on the premises during her absence. However, she did not leave without first imparting a warning. "No matter what happens, do not go into that room," she cautioned, indicating with a twisted finger a red door the garrulous religious traveler had earlier failed to notice.

The pilgrim nodded his head in enthusiastic assent, hoping to further loosen the old woman's purse strings with his trustworthiness. Unfortunately, the seed of curiosity had already been planted and after her departure, he could think of nothing but the door and the mysteries contained behind it. Without any fire, the icy daggers of wind sluicing through the unpatched roof had become even more formidable, and the shivering religious trekker took to stamping about in an effort to keep warm. With each clippity-clomp of his sandaled feet, the forbidden door took on the guise of a harlot, beckoning him nearer and nearer its red-painted presence. Summoning up the courage to place his hand against it, he heard the aged granny's premonitory refrain echoing in his ears. Suitably chastened, the pilgrim returned to his post before the cold hearth, his heart hammering with the realization that his hostess was due to return at any moment and would likely be very angry at finding her generous hospitality rewarded in so thankless a fashion—in which case he could kiss goodbye any chance of a few coins being thrown his way.

Only the old woman did not return. As the darkness outside the ruinous little inn grew thicker and blacker and, indeed, more menacing, the religious traveler began to feel uneasy at having been left on his own for so long. Although concerned for the absent proprietress's welfare, it was his own that concerned him the most. He kept hearing a mournful howling—a howling that became louder and more lamenting with each passing minute. Yet rather than being the sound of the wind gusting through the vast empty plain, it seemed to be coming from behind the red door. If he did not learn what lay on the other side, he would go completely mad. Besides, what possible harm could it cause? As long as he did not leave any evidence of his presence, the moth-eaten granny need never even know he had peeked.

The curious fellow moved with trepidation toward the mystery door, steadying himself with a series of deep breaths before placing the perspiring palm of his hand against the paper surface. *The old woman probably stores her fortune in here*, mused the pilgrim, fully expecting to be greeted with dust-covered sacks of coins. Instead he discovered what appeared to be the inn's one and only guest room.

And indeed, the wizened old proprietress had not lied when she claimed to be fully booked for the night. For shackled to a wall was an assemblage of guests, all young men of extraordinary pulchritude and vigor. Their muscled flesh had been partially covered with a supple black hide that stretched across their brawny backs and chests like a second layer of skin, offering little in the way of protection to those parts traditionally in need of protection. The contrast of dark against light further accentuated the areas that had been left exposed, as if the intent was to call attention to them. While this was an incongruous enough costume by itself, even more so were the ornamental accessories accompanying it. Bracelets of an unpolished iron encircled the mighty wrists and ankles of each of the inn's guests. A chain constructed from the same iron had been attached to these cinching cuffs, thus preventing the wearers from straying beyond the confines of the mean little room.

Upon seeing the curious pilgrim peering in at them, the young men began to gesticulate wildly about, the chains keeping them imprisoned rattling and clanging with enough noise to summon the old woman back from wherever she had vanished to in pursuit of firewood. Several attempted to call out to their would-be rescuer, their hopeful faces swelling purple with the effort. For a braided cord of hide had been fitted between their lips, muffling all sound save for the slightest of incoherent murmurs and the occasional frustrated wail.

One of the room's tethered occupants remained slumped by himself in a corner, making no effort to join the inarticulate pantomimes of the others. He was far handsomer than his fellow companions in both face and form, with an athletic chest and backside that had been generously marked with red stripes of varying degrees of intensity and deliberation. Like the establishment's more effusive guests, he, too, had come to be attired in only the most inadequate of vests fastened in the front with cords of the same hide as that which subdued his mouth. The garment failed dismally to safeguard his lower portions, which, despite the cruelty of the temperature, had been left totally bare and vulnerable to the elements. As a direct consequence of such abbreviated costuming, the sturdy muscle of his manhood was plainly visible to all, and it remained in a state of perpetual agitation, the ring of plaited hide embracing it at the root having inspired a severe engorgement of blood to occur. The condition looked quite painful, judging by the moans of those afflicted.

For once the pilgrim had finally unfixed his disbelieving eyes from the lethargic figure in the corner, he discovered that the others suffered from this discourteous malady as well. Indeed, the braided rings of hide encircled the upstanding members of everyone in the room, lending a livid and not altogether unappealing purple cast to these thickened pillars of flesh. Several of the shackled young men clutched themselves in poignant anguish, their eyes rolling upward in their sockets as the lustrous black hide of their vests and those of their immediate neighbors became splattered with a thick white froth, which dripped slowly down the robust cylinders of their thighs. Stepping forward, the religious traveler reached out a hand toward the man nearest him, hoping to provide some comfort. As his tremulous fingertips caressed the bulging arc of flesh held imprisoned by its plaited ring, he found himself being sprayed with the same spumy substance that stained the captive's costume and those of his unfortunate comrades. As if in sympathy, the pilgrim put forth his own contribution, discharging it discreetly within his loose-fitting garments. Nevertheless, his corresponding cry of pleasure was anything but discreet, and he stuffed his fingers inside his mouth to quell it, inadvertently tasting the pleasure of another.

Horrified by his actions and what they had brought about, the pilgrim looked down at his sandaled feet in shame, only to be even more horrified by what he saw on the floor, for its sticky surface had been littered with inspirational pamphlets just like those he carried about the country with him. With his future suddenly laid out before him, he fell backward in a panic, his frantically pumping elbows jabbing holes into the flimsy red door and leaving irrefutable evidence that he had seen inside the forbidden room.

Collecting his rucksack containing his precious pamphlets and his chronically empty cup, the pilgrim dashed out into the chilly night, leaving behind the lurid montage of his enslaved brothers. However, he would not even reach the broken bamboo gate before a loud cry pierced the silence. From the far side of a dead tree appeared the old granny, her ancient form squeezed into a corset of buttery black hide. A cat-o'-nine-tails swung from one withered arm, cracking dangerously through the air. "Stop!" she screeched, her once-feeble voice like rusted nails being hammered into the pilgrim's ears. The kindly, crinkled face she had worn for her unsuspecting guest had melted away, revealing the sadistic visage of the Goblin of Adachigahara.

The religious traveler's journey-worn legs sprouted invisible wings and he ran like the wind, the tails snapping closely and threateningly at his heels and sending up an explosion of sparks from the frosty ground. He knew now that the old woman's warning had been intended to lure him into that vile lair, where she planned to catch him in his spying and make him a prisoner. Indeed, two empty sets of irons awaiting the wrists and ankles of some unfortunate soul had been set to one side, eager to be used. How many other unsuspecting pilgrims had come knocking on the door of this dwelling of the damned in expectation of a donation?

The terror-stricken fellow ran and ran until a pink dawn began to break over the great plain of Adachigahara. He ran until not a scrap of flesh remained on the bloodied soles of his feet. Only when the white of his bones showed through did he stop. Although the goblin had vanished into the blackness of the night, her eerie wails continued to haunt him — as did those of the men he had seen imprisoned behind the red door. To think that he had been so close to becoming the fettered amusement for the inn's godless proprietress. Why, she had not even bothered to read one of his inspirational pamphlets!

The next place the pilgrim came to would be the place where he chose to spend the remainder of his days, but not without first setting fire to his remaining pamphlets in symbolic thanks for being spared such a fate. Here he met many others like himself, all of whom had managed to escape from the Goblin of Adachigahara. Indeed, some still wore their plaited rings of hide and appeared not to mind in the least when the newest among them stroked their straining flesh to a frothy fulfillment.

For the pilgrim could not so easily forget those he had left behind. ❧

RAPUNZEL

Most familiar to us by way of Germany and the Brothers Grimm, "Rapunzel" originated many centuries earlier in Mediterranean Europe. Perhaps the farthest back it can be traced is to the ancient Greek folktale "Anthousa the Fair with Golden Hair." Despite its already lengthy past, the possibility remains that the rudiments of this so-called puberty tale may stretch all the way back to the primitive societies living in the days before recorded history.

For long before the *Kinder- und Hausmärchen* or the tales of the ancient Greeks, it had been common practice among tribal societies to confine a young girl of Rapunzel's age inside a "puberty hut" during the time of her menstruation. In their construction, these structures often took the form of a tower. Most ancient cultures practiced some manner of isolation of a young girl, separating her from the community at the first onset of her menses. She might be placed in the hands of the elder women of the tribe, who then prepared her for womanhood. Indeed, Rapunzel's confinement within a tower took place at the age of puberty — with her guardian being an old woman. In Mediterranean versions of the tale, the old woman who takes the girl from her parents is no nurturing mentor, but a flesh-eating cannibal. So gruesome a character could provide further evidence of Rapunzel's connection to primitive societies, for cannibalism was a part of the belief system and social reality of these cultures, which may have practiced the consumption of human flesh in puberty or religious initiations or even as a result of famine.

By the time of the Grimms, the cannibal character had evolved into a witch/enchantress. In their earlier renderings of "Rapunzel," the brothers, rather than concluding with the shearing off of the girl's hair, allow the story to continue with Old Gothel using the shorn tresses to lure the character of the prince into the tower. Seeing this hideous impostor in place of his beloved, the prince leaps from the window, losing his eyesight in the fall. For many years he blindly wanders the desert into which Rapunzel has been banished, along with her twins. Upon their reuniting, Rapunzel's tears fall into the prince's eyes, restoring his vision.

As the Grimms continued to revise their story, this second part would eventually be lost, along with any references to procreative matters. Yet this was not the case in the "Rapunzel" appearing in the first edition of the *Kinder- und Hausmärchen*. In referring to the prince's visits to the tower, the Grimms wrote: "The two lived joyfully for a time, and the fairy [witch] did not catch on at all until Rapunzel told her one day: 'Tell me, Godmother, why my clothes are so tight and why they do not fit me any longer.'" Here is a blatant indicator of Rapunzel's gravid condition—an indicator that in subsequent versions loses its initial punch as the issue of overly tight clothes evolves into the anger of the witch caused by having been told by her ward that she is a good deal heavier to pull up into the tower than the handsome prince. Deeming the tale unsuitable for children, the brothers moved to clean up any objectionable content, which included the apparently unwed and pregnant state of the protagonist.

Although the Grimms thought "Rapunzel" came from an eighteenth-century novelist who heard it from a member of the common class, the German text they adapted was actually a translation of a French literary tale composed by a lady-in-waiting at the court of Louis XIV—which she in turn based on a French folktale. In Charlotte de la Force's story "The Maiden in the Tower," the beautiful Persinette finds herself confined inside a tower to prevent her from being carried off and, no doubt, ravished. Yet ravished she will be, as Mlle. de la Force makes no secret of the fact that the unwed Persinette becomes pregnant as a result of the daily visits of a prince.

Indeed, sex and eroticism would make an appearance even before the arrival of the French literary tale. In Giambattista Basile's story of "Petrosinella" from his volume *Il Pentamerone*, the prince maintains no qualms about the partaking of fleshly pleasures from Petrosinella as "…he sated his desire, and ate of that sweet parsley of love." (Note that in some versions, *Parsley* is also the name for the protagonist, perhaps providing a duel meaning.) Be that as it may, by the time the tale of "Rapunzel" fell into the bowdlerizing hands of the Grimms, any such feasting had been turned into sexual famine.

Since no man would likely scale the wall of a tower just to hear a song, I have revived the erotic spirit from Rapunzel's early days, for I could not allow such masculine efforts to pass unrewarded. ❦

Rapunzel

IN A PASTORAL LAND OF GREEN WHERE nature's bounty thrived in abundance, there lived a husband and wife. Although it was their greatest wish to have a child, the fertility of their surroundings did not seem fated to extend to their household. To ease the pain of her emptiness, the wife took to blanketing her sorrows in food, growing outward in girth until her husband thought she could grow no more. Indeed, his wife had discovered that there was more than one way to fill a hollow belly.

By some coincidence, the farmhouse located directly adjacent to the couple's cottage boasted a splendid orchard that had won many awards. It contained the ripest and tastiest of fruits whose delights were enjoyed solely by its lone caretaker, an unsightly crone who went by the name of Gothel. With such choice edibles only a few steps away, it was inevitable that a certain neighbor should find herself obsessed with the desire to visit this rich piece of earth and partake of its verdant contents. Of course it also stood to reason that easy access could not be gained to a parcel of such wondrous fecundity. A high fence topped with barbed wire surrounded it that not even the heartiest and bravest dared venture to climb. For it had been rumored that this orchard belonged to a witch of great power...and an even greater temper.

One morning as the wife stood before an upstairs window gazing longingly down into the perfect rectangle of green on the far side of the fence, her eyes suddenly alighted upon an alligator pear tree. She cried out in what sounded like a fit of agony, for she preferred the alligator pear to even the sweetest of cream cakes brought daily to her by her thoughtful husband. The leathery-skinned fruits dangling weightily from the branches called to her, boasting of the delicious buttery meat that lay hidden beneath — a buttery meat that appeared to be going to waste, the owner of the orchard having made no attempt to harvest any. Every day this bereft neighbor could be seen hovering at the window, the imagined taste of alligator pear on her tongue turning her into a mere ghost of herself.

Returning home one evening with a box of fresh cream cakes — only to discover the previous day's cream cakes sitting out on the kitchen table uneaten — the woman's husband could bear no more. "What ails you, Wife?" he prodded gently, believing it to be the absence of the child they could not have. He would be quite taken aback by the explanation for his spouse's misery — that being her tearful proclamation that she would die if she did not receive at least a tiny serving of the savory alligator pear growing within the fenced orchard. It should be noted that the man loved his wife very much and that it tore at his heart to observe her wasting so pitifully away. Preferring her former buxom self to what now lay beside him in bed each night, the husband decided that he would happily risk the wrath of Old Gothel the witch, since *anything* had to be better than the skin and bones into which his good and faithful helpmate had turned. He could not endure another night of reaching out and sinking his fingers into the flattened disks of her breasts and the concave pit of her belly where there had once been layers and layers of plush, jiggling flesh.

Under gloaming's protective cloak, the husband climbed over the barbed-wire fence, cutting himself to shreds in the process. Although all remained quiet at the farmhouse, he made haste as he plucked from the bountiful tree an alligator pear for his wife's supper. With bleeding hands, he delivered it to her like a bouquet from an enamored suitor, basking in the brightness of her smile as she prepared from it a salad and ate of it joyously. Alas, so modest a sampling only piqued the woman's appetite for more, and by the very next twilight the husband could again be seen scrambling over the high fence separating the two properties, knowing that he would not be granted a moment's peace until his wife had finally had her palate for the fruit satisfied.

Perhaps good fortune had been at his side the previous day. As for the occasion of his second visit to the forbidden orchard, fortune apparently chose to be elsewhere. The lacerated fellow had barely finished gathering his leathery spoils when all providence took leave of him. "Halt, thief!" came a voice so horrible that it felt as if hundreds of hot needles were being thrust into the hearer's ears.

The terror-stricken husband straddled the tall fence with great precariousness, with one trembling leg dangling toward the orchard and the other toward freedom, the barbs jabbing purposefully into the crotch of his trousers. Yet he would not have been able to flee if he tried, for the hideous figure of the orchard's owner held his foot tightly within soil-encrusted fingers. "Please, Madam, have mercy on this poor soul!" he pleaded. "I am here on behalf of my dear wife, who is near to death with longing for a taste of this fine alligator pear."

"Near to death, say ye?" echoed the keeper of the alligator pear tree.

The man nodded sadly, praying that the old witch's heart could not possibly be as ugly and malevolent as her face.

"If such a claim is true, I may be of a mind to offer my charity."

Weeping with relief, the grateful husband thanked his gap-toothed capturer and proceeded to shift himself back in the direction of home.

"*On one condition,*" added Old Gothel in an ominous tone.

The alligator pear thief froze, dreading what would be coming next. Indeed, it was not considered prudent to strike a bargain with a witch, especially *this* witch.

"Ye must bestow unto me the child that shall be born of your wife."

Out of fear and desperation and the fact that he had just been caught in the act of stealing, the husband readily agreed. Despite an icy quiver of foreboding in the vicinity of his testicles, he felt confident that his promise would come to nothing. In their many years of marriage, his wife had never once been able to conceive, no matter how frequent or carefully timed their nocturnal encounters. Therefore he returned safely home with the precious alligator pear, pleased at the oh, so clever bargain he had struck with the foolish hag next door.

Within three-quarters of a year an infant was born to the couple—a delightful baby girl who emerged from the womb complete with a full head of golden locks. No two people could have been more astonished by her arrival. By this time, the husband had forgotten all about the silly pact he had made with their green-thumbed neighbor. However, Old Gothel had *not* forgotten and within a matter of days appeared at their door to lay claim to her half of the bargain. The wife had been consuming alligator pears from her orchard at an alarming rate—a fact that could not be denied by the new parents. Conferring the name of *Rapunzel* upon the gurgling infant, the witch took her back with her over the high fence, the little one never again to be seen by the couple who had given life to her.

Rapunzel was a beautiful child — her beauty so striking that it actually seemed to emphasize the ugliness of the individual who had taken over her care. When the girl reached the age of twelve, Gothel shut her up inside an abandoned tower set deep in the wilderness, no longer able to tolerate being daily cuckolded by such physical perfection. On those occasions when she visited her banished ward, she called up to her from below: "Rapunzel, Rapunzel, let down your hair!" This would be the agreed-upon signal for the girl to assist the witch, for Rapunzel possessed a head of hair that had grown so long throughout her many years of solitude that it could easily suffice as a rope. Since the tower had neither steps nor door, she cast these golden plaits out the window some twenty ells below to enable Old Gothel to climb up. The witch had been the only mother the girl had ever known, therefore she was most eager to have her company.

Rapunzel's beauty continued to flourish as she blossomed into young womanhood, resulting in a conspicuous lessening of visits from the evil one who had wrenched her from the adoring arms of her parents. Out of boredom and loneliness, the girl sought to pass the endless hours of the day by entertaining herself with the rhythmic lyrics that played inside her mind. She often spent entire afternoons in this way, hopping from foot to foot and stabbing the air with her fingers. On one of these afternoons a local survivalist had been out riding in search of his dinner when he heard a voice of such sweetness and purity that he could go no farther. Tethering his horse to a tree, he settled himself on a patch of scrubby grass, his heart soaring with love for the voice's unseen female owner as he listened to her stirring song.

> *Yo!*
> *Whassup?*
> *Don't gimme no shit,*
> *Motherfucker!*

And indeed, the voice belonged to none other than the beautiful Rapunzel. So moved was the horseman that he arose from his listening place and encircled the tower several times in search of a way inside its crumbling walls, baffled to find none. He returned home to his cabin in anguished frustration, only to ride back to the forsaken tower the very next day, and the next as well, his heart tormented by the curious cadences coming from within—and stirred by the young woman he imagined to be their composer.

One afternoon as the horse-riding survivalist sat listening to his favorite rapstress, he witnessed the arrival of a horrible creature. Never before had he laid eyes on such a misshapen form or a countenance of such utter hideousness. Frightened that she might see him and place upon him an evil hex, he secreted himself behind a large sycamore, his camouflage fatigues blending him into his surroundings as he kept a watchful eye on the witch who hobbled toward the ruinous tower, and hence toward its musical mysteries. The voice caressing his appreciative ears continued to haunt him, and he took comfort from pressing himself against the rough bark of the tree, moving in rhythmic concert with each exquisite word. However, the restless young man quickly discovered that what had originally brought comfort would instead bring agitation, and he all but drove to tatters the front of his fatigue pants in his quest for relief.

"Rapunzel, Rapunzel, let down your hair!" bade a voice that flayed the tender insides of this concealed music lover's ears and proved as offensive in nature as the voice coming from the tower had been pleasing. The rap abruptly ceased as two golden ropes dropped down from out of an indistinct little opening set high up in the tower wall. The horseman nearly kicked himself for his folly, for in his single-minded search for a door, he had neglected to notice the presence of the window. He watched as the hands of the crone grabbed hold of the braided cords and employed them as a means to climb up the tower's ruinous exterior, at which point she leapt through the window.

After several days of stealthy observation, the young survivalist arranged to return on his horse before twilight, certain he would go mad if he did not meet the rapstress whose rousing words had forced him to rub himself to a frenzy against the coarse bark of a tree. Satisfied that the grotesque creature who had visited in the daylight would not be returning in the eve, he placed himself directly below the little window and called: "Rapunzel, Rapunzel, let down your hair!" And like clockwork the golden ropes were flung out, this time to be seized by a masculine pair of hands.

The figure climbing boldly in through the small opening heretofore reserved exclusively for Old Gothel's entry led Rapunzel to cower against the wall in fear and confusion. Thanks to her many years of confinement by the witch, she had never set eyes upon a man. Nevertheless, her handsome visitor spoke so softly and lovingly to her that her unease vanished, especially when he implored her to sing for him. Indeed, Rapunzel took tremendous joy in her little raps and launched into one at every opportunity. Unfortunately, Mother Gothel did not like for her to sing and would always issue a stinging slap across the mouth whenever she caught the girl doing so. Yet this stranger was kind of heart and pleasing to the eye — of *course* she would sing for him!

A rhythmic cadence began to issue from Rapunzel's graceful throat, rising and falling in pitch while gaining in strength. Its devotee instantly recognized it as the rap he had heard on that first day he had hidden himself behind the trunk of the sycamore. All at once a familiar sensation seized hold of him. Seeing nothing resembling a tree in the tiny room of the tower, he installed himself directly behind Rapunzel, pressing the front of his camouflage fatigues against the pleasing roundness he encountered there. It felt far nicer than the coarse, unyielding bark of the sycamore to which he had grown accustomed. Why, there was even a convenient and warm groove into which he could fit himself most comfortably and agreeably.

Happily situated, this visitor to the tower loosened Rapunzel's hair from their restrictive plaits, freeing up the long tresses of gold. With her voice filling his ears and her silken locks filling his hands, he forged ahead, thrusting forth his pelvis and raising himself up onto the very tips of his combat-booted toes, each note inspiring its appreciative listener to rub harder and harder and faster and faster. Indeed, the more force he exerted, the more passion the lyric seemed to possess, and before long Rapunzel would be rapping with all the force of a gale wind.

> *Yo!*
> *Whassup?*
> *Don't gimme no shit,*
> *Motherfucker!*

Like his earlier encounter with the sycamore, the young survivalist's comfort swiftly turned to agitation. Yet still he did not cease from his strange gyrations, for he sensed that relief would very soon be his—a relief that promised to be a good deal more satisfying than any that could be gotten from a mere sycamore. Within moments a powerful explosion took place, sending Rapunzel's musical admirer soaring high into the cloudless sky. He whirled about like a falcon in flight, swooping upward on a current of air, then dropping back down again. The aqueous roiling of seed taking place in his congested testes erupted in a tempestuous storm, flooding his fatigue pants and leaving behind a masculine signature that even their camouflage pattern would fail to conceal. Never had the survivalist experienced such a wild journey! It was then that he made the fateful decision to visit this enchanting rapstress each and every twilight, regardless of the perils involved.

Rapunzel, too, desired her intrepid suitor's return, wishing only to sing for him and him alone. From this day forward her throat refused to release a single note until the handsome horseman came to claim his place behind her. So happy had she been made by his secret visits that one day when Old Gothel was paying a call, the euphoric girl suffered a devastating slip of the tongue. The witch had taken a particularly long time in reaching the window, placing a nearly unendurable burden on Rapunzel's golden plaits. "How is it, Mother Gothel, that you climb so slowly while the good horseman moves with the swiftness of a deer?"

"Wicked child!" shrieked the witch. "What is this I hear? Ye have betrayed me most grievously, and for this I offer punishment." Seizing Rapunzel by her golden tresses, Old Gothel removed a pair of gardening shears she always kept handy in the pocket of her smock and severed the plaits clear down to the pale white of their transgressor's scalp.

Rapunzel collapsed to the floor, her fingers clutching hopelessly at the fine filaments of hair that lay all around her like sunlit sheaves of wheat. With a satisfied cackle, the witch leapt from the high window, landing unharmed on the scrubby grass below. "Ye shall die an old maid!" she cried victoriously, taking pleasure from her cruelty. In fact, it was highly probable that these vicious words would come to pass, since many years would be required for Rapunzel's lustrous tresses to grow back to the glorious length they had once been—and by then it would be too late for *any* man to come courting.

Be that as it may, there was one thing that Old Gothel the notorious bargainer had not bargained on. That same day the young survivalist returned before twilight to the crumbling tower in the wilderness. "Rapunzel, Rapunzel, let down your hair!" he called from below, his heart pounding in anticipation of the rhythms that would soon be filling his ears and the rhythms that would likewise be filling his loins. Hearing his voice summoning her, Rapunzel touched the stubbly wasteland of her freshly shorn head, devastated by the loss of her beautiful locks. Yet her love for the handsome horseman could not so easily be thwarted. For in her rage, Gothel had overlooked some locks as fine and golden as those that had once adorned Rapunzel's head.

Placing herself before the little window, the girl raised up her skirts, thus allowing the cascade of golden curls previously hidden from view to tumble down to her waiting lover. Grabbing hold of this fragrant, silken ladder with his hands, the young man climbed up the exterior of the tower...where he and Rapunzel remained till the end of their days. Indeed, the most pounding of raps could be heard both day and night, their singer never tiring of singing them, or their listener of listening. Their aficionado would even add his own contrapuntal cadences, accompanying each word by scratching with his penknife against the broken-off bark of his favorite sycamore.

Yo!
scratch —
Whassup?
scratch —
Don't gimme no shit,
scratch —
Motherfucker!

As for the loss of Rapunzel's head of golden tresses, this did not make her in any way wanting to the handsome survivalist. In fact, he barely noticed their absence. For with Rapunzel's every rap, his fingers joyously entwined themselves within the spirally tresses of gold growing beneath her skirts as he rubbed himself silly against the delightfully grooved roundness he found at her back.

And not even Old Gothel the witch could climb up to stop them. ✖

THE SWINEHERD

Scandinavian literature has long been fraught with extremes—
extremes that likely take their cue from climate and geography.
As one who found his inspiration from such extremes, Hans
Christian Andersen would become the individual most commonly associated with the folktales of Scandinavia. A favorite
story of the king of Denmark, "The Swineherd" was often given
a royal recitation by the author himself, for Andersen's tales
charmed one and all.

Unlike his nineteenth century German contemporaries
and friends Jacob and Wilhelm Grimm or his European predecessors, Andersen would be the first writer of fairy tales to come
from the humble class for whom the oral telling of tales was a tradition. Although a number of his works had been claimed by him
as a product of his own imagination, he was known to have
crafted stories heavily influenced by the folktales and legends
told to him in childhood. Of those most thought to be original
creations (and some that were not), many end on an unhappy
note, apparently influenced by the Dane's personal life. Indeed,
themes of suffering and misery appear in abundance all throughout his tales, including "The Swineherd." Unlucky in love,

perhaps Andersen incorporated his own unsuccessful romantic experiences into his work.

Basing his "Svinedrengen" on the folktale "The Proud Maid," Andersen discovered that his source material contained parts he considered unsuitable for his readers—such as the female protagonist's allowing her suitor to spend a night in her bedchamber and, later, in her bed. Many versions of the story show the princess trading her chastity for objects of gold, which Andersen (likely influenced by the religious climate of his country and the moral tastes of his editors) changed to the more innocuous kisses. A woman's desire for material possessions—a desire that eventually leads her into trouble—has become a well-established theme in the folktales of Scandinavia. The message in "Svinedrengen" appears to be that a woman will dispense her favors for the mere possession of a trinket. Of course, proud princesses with a love of the superficial are not exclusive to Hans Christian Andersen. In "King Thrushbeard" by the Grimms, a disguised suitor attracts a spoiled princess with the aid of a golden wheel that makes music, much like the waltz-playing rattle of Andersen's swineherd. Indeed, it happened that the Dane's tales held such appeal to their nineteenth century audience that some would be passed on in oral form, only to turn up in the subsequently published work of the Grimms.

Two centuries before Andersen wrote "The Swineherd," there existed a counterpart not only to his work, but also to the folktale that inspired it. In Basile's "Pride Punished," a king rejected by the proud princess Cinziella alters his appearance and takes employment in the palace gardens, whereupon he entices Cinziella with a robe adorned with gold and diamonds in return for sleeping one night in her apartments. The disguised king next tempts the princess with a beautiful dress, if only he may sleep for one night in her antechamber. Lastly the disguised king offers Cinziella a special undervest in exchange for one more night in her room. Having thrice agreed to his terms, the princess draws a line on the floor to separate them. However, no line can deter her determined suitor. "The king-gardener awaited till she was asleep, and thinking it was high time to work in the territory of love, he arose from his seat, and laid himself down by her side, and before the mistress of the place was well awake, he gathered the fruits of his love...." And such lusty activity apparently continues as Cinziella witnesses her belly growing rounder by the day. Humiliated by her pregnancy, she runs off with the man she believes to be a gardener—a man who forces her to suffer numerous indignities for her initial rejection of him.

Rather than meting out various forms of punishment in the manner of Basile or the Grimms, Andersen's swineherd prefers to do so by revealing his true royal identity, even as the princess laments her loss of the prince who once courted her, thereby prompting his declaration of contempt. For the princess has rejected an honorable prince, yet kissed a common swineherd just to gain possession of a toy. Perhaps the socially dejected Andersen has slipped a message into his tale. In the swineherd's attempts to be accepted into high society, the shallowness of this very same society has been exposed.

Nevertheless, a good deal more will be exposed when the swineherd in my version demands his hundred kisses from the young woman with whom he has fallen in love. ❧

The Swineherd

I N A TIME OF SPORADIC WARFARE AND
political upheaval, there lived a young gentleman of title who possessed a great wealth of
appearance. Alas, such wealth fell short of extending
to his noble pockets. The coffers belonging to his
family echoed emptily in comparison to the bountiful
coffers of his aristocratic neighbors, who, unlike him,
did not find themselves obliged to throw open the
doors of their stately homes to visitors for an entry fee.
To compensate for his financial shortcomings, he
always needed to be cleverer than others in his
endeavors, especially when those endeavors involved
wooing a potential bride.

Being of an optimistic character, the bachelor
nobleman saw no reason why his lack of riches should
thwart him in his quest. He knew of others who had
married successfully with less wealth, therefore he felt
certain that many a fine lady would be pleased to
accept his proposal. Unhappily for this marriage-
minded gentleman, the bewitching daughter of a
notorious warlord for whom he had set his cap could
not be counted among them. Indeed, there were those
who might have said that by offering his heart to one

so far out of reach the gentleman invited the lady in question to trample upon it.

In a small patch of garden he tended himself, the nobleman had cultivated a very rare plant that came from the distant fields of the tropics. Unlike the more commonly held varieties, its leaves and clusters of greenish flowers when dried and touched by flame emitted a fragrance so sweet that anyone who inhaled it would instantly forget both sorrow and trouble, regardless of their gravity. The nobleman also had a special pipe whose wood he had carved and painted so beautifully that it put the finest works of art to shame. Since these were the most valuable of his worldly possessions, he decided to fashion by his own hand two silver boxes into which he would place these treasures and have them presented as gifts to the unmarried daughter of the warlord. Having a flair for the theatrical, he made the boxes oversized so that their contents would be even more of a surprise to their recipient. For the nobleman had quite set his foolhardy heart on wedding the young lady, with whom he had fallen desperately in love the moment he had seen her snapping her scourge at the vanquished townspeople as she passed through the pillaged ruins of the city on the uniformed arm of her father.

The warlord's daughter was busy improving her technique on the already scourge-toughened backsides of her handmaidens when a pair of servants brought the nobleman's offerings up to her. Seeing the large silver boxes, she clapped her hands together in delight. "Oh, I do hope one of them contains a new pillory!" she cried, for she very much wished to install one in her room. Yet no sooner did she hoist up the gleaming lid of the first box and discover its contents than her mouth shifted into a petulant pout—a pout that bore the beginnings of a dangerous grumble of discontent.

"The box itself is quite prettily constructed," offered one of the handmaidens, hoping to stave off another of the young woman's infamous temper tantrums. "In fact, that filigree work is the finest I have ever seen." Although little more than a servant, she knew a great deal more of such matters than her mistress, the handmaiden's late father having been the deposed monarch in whose household the warlord's family now lived.

"Aye, it is uncommonly lovely," remarked the warlord with effusive jocularity as he entered the room, sharing a similar hope to that of the handmaiden who had just spoken.

The warlord's disappointed daughter dipped a hand inside the intricately tooled box to touch the leafy plant. As her fingertips brushed against the clusters of greenish flowers, she yelped as if stung by a bee. "What is this ugly thing? Surely I cannot be expected to allow this to take the place of my trusty nettle scourge?"

"We should say not!" chimed the handmaidens, knowing it was best to agree with their capricious mistress. Nevertheless, they gazed at the gift with bittersweet forlornness, for its leaves would have been preferable to the stinging nettles they were made to endure.

"Now, Daughter, perhaps we should investigate what awaits us in the other box before we allow our tempers to get the better of us," admonished the warlord with a long-suffering smile. He wanted only for these proceedings to be over and done with so that he could return to the important business of seizing territory.

With the raising of the lid of the second box, the pipe that had been placed inside with such tender care by its owner came into view. Its exquisitely carved presence stilled the tongues of all those in the room. For a moment it appeared that no one could find fault with this gift, until the warlord's daughter ascertained that the pipe was not made of painted porcelain, but rather of ordinary briarwood. She immediately ordered its return, dispatching along with it a message to the gift-bearer indicating that she would not *under any circumstances* permit a miserable worm like himself anywhere near her. Why should she bother with the likes of so inconsequential a suitor when she had turned away far better from her door? As for the plant, she gave it to the cook, who chopped up its leaves and mixed them into the bread that would be baked for that evening's supper.

Having nothing to lose but his manly pride, the enamored nobleman refused to let this curt rebuff discourage him. If anything, it made him even more determined to ingratiate himself with the warlord's daughter. The young woman's mean disposition had long been a popular topic of conversation at many supper tables, and this most recent indication of it simply confirmed that he had made the right decision in settling upon her to be his bride. Hence this undaunted suitor decided to modify his courtship tactics, since it had become apparent that his status as a nobleman was of little consequence.

After selectively blackening the contours of his face with boot polish and placing on his head a tattered old cap he bought off the head of a passing vagabond, the nobleman journeyed to the former palace of the ousted monarch to inquire of work. Because so many had already been rendered into poverty since the arrival of the warlord, every post was filled save for that of the warlord's swineherd. Although the prospect of spending his days and nights in the company of pigs did not exactly inspire joy in the young gentleman's heart, he accepted the position, only to find himself being led to a mucky little stall directly adjacent to the pigpen—the room that was to become his new home.

When not tending pigs or shoveling dung, the new swineherd spent his time fashioning a cane from the local hickory, which he imbedded with beads made out of clay baked to a hard finish inside the cast-iron stove that provided his sole source of heating and cooking. All around its gracefully turned handle he attached a string of tiny silver bells that, when turned at a certain angle, played the most jolly of melodies. But perhaps the most distinctive quality of the musical cane was its amazing ability, just by grasping its handle, to allow one to hear the whistling whack of wood on flesh produced by every cane in every household in the city. Surely such a clever creation would be hard to resist.

One rain-freshened afternoon while the daughter of the warlord had been taking a turn in the palace grounds with her handmaidens, she heard the playing of music. Although not unusual in and of itself, the fact that it seemed to be coming from the pigsty *was*. Indeed, what transpired next would rouse her interest to impassioned proportions as the music became abruptly supplanted by the unmistakable sound of hickory hitting flesh. Panting with excitement, the warlord's daughter ordered the most attractive of her handmaidens to seek out the new swineherd, for she very much desired to own the instrument that created such sublime sounds and was prepared to pay a goodly sum for it. However, the musical cane could not be purchased for any amount of gold. After several minutes of failed negotiations, the thwarted handmaiden returned to her mistress, a furious flush staining her plump cheeks.

"Well?" snapped the warlord's daughter, who was impatient to get on with the proceedings. "What is the swineherd's price?"

"I dare not say," stammered the handmaiden, her neck turning as red as her face. "For it is very naughty."

"Oh, for pity's sake, I do not have time for such foolishness! You may whisper into my ear if it is so difficult to speak of it aloud." And so the embarrassed messenger revealed the swineherd's price: ten kisses from her mistress's lips.

Clearly such a price could not be paid, for no daughter of a successful warlord would ever condescend to kissing a common swineherd. Upon being informed of this impudent proposition, the affronted young woman went storming off in the direction of the palace. At that moment the bells on the cane chose to play their special music, followed by yet another rhapsodic session of wood against flesh. Envisioning all those upraised backsides quivering with each biting kiss of the hickory, the warlord's daughter spun about on her heel and grasped the startled wrist of the handmaiden who had spoken with the instrument's maker. "Ask that cheeky swineherd if he would be satisfied with ten kisses from my handmaidens," she demanded. If he had any sense, the mud-caked brute would consider a kiss from the lips of *ten* women a superior bargain to the kiss of one.

The daughter of the warlord did not seem to realize that it was her lips alone that the lovesick swineherd desired most, therefore her latest proposal would also be met with rejection. Indeed, she was growing extremely annoyed with the pig-man, whose stubbornness only strengthened her resolve to own the instrument capable of such dulcet tones and — if the fantastical story told her red-faced handmaiden could be believed — capable of making her privy to the activities of every cane in every household in the land. With no other choice remaining, the warlord's daughter accepted his terms. For them to be administered with the least amount of indignity to herself, she required that her handmaidens form a circle around the two of them and open out the folds of their skirts so that no one could view this scandalous kissing of the swineherd.

Finally face-to-face with the presumptuous underling whose talented hands had fashioned the musical cane, the daughter of the warlord was astonished to find that the fellow was by no means as grubby or repulsive as she had anticipated. "Very well," she snapped, the corners of her mouth twisting downward with a disgust not entirely genuine. "Let us get this disagreeable business over and done with."

Just as the warlord's daughter took a step forward, the swineherd's mud-stained breeches dropped to his ankles. An object resembling the imperial scepter her father had ripped from the monarch's dead hand pointed up at the cloudless sky, swaying unsteadily from its weight. For some mysterious reason, the swineherd had stuck a very large purple plum on the end of it, which probably accounted for so much unwieldiness. Curious though she was to learn why a common keeper of pigs should go about with a piece of fruit attached to the lower half of his person, the warlord's daughter refused to flatter him with such inquiries. Yet she did put forth the issue to one of her handmaidens, only to be informed with an embarrassed giggle that what the mistress had before her was *no plum.*

"And now for those kisses you promised?" prompted the swineherd, unable to drag his eyes away from his intended bride's stern mouth. He thrust his pelvis forward, prompting the weighty protrusion at the end to bob up and down. Its throbbing contours had grown so fat and purple that it looked in danger of bursting, in which case the young woman's fine frock would be ruined — an occurrence that would have been difficult to explain to her father, who had acquired the pale-yellow silk for his daughter during his recent annexation of Manchuria.

Such concerns for her garment began to appear ever more likely to come to fruition once the warlord's daughter realized that the ten kisses the presumptuous swineherd demanded as payment for the musical cane were not to be bestowed upon his lips as she had assumed, but rather upon the bloated specimen thrusting out from his pale loins. Perhaps this need not be so terribly unfortunate, however, since she found it preferable to lavish her kisses upon this robust offering than upon the mouth of a strange man—especially one who earned his keep tending pigs all day. Thus cloaked in the shelter of her hand-maidens' skirts, the warlord's daughter went to her knees before the expectant swineherd. Had her father discovered her in such a pose, he would have sent her off to tend soldiers savaged in battle, not to mention stringing up the poor swineherd from the nearest tree and letting him dangle by the neck until dead. Yet, whatever the risk to herself or another, she simply had to own the musical cane.

The rigid set of her lips relaxed and softened as the young woman pressed them warily against the wildly bouncing object with which she had been presented. The exhilarating warmth from her breath inspired it to dance about with such recklessness that she would be forced to grab hold of the stout stave with both hands just to keep it still. As it turned out, the swineherd tasted so pleasant that the daughter of the warlord had no difficulty in fulfilling the remainder of their bargain. With kiss number ten still shimmering upon the purple flesh of the pig-tender, she snatched up the musical cane and ran off, her concerns about stains to her frock forgotten.

For the remainder of the day, the warlord's daughter and her handmaidens entertained themselves by dancing to the tunes of the musical cane and taking turns grasping the handle until scarcely a cane remained in the city whose lusty activities were unknown to them. As one might have expected, it did not take long for the capricious young woman to grow bored with the game, not to mention irritated with her handmaidens' silly titterings over the private lives of the townspeople. Not even the repeated application of the cane to their reddening backsides could return her to the spirit of things. No matter how hard she tried, the warlord's daughter could not banish the image of the swineherd from her mind...or the taste of him from her lips.

In the meantime, still more miraculous creations would be forthcoming from the pigsty. The nobleman-turned-swineherd refused to sit idle for a single moment. Over the next several weeks, a great deal of sawing and hammering could be heard, keeping the warlord's daughter tossing in her bed at night. Needless to say, her curiosity had been piqued to such a level that she dispatched her most trusted handmaiden to spy on the nocturnal activities of the swineherd. Fatigued from spending all day meeting the demands of her mistress's new cane, this chosen emissary promptly fell asleep outside the pigsty window and would have no information to impart in the morning.

Since being in the employ of the warlord, the swineherd had heard of the daughter's desire to own a pillory into which those whom she deemed in need of punishment could be locked. Having already enjoyed a fair amount of success with the musical cane, he decided to set about constructing one, confident that the finished product would win her over completely. For this would be no ordinary pillory, but one that replicated the cries of those locked into pillories all throughout the land. To make it as attractive as possible, the swineherd melted down every last piece of silver in his pockets, applying this glittering liquescence as trimming for the framework. He also took special care to buff away any roughness inside the holes carved out for the hands and head, hoping in his heart that his own might one day be fitted into them.

While out for her usual constitutional with her handmaidens, the warlord's daughter thought she could hear the tortured groans of men and women originating from the muddied recesses of the pigsty. She came to an abrupt halt, causing one of the more distracted of the handmaidens to collide with her. "What is that exquisite sound I hear? I simply *must* own the instrument that is the source of such delight!" She gave a push forward to the handmaiden who had trod on her heels. "Clumsy oaf, go and ask the swineherd what he wants for it. Only this time I shan't kiss him."

The handmaiden disappeared inside the pigsty, only to reemerge with a furious flush on her cheeks. "Oh, Mistress, now the beastly swineherd desires from you a *hundred* kisses!" she wailed, her umbrage so great one might have thought the demand had been made of herself.

"The fellow must be mad," declared the warlord's daughter. "Who does he think he *is* to request such a thing?" And indeed, she genuinely believed that this time the talented swineherd had gone too far. With a disdainful toss of her head, she went striding back toward the palace, the handmaidens hastening after her in a flurry of ruffled white. However, she did not even reach the ivy-covered colonnade before the mournful strains of an agonized wail teased her ears. "Hmm…perhaps a kiss is not such a costly price to pay for so magical a contrivance," she murmured. "Very well. You may inform the swineherd that I shall grant him *ten* kisses. As for the other ninety, they must come from my handmaidens."

"But we do not desire to kiss the swineherd!" protested the handmaidens in horrified unison.

"I assure you, it is not so disagreeable as you may imagine," replied their mistress with a secret smile.

As before, the pillory's marriage-minded creator could be neither tempted nor negotiated with. "If your mistress wishes to own the pillory, then she must grant me one hundred kisses," he stated resolutely. "I shall not accept a deputy in her stead." The swineherd knew he was pressing his luck, yet he would have done anything for such a bounty of kisses from the warlord's daughter.

And so the bargain was struck. A pillow would immediately be secured, the dispensation of a hundred kisses certain to place a considerable strain upon the knees. Without needing to be told, the handmaidens gathered in a circle around their mistress and the swineherd, fanning out their skirts to ensure that the activities occurring therein could not be monitored by passersby. Secure in her privacy, the daughter of the warlord found herself oddly flustered at once again being confronted with the swineherd's prodigious offering, for it had been revealed to her before she had even gone to her knees.

The handmaidens counted off each kiss aloud so that this impertinent tender of pigs would not be given any more than his agreed-upon due. Nevertheless, it soon became too difficult to keep a running tally, as each kiss lingered longer and longer than the last, their bestower's lips shining with the sweet juices they had inspired. The warlord's daughter executed her side of the bargain with unladylike relish, repeatedly squeezing her thighs together and riding the heel of her slipper as she alternately sipped and slurped the swollen purple object presented to her, unconcerned with the rude sounds her mouth made or the disconcerting effect it had upon those who listened. Indeed, the daughter of the warlord drew on the swineherd with such ferocity that he let out a tremendous roar, his legs folding in upon themselves — and still she refused to cease from her kisses. Even after the aggrieved pig-man had crumpled to the ground in anguish, she could be seen clutching his depleted flesh, her tongue fluttering to and fro within its drooling little cleft long after her handmaidens had called *"one hundred."*

Unbeknownst to the participants or their con-
spirators, the warlord had been seated at an upstairs
window planning the tactics for his next invasion
when he became distracted by the commotion occurring in the vicinity of the pigsty. Annoyed at having
his concentration interrupted — for it so happened that
the land he planned to invade was, by coincidence,
that of the nobleman-turned-swineherd — he set aside
his work to investigate the reason for this disturbance.
Certain that some devilment was in the works, he
crept up on the ring of women until he had gotten
close enough to peer over their heads. Observing his
daughter crouching over the groaning swineherd
whose breeches lay suspiciously rumpled about his
ankles, the warlord slipped off a shoe and set about
striking the handmaidens on the tops of their bon-
neted heads. "What is this mischief?" he bellowed as
he made his angry way toward the center of the circle.
However, no sooner did he reach the source of his
daughter's disgrace than he slumped forward, his
heart giving out, and he fell lifeless to the ground.

It would have seemed fitting that, with the
unexpected death of the warlord, the swineherd
should have chosen to disclose the truth of his situation to the warlord's daughter and return with her to
his home. Instead he remained silent, preferring to
reside with her at the palatial residence of the
deceased warlord. The nobleman continued to wear
the garments of a common swineherd, the muddied

breeches of which would frequently be loosed so that the new warlord (the daughter having taken over from the father) could apply the musical cane to his backside all through the day and long into the night as he stood with his hands and head locked into the glittering pillory he had built.

For what better form of annexation could there be? ❧

THE SHOES THAT WERE DANCED TO PIECES

Tellers of folktales have always been known to bring their personal experiences as well as their social environments into their stories. Although the peasant narrator generally reigns as supreme, there exists yet another voice — a voice belonging to one who has experienced the battlefield. Such a voice can be heard in the soldier's tale called "The Shoes That Were Danced to Pieces."

Equally well known as "The Twelve Dancing Princesses," the story tells of a poor discharged soldier who manages to rise in status by using his ingenuity, gaining for himself not only the crown, but also a beautiful princess. This type of tale likely arose from the inspired imaginations of the many soldiers all throughout history who, on finding that their services were no longer required, had nothing remaining to them except a life of poverty. Ergo, the creation of stories like "The Shoes That Were Danced to Pieces" provided these soldiers with adventure and a means of once again being useful, even if only within the boundaries of folktale reality.

Exclusive primarily to Central Europe, the tale is believed to originate in Russia. More than a hundred variants of "The Shoes That Were Danced to Pieces" have been recorded, the majority reaching from Serbia to Finland, which makes its diffusion quite limited when compared to other European folktales. Although scholars consider it doubtful that the story of the princesses and their worn-out shoes came into existence any earlier than the seventeenth century, elements occurring in the tale already have their antecedents in works of antiquity. The presence of the underground tree bearing jewels from which the soldier takes a sampling can be seen in the four-thousand-year-old Sumerian epic of the Mesopotamian ruler Gilgamesh. Like his more modern-day counterpart the soldier, Gilgamesh must make his way through an underground world, crossing over waters and encountering along the journey vines and bushes that bear jewels instead of fruit. And indeed, the tale may reach back farther yet by way of the coat the soldier wears to make himself invisible — an element indicating a possible connection to the folklore of primitive cultures and their belief in metamorphosis and magic.

Most familiar to fairy tale fanciers will be the version put forth by the Brothers Grimm. Coming upon elements of their story "The Twelve Dancing Princesses" in their travels throughout various regions of Germany, the Grimms found that not every story contained twelve princesses. One version involves a princess who supposedly wears out twelve pairs of shoes. They are in turn repaired by twelve apprentices, the most curious of which hides beneath her bed to learn how so many pairs of shoes could possibly be worn out by one wearer. In so doing, the apprentice discovers the existence of eleven other princesses, leading to the inevitable reward of being allowed to marry the first. In another version collected by the Grimms, three princesses wear holes into their shoes, thereby inspiring the announcement that anyone who can solve the mystery of the worn shoes will receive the hand of the youngest in marriage.

Present here for the first time is the character of the soldier who pretends to drink the drugged wine given him by the princesses — an element that became permanently incorporated into the tale by the Grimms, along with the gruesome disposal of those who tried and failed to solve the mystery of the worn-out shoes.

Indeed, Victorian editors would have a difficult time with the fatal and unjust disposition of the candidates who failed to learn where the princesses went at night. For the concept of those who strove yet failed despite their valiant efforts was not a theme held in particularly high regard by the Victorians. Nonetheless, these very same editors who objected to the dismal fate allocated the many candidates did not appear to pose any objection to a soldier's surreptitious spying on the intimate doings of beautiful young princesses or the princesses sneaking off in the night to meet with young men. Perhaps the bolting of their bedroom door by their father had been intended as a means of protecting their virtue, since surely a good deal more than a dance was on the princesses' agenda...as it would be for the young women in my version. ❧

The Shoes That Were Danced to Pieces

HIGH IN THE CARPATHIAN MOUNTAINS where counts came a dime a dozen, there lived a wealthy widowed Count who had for his pride and joy twelve daughters whose smiles warmed their father's heart. Concerned about untoward influences affecting the wholesome innocence of their lives, the Count insisted that his toothy offspring share the same bedchamber. Fortunately, it was a very large room with space enough to accommodate twelve satin-upholstered beds, which had been custom made from the finest mahogany and trimmed with bronze. Each evening at twilight, their father locked the young Countesses in, placing the one and only key within the pocket of his cape, thus ensuring that no one could go in or out but he himself.

Despite these paternal precautions, something always seemed to go seriously awry. For just before sunrise when he unlocked their bedchamber door to check on his daughters before retiring for the day to his own bed, the Count discovered that the soles of their shoes had become worn through from their nocturnal activities — activities that had evidently

been of so strenuous a nature that twelve corresponding pairs of underdrawers lay discarded beside their
owners' beds, one damper than the next. The continually thwarted Count was eventually forced to post a
notice in the village, announcing that any man who
learned where his twelve daughters went at night
would be granted the countess of his choice to take for
his wife *and* — upon the father's death — would inherit
vast wealth. As with most bargains of the day, there
was a slight caveat to this generous proposal: Not only
had the Count already lived for many centuries and
would likely live for many more, but if the man who
offered his services had not made the discovery inside
of three nights, he would have every drop of blood
drained from his body.

Within hours of the notice's posting, the son of
the burghermaster presented himself at the castle. A
notorious gambler, he owed money to nearly everyone in the village and had twice suffered a broken
nose as a result. He was immediately assigned a small
room across from that of the twelve Countesses in
which a pine box had been conveniently placed for
him to rest. So that the Count's ungovernable daughters might be more effectively observed, the door of
their bedchamber would be left fully open, placing
their every activity within plain sight of this sentinel.
Indeed, the burghermaster's son took considerable
delight in watching such fine young ladies dashing to
and fro in petticoat and chemise as each performed

her toilette, for the twelve Countesses possessed figures of great allure that not even the modest cloak of
their undergarments could hide.

Although such visual pleasures had never
before been made so readily available to him, this new
arrival had undergone a tiresome journey from the
village, and his eyelids began to droop with heavi-
ness, bringing with them an unwanted slumber.
Having found no coachman willing to transport him
to the Count's castle, he had had to walk the distance,
most of which was uphill. Only the rising of the sun
could finally prize the burghermaster's son out from
his sleeping box. The following morning he awakened
rested and refreshed…until suddenly he remembered
the reason he had come to the castle. Stealing into the
bedchamber of those over whom he had been
assigned to keep watch, he was greeted with the reas-
suring image of the twelve Countesses sleeping
peacefully in their mahogany beds, a toothy smile of
contentment on their pale faces. Alas, their guardian's
relief at his findings would be very short-lived.

For abandoned alongside each sister was a pair
of shoes, all of which had fresh holes worn into their
soles. Stuffed carelessly inside the left foot of each was
what at first glance appeared to be a kerchief.
However, a more thorough investigation revealed not
kerchiefs as originally thought, but ladies' underdrawers. The burghermaster's son pulled them out one by
one the better to examine them, his fumbling fingers

encountering a mysterious dampness upon their silken gussets. So intrigued was he by his findings that he took the pair assigned to the shoe of the youngest of the twelve Countesses back with him to his quarters to contemplate it at his leisure. And so it would be on the second and third nights as well, which explained how this luckless betting man came to be bled dry.

Be that as it may, there was always some desperate soul willing to risk his life-giving fluids for a chance at possessing great wealth in his pockets and a beautiful young bride in his bed. Indeed, both tradesman and peasant would be left with an emptiness in their veins, thereby necessitating a continuous supply of pine boxes to the castle. For not only did they function as beds, they could be utilized to bury their users in as well, proving the ultimate in multipurpose efficiency for the economically minded Count, who, it should be noted, had not accumulated his fortune by being a spendthrift.

One day a soldier passing through the village heard of the Count's unusual proposition from an old woman selling garlic in the marketplace. No longer in the sweet bloom of youth, he found the prospect of seizing tremendous riches greatly appealing. A wound incurred during the heat of battle had prevented the soldier from remaining on in service, leaving him in a position of poverty and lowly status. He beseeched the garlic seller to direct him to the castle until she grudgingly obliged, albeit not without first issuing a garlic-breathed warning: "You must refuse to eat or drink anything the Count's daughters offer. For if you fall asleep, your blood will be let by the close of the third night!" Apparently taking pity on him, the old woman placed a cloak of the blackest and most supple rubber across his arms. "Wear this and you will be protected from evil."

In appreciation, the soldier bestowed upon the marketwoman the one thing of value he owned: the silver crucifix he wore around his neck. Then he set confidently off on the road to the castle. Like his inauspicious predecessors, he would promptly be conducted into the little room across from the bed-chamber of the Count's daughters. Accustomed to sleeping rough, the soldier found no fault with his accommodation. As darkness descended over the Carpathians, he lay in repose inside his pine box, observing the twelve Countesses through a crack in the wood. The moment the eldest came toward him with a cup of what looked to be wine, he began to snore loudly and with great enthusiasm, for he thought it best to heed the old garlic-seller's advice. With cup in hand, the Countess returned to her eleven sisters, whereupon they tittered merrily, no doubt heartily sorry for the doomed fellow who, at the con-clusion of the designated three nights, would be obliged to spill his blood.

With the soldier snoring safely at his post, wardrobes and cupboards were flung open and garments were draped over every available surface. The Countesses dressed both themselves and each other, dancing gaily about on shoes whose soles had yet to experience wear. Despite such girlish gaiety, the youngest of the Count's daughters did not act nearly so carefree as her siblings. "Sisters," she addressed them portentously, "I fear an obstacle shall be placed in our paths on this eve."

"What nonsense!" retorted the eldest. "Can you not see how the fool sleeps?" She indicated the slumbering soldier, who had not altered his position since dusk. One might even have imagined him dead were it not for the guttural snorts and rattles emanating from the pine box. To make certain all was well, the sisters performed a closer inspection of their inharmonious sentry. Confident that he posed them no threat, they returned to their bedchamber, forming a line before a painted landscape of an ancient necropolis whose ghoulish iconography had sent shudders through the soldier on his arrival. The first-born rapped her knuckles thrice against the gilt frame and the immense canvas swung inward, revealing the entrance to a passageway. Although many castles had been designed with such secret labyrinths, it was the Count's servants whose persistent indolence prevented this particular one from being sealed up. With toothy grins, the twelve Countesses vanished into the black tunnel, the oldest going first, the youngest last.

All the while, the ostensibly slumbering soldier had witnessed everything, including the very pleasurable sight of the sisters' disrobing. Why, his famished eyes had roamed over vistas the likes of which had never been theirs to roam! With such fleshy scenarios still vivid in his mind, he undressed down to his boots before fastening at his neck the cloak of black rubber the old marketwoman had given him—only to discover that it rendered him completely invisible. Armed in his protective garb, the fearless soldier followed the Count's giggling daughters into the cobwebby darkness and down a succession of narrow steps. The smell of the rubber and the feel of it against his bare skin proved unexpectedly stimulating and in his distraction, he accidentally trod on the hem of the youngest's gown. "Eeek! Who goes there?" she shrieked, swatting her hands about as if to ward off an overly persistent bat.

"Hush, you silly!" hissed her sisters in annoyance. For they needed to remain absolutely silent until they had left the castle grounds and, most especially, the range of their father's highly acute hearing.

The twelve Countesses and their unseen pursuer emerged from the musty passageway into a small family graveyard whose ancient and crumbling tombstones lay in the moonlit shadows of trees. Unlike ordinary trees one might encounter in any graveyard, these arboreal specimens were dappled with shiny leaves of silver. The soldier decided to collect one as a token, figuring that he could secure a good price for it in the village in the event that matters did not conclude as favorably as he hoped and a hasty escape proved necessary. As he reached up to break off a leaf, the sound of its stem snapping fractured the stillness, alarming the already-alarmed younger Countess. "Sisters, did you hear?" she cried.

"Shush! It is only the sound of a gun being fired at a werewolf," scolded the eldest.

"Must you always be such a ninny?" reproached another sister, her sharp eyeteeth gleaming in the darkness.

The graveyard eventually opened out into a slightly larger graveyard whose leaning tombstones were overhung with trees containing leaves that appeared to have been hammered from gold. Regretting that he had not gathered for himself more of the silver, the soldier happily settled for a token of the gold, since it would fetch an even greater price than its more modest predecessor. Hearing the loud crack the stem made when broken, the youngest Countess jumped in fear, only to do so again when she and her sisters entered a graveyard of immense proportions whose more recent tombstones were eclipsed by trees that dangled glittering diamonds like ordinary raindrops. Having lived a life without anything of value in his pockets, the soldier wished to acquire a sampling of this as well. Indeed, with graveyards such as these in his environs, no wonder the Countesses' father possessed enormous wealth.

Having by now resigned himself to spending the entire night stalking the Countesses through graveyards, the soldier was startled to see the sparkling water of a lake at the terminus of this dominion of the dead. A dozen rowboats had been moored along the pebbly shore, and at each of their helms sat a handsome young squire, all of whom held a cudgel in their laps to ward off any blackguards who might happen by. As the twelve sisters fanned out to join their waiting sweethearts, the rubber-cloaked soldier attached himself to the youngest and, in his opinion, the prettiest. Since arriving at the castle, he had grown quite enamored of the little Countess, who seemed so much more ingenuous than her older and toothier siblings.

The boats and their occupants cast off toward the opposite shore of the lake, where the sound of music and laughter could be heard. Lagging far behind was the young Countess, whose robust companion rowed with unexpected difficulty, a labored sweat breaking across his smooth brow. On this particular evening the vessel felt unusually heavy—a phenomenon that he blamed on a fatigue brought about by too many nights of carousing with the Countesses, rather than on the presence of their invisible stowaway. As the rowboats touched land, the sisters took off in a run along the beach, taking care not to move too swiftly for fear they might outrun their handsome escorts. Furthermore, the pebbles hurt their feet, the soles of their shoes not having been intended for such rough terrain. Seizing the Countesses in their arms, the squires raised up the hems of their gowns, bringing into exposure their underdrawers, the already-dampened gussets of which were immediately drawn to one side. In this manner each couple danced on the shore, although instead of the partners being face-to-face and palm-to-palm, the gentlemen stood behind the ladies in close tandem.

In his position of newfound invisibility, the soldier could move freely among the twelve dancing couples with no concern for being made a victim of the squires' weapons, for, indeed, some of the larger ones looked quite menacing. Admittedly lacking in the social graces, this unseen spectator considered their jerky dance steps most peculiar and not at all in keeping with the elegant style he expected from those of their station. Yet perhaps even more peculiar was the fact that the squires insisted upon hiding their cudgels inside the disturbed gussets of the Countesses' underdrawers. Each charged forth with warlike impunity, his handsome features distorted with the effort of lodging his armament as deeply as possible before moving on to impale the next eager sister. Those gentlemen of a less robust physical nature paused to rest in between and give their spent weapons an opportunity to return to their former defensive mode, leaving their female partners swaying and shuddering in a solo dance before yet another squire moved in to claim them. The soldier placed himself before his favorite of the Count's twelve daughters so that he might get to the crux of the matter, the crude objects in the squires' care offering a bitter reminder of how skillfully he had once wielded a bayonet in battle. In his opinion, such masculine horseplay would be certain to result in serious injury to the Countesses, if it had not done so already.

Indeed, the youngest moaned wretchedly as she shimmied beneath the imprisoning arms of her dance partner, who had lifted her completely off the ground, leaving her legs to dangle beneath her upraised skirt. She clutched her ruffled bosom in distress, pleading with the grunting and grimacing squire to release her from her misery lest she die before the next sunrise. However, the fine fellow appeared not even to hear her. Instead he stepped up his vicious attack until the Countess began to howl like the creatures of the night of which her father was so terribly fond, her pointy eyeteeth bared to the moon. Before the concerned soldier could intervene on her behalf, he spied a tiny hole that had been forced into view by the retracted silk of her underdrawers. Although at first glance it was black as pitch, a closer inspection showed it to be as red and flamboyant as the poppies he had encountered in his desert travels. It was here that the squire's great cudgel vanished time and time again—as did those of his male companions, all of whom seemed to have the same effect upon the frantic young Countess. As the rubber-cloaked soldier proceeded to monitor the other dancing couples, he noted that all twelve of the Count's daughters sported a similarly outfitted hole.

The revelry went on well into the small hours of the morning until even the moon itself had gone to bed. Each squire performed this awkward dance with each Countess until all parties had been happily paired together, the wolfen howls of the sisters and those of the squires creating an eerie symphony of night music. Despite such equitable arrangements, there were those who desired a second dance with a partner already known to them. The eldest Countess, in particular, was shockingly bold in making her wishes manifest. Before the night was through, she had enjoyed two or three dances each with all twelve squires, hanging forward over the bridge of their arms as they swung her wriggling and baying figure about, her sharp teeth snapping at the air. Unlike her greedier older sister, the youngest seemed modestly content to partake of one promenade per squire, after which she dropped to the pebbly ground in quivery exhaustion, the soles of her shoes worn clear through to her feet. As she occupied herself readjusting the disarranged gusset of her underdrawers, the soldier would once again be granted a glimpse of the little mystery hole the dozen squires had used. To his astonishment, it had grown as large as the one belonging to her eldest sister.

The pink light of dawn was almost upon them by the time the squires rowed the dance-weary Countesses back over the lake. As the rowboat in which he had been traveling approached its pebbly moorings, its invisible mariner jumped out, charging ahead of the Count's daughters and reaching his quarters before the first-born had touched the tattered bottom of her shoe to the top-most step in the secret passageway. Flinging himself into his pine sleeping box, the soldier let loose with his most boisterous snores, his heart pounding furiously from his exertions and the curious events he had witnessed. Fortunately, the sisters had no reason to check on their unwanted sentry, who had forgotten to remove his rubber cloak and thus would have been invisible to them anyway. They instead fell into their mahogany beds in lifeless slumber, their battered shoes and moist underdrawers forgotten on the floor beside them.

Following in the wake of his unsuccessful forerunners, the soldier also made the tantalizing discovery of the dampened wisps of white that lay crumpled up within the left shoe of each Countess. Something compelled him to try on the pair belonging to the youngest, which hugged his masculine curves and lumps with the snugness of a fine glove and left him gasping for breath when he ran his hands over himself in an appreciative caress. He so enjoyed the delicacy of the silk beneath the putty-like feel of the rubber that he sampled them all, since they proved so much more pleasing against the skin, what with their pretty owners a mere arm's length away. Indeed, this fallen warrior all but scraped his battle-scarred knees to bleeding, so much furtive crawling about the floor did he do in his self-appointed quest for fulfillment.

On the second night of his stay beneath the Count's roof, the soldier again feigned sleep so that he could slip back into the black rubber cloak and pursue the unsuspecting Countesses to their illicit assignations. Only now, rather than collecting silver or gold or diamonds, he had a far more valuable token in mind.

When the moment arrived for him to be summoned before the Countesses' father, this former combatant went armed with his precious leaves, which he presented to the Count, along with a circuitous explanation of the lake and the twelve boats and the twelve squires whose handsome presences had rowed them. He spent an inordinate amount of time belaboring details of lesser consequence such as the quality of pebble on the shore and the motion of wave on the lake, even going to the trouble of describing the color of the moonlight. Despite his anger, the Count was relieved to have finally received an explanation for the disgraceful condition of his daughters' shoes and underdrawers…although he was not given the exact specifics of the dancing that had taken place or the cudgels that had been wielded with such impunity by his daughters' dancing partners. For it appeared that the soldier had come to an arrangement with the Countesses.

The Count next called upon his recalcitrant offspring, who, in the face of the evidence against them, were obliged to confess. Apparently satisfied, he instructed their garrulous sentry to select for himself a wife from among the twelve. It would not be an easy choice to make. Each of the sisters possessed considerable appeal in face and figure, although in the soldier's eyes their smiles left a great deal to be desired. It might be thought that he would have taken for himself the youngest, since he had so admired her vernal artlessness, not to mention the poppy-like redness of her little mystery hole. Yet instead he claimed the eldest as a bride, her boldness and commanding nature offering him a battle he very much desired to fight with his bayonet — even if it was *not* so stalwart as a squire's cudgel.

The couple took for themselves a private apartment in the castle, one located near the bedchamber now occupied by the eleven remaining Countesses. With the Count's troubled mind at peace, his daughters resumed their nocturnal activities with the complicity and silence of their new brother-in-law, who was most eager to make good upon his bargain.

Night after night, the sisters stole away to meet the handsome young squires at the lake, only to return before dawn, at which time the soldier would be waiting to collect from each of them his token. Unlike a glittering memento of silver or gold or diamond, the token he wished to extract from his sisters-in-law commanded a value well beyond that of the monetary. Indeed, he did not need to await his father-in-law's death to become a wealthy man, for he attained his riches in other ways—and that is how it came to pass that the soldier acquired such an extensive collection of ladies' underdrawers. ❧

THE EBONY HORSE

A tale of the exotic East, "The Ebony Horse" can be found in *The Thousand and One Nights,* or, as it has come to be more commonly known, *The Arabian Nights*—an anthology of tales assembled from remote parts of the Islamic world over several centuries. Although admired by the West as a work of literature, *The Arabian Nights* has always been held in low esteem by the Arab world. In fact, were it not for the Europeans, it might never have made its way into our literature.

"The Ebony Horse" is one in a series of stories told over a thousand nights by Princess Shahrazad to her husband, King Shahryar. The princess used such stories as a form of entertainment and distraction and—most importantly—as a means to keep her life. For these stories served to prevent her husband from continuing with his pastime of marrying a different woman each night and, after taking her virginity, beheading her in the morning. Having discovered his first wife in sexual dalliance with a blackamoor slave, the king vowed to take no more chances. After experiencing a night of erotic pleasure with a steady succession of wives, he ordered them all put to death. However, he would soon run out of marital candidates as

"...parents fled with their daughters till there remained not in the city a young person fit for carnal copulation." Fortunately for all parties concerned, by the time Shahrazad finishes spinning her tales, she will have borne the king a son—and will thus be spared the fate that befell so many of her sex.

Much speculation exists as to the true origins of *The Arabian Nights*. Although the flavor of the work is distinctly Middle Eastern, with the core of the collection believed to represent medieval Cairo, its earlier tales, such as "The Ebony Horse," likely originated in either Persia or India, only to be passed down from generation to generation in the oral tradition by the storytellers of the Arabs, Egyptians, Iraqis, and other Mohammedan peoples. Over time, more and more stories came to be added, and by the fifteenth century the collection had been set down in manuscript form.

Yet, many centuries before the tales in *The Arabian Nights* even appeared in the Arabic language, they may already have lived in print. In the *Hezar Efsan* (A thousand stories) from Persia, the frame story also consists of a king who puts each of his wives to death, only to be distracted from this practice by his latest wife Shahrazad—a concubine of royal blood who keeps her husband entertained for a thousand nights with a series of stories. Despite its parental connection to *The Arabian Nights*, the *Hezar Efsan* likely has its own parent in India. The idea of framing stories within stories to provide a pretext for their telling is widely regarded as an Indian invention.

The Arabian Nights eventually made its way to Europe, undergoing various translations and revisions to suit the tastes and mores of the day. Just as Charles Perrault and the Brothers Grimm stamped their personal imprints on the folktales of Europe, so, too, would the translators who chose to tackle *The Arabian Nights*. Since many of the stories had been composed during the golden age of Baghdad—at the time a city of both pleasure and a marked licentiousness among the upper classes— the Middle Eastern reader would not need to look very hard to locate seduction, adultery, incest, and orgies on its pages. But all this would change, along with much of the integrity of the tales, as Western scholars of the eighteenth and nineteenth century got their hands on the Arabic manuscripts. Although the original work treated matters of sex in an uninhibited manner, such frankness was deemed unacceptable by the "modern" reader. A gulf existed between standards of morality and taste in Eastern and Western cultures—a difference made all the more intense by the developing prudery of middle-class readers, which prompted a continual expurgation of sexual content in *The Arabian Nights*. Nevertheless, one translator refused to shrink from such frank sexuality. In reaction to the Victorian prudery of his day, author and explorer Sir Richard Burton decided not only to include, but even to *emphasize,* the erotic content in the tales, thereby making his work the closest to the original.

Considered one of the oldest stories in *The Arabian Nights*, "The Ebony Horse" appears to be of Persian extraction and may be a survivor of the *Hezar Efsan*. Although not as sexually infused as some of the neighboring tales, it is not without the occasional erotic passage. Unlike his blushing predecessors, Sir Richard seemed to relish such passages, especially those describing the prince's desire for the beautiful princess. "...[T]he fires of longing flamed up in his heart and pine and passion redoubled upon him. Grief and regret were sore upon him and his bowels yearned in him for love of the King's daughter...." Such extravagance of language cannot easily be found in similar works. This literary style would prove quite popular as more and more readers (and even a few writers) came to discover the lure of the exotic and, indeed, the erotic in *The Arabian Nights*. ஃ

The Ebony Horse

I N A LAND OF GOLDEN DESERT SANDS THERE
lived a great and powerful sultan named Sabur.
He was much loved by his people, such that each
year the day of his birth came to be celebrated with
more lavishness than those that had gone before. As
he sat upon his jeweled throne surrounded by his
loyal courtiers, dervishes would dance, slave girls
would serve, and cooks would proffer exotic victuals
capable of pleasing the most fastidious of imperial
palates. So revered was the Sultan that on his birthday
every road in the empire stood littered with gifts, each
finer than the next. But on the day marking his fifty-
fifth year, one gift surpassed all the others.

An old sage who dwelt in the cave of a mountain presented himself to the Sultan, bowing with
extravagant ceremony to kiss the ground between
Sabur's large feet. On this special occasion he had
brought a life-sized horse carved from the finest
ebony, with eyes of glittering diamonds and a mane
and tail created from the cocoon of the silkworm, the
quality of which surpassed even that of the Sultan's
best robes. The tooled red hide of the saddle, bridle,
and stirrups had been inlaid with gold and every

precious jewel that could be cut from the earth. "Your Majesty, this horse has the power of flight. It can leap higher than a rainbow and cross the seven seas," boasted the sage, his claim generating no less than a few scowls of disapproval.

"If what you say is true, then I shall reward you with your dearest wish," replied Sabur with an amused smile, convinced that this unctuous braggart was endeavoring to get the better of him.

Upon hearing these words, the sage leapt up with startling agility onto the ebony horse. Rotating a peg hidden beneath the saddle, he flew off through the arches of the palace gallery and high into the pinkening sky. By the time he returned, the Sultan was beside himself with excitement at the notion of possessing the splendid horse. In his eyes, no wish would have been too grand to fulfill. Therefore when the sage requested the one thing of value belonging to the Sultan, it could not be denied. As a result, Sabur's only daughter came to be promised to the sage in marriage.

Outraged by this impetuous peddling of his young sister, the Sultan's son found himself obliged to intervene in this unwholesome bargain, fearful that the outcome would not bode well for his unworldly sibling. "Father, this wicked man is a common sorcerer. Surely you cannot trade your precious daughter for a toy horse?" Kamar al-Akmar protested in horror.

Sabur raised a hand to still his son's heartfelt remonstrations. "A sultan's word is his bond — and my word has been given. Perhaps you might elect to ride upon it yourself to determine if your opinion is in need of altering," retorted the Sultan, who did not take kindly to having his decisions questioned.

All the while, the old sage had been standing silently by, cloaking his instant hatred of Kamar behind a habitually sour visage. "Simply turn this little peg and you shall partake of journeys it would require ten lifetimes to experience," he croaked, grinning yellowly and bowing toward the young Shahzada with false respect.

Being of a fair mind, Kamar al-Akmar felt himself relenting. And indeed, no sooner did he climb up onto the saddle and touch his fingers to the peg the sage had indicated than the ebony horse went bounding off over the gallery and high into the desert sky. At first he enjoyed this amazing sensation of flight, but the heights he reached and the speed with which he traveled soon became too much for a young man created from flesh and blood, regardless of its royal content. The panicked Shahzada barked out a series of frantic commands, his words failing to penetrate the horse's delicately carved ears as all he had ever known faded to an ochre haze beneath him.

As the shadows flickering upon the marble walls of the palace became absorbed into the night, the Sultan grew increasingly concerned. He ordered his slaves to fetch the old sage, who claimed that nothing could be done. "The good Shahzada departed with such swiftness that I did not have an opportunity to explain to him about the second peg," he shrugged in exaggerated dismay, his black heart swelling with joy at Kamar al-Akmar's apparent misfortune. Only, rather than being allowed to console the Sultan with hollow declarations of sympathy, the sage found himself banished to a cell, where he would spend his tenure being whipped by the palace slaves. Since they were so often whipped themselves, they took great satisfaction from inflicting pain upon the body of another and performed their task far beyond their ruler's most stringent expectations. Needless to say, the Sultan's earlier matrimonial promise of his daughter was promptly rescinded, thereby further blackening the sage's heart and setting him toward what would become an unwavering path of revenge.

By this time, Kamar had traveled a considerable distance and, while battling to control the ebony steed, he called upon Allah to bring him back down to safety. It was then that his furiously searching fingers alighted upon a corresponding peg located to the far side of the saddle—a peg so seemingly insignificant that one might have thought its presence was not meant to be detected. His fingertips barely grazed it before he discovered himself plunging perilously toward the converging rivers of the Tigris and the Euphrates. Further adjustments managed to slow the wooden beast's progress, and the young Shahzada was soon journeying at a more leisurely pace, marveling at the vast desert landscape laid out below him. As the veil of night cast itself over him, he was drawn toward the shimmering lights of Sana, where he had seen a magnificent palace whose marble exterior still glowed with the heat of the now-sleeping sun. Certain that he would be welcomed here, he maneuvered the ebony mount steadily downward, landing atop a flat portion of roof.

Since the hour had grown quite late and was thus not an appropriate time to presume upon the hospitality of strangers, Kamar al-Akmar stole into the palace via a carelessly unbolted door, moving with winged feet along the polished marble floors of the topmost corridor in search of sanctuary. Just when he despaired that he would never locate a place to rest his weary body, he arrived at a small vestibule. A slave stood guard outside, fast asleep on his bare feet. Tiptoeing past so slowly that he did not even disturb the air, Kamar drew aside the heavy velvet drapery concealing the entranceway, discovering a private bedchamber.

Commanding the center of the room stood a round bed constructed from the rarest pink-hued agate and studded throughout with the same precious gemstones that adorned his father's crown. Flames from a bevy of candles repeated themselves in miniature within the brilliant reds and greens and blues, giving the illusion that the source of light originated from the bed itself. Little else in the manner of furnishings appeared to be present, which only made this solitary specimen for sleep all the more spectacular to its observer. Voile curtains hung in a graceful drape from a canopy of intricately carved rosewood, and they fluttered slightly at Kamar al-Akmar's approach. They had been tied back in one place with a gleaming silken cord, as if offering to him an invitation.

And he would accept it most gratefully, for just behind these curtains was the most enchanting creature the young Shahzada had ever seen. The one he gazed upon could be none other than the famous Shahzadi of Sana—Shams al-Nahar. Kamar had heard a good deal spoken of her legendary golden hair and tiny white hands; they had been the subject of many a male dream in empires far and wide and in dreamers both young and old. The Shahzada all but dropped to the floor in a faint as he spied the beautiful Shams lying in graceful repose upon her back, her perfect alabaster form untainted by cloth save for a gauzy veil concealing the lower portion of her face. A pair of half-lidded eyes the color of smoke had been caught in a trance-like state as two pretty slave girls knelt over her, dutifully administering to their beloved Shahzadi. They wore scarcely more than their highborn mistress, their own veils having been pulled immodestly down to reveal mouths with lips as lush and red as fine wine and nearly as wet. From what this stealthy encroacher could discern, the duo appeared to be bathing the Shahzadi with their tongues, as Shams al-Nahar possessed skin of a remarkable delicacy that would have been marred by the common crudeness of a sea sponge.

Kamar watched in spellbound silence as the slaves licked slowly up along the silken lengths of each lovely thigh, urging them gently apart to gain access to the innermost potions. The Shahzadi sighed softly as they worked, the sighs turning into low throaty moans as the diligent pink tongues of her two attendants moved toward a dainty little pleat located at the junction of her outspread thighs, at which point the pale swell of her belly began to undulate like waves on a storm-tossed sea. The cleft flesh reminded its captivated beholder of a cowry shell that a visiting ship's captain had given his childhood self, although this version proved far superior in every respect. Why, one could almost liken the slender seam running through it to a tiny mouth—a mouth that, unless the Shahzada was greatly mistaken, actually smiled at him.

Indeed, the closer the two slave girls got to this special place, the more force with which Kamar al-Akmar's heart beat. Encouraged by his friendly reception, he placed himself to the farthest end of the bejeweled bed and, with furtive deliberation, raised up the voile curtain to better observe the enchanting Shahzadi's evening bath. For the first time in his privileged life the Shahzada actually found himself envying those of menial status, for it did not seem so terribly unpleasant to pass one's days attending a mistress in possession of such beauteous attributes. He started to tremble as the slaves' feline tongues reached the charming little pleat between the Shahzadi's thighs, the trembles graduating into violent shudders when each placed a well-acquainted thumb along the polished sides, drawing them tenderly and lovingly asunder.

Out from this artificially widened rift grew the petal of a rose, its pink more vibrant and lustrous than any Kamar al-Akmar had ever come across in his journeys. It bloomed with all the vernal freshness of a new spring, offering up a perfume as subtle as it was sweet. A breeze blew across the silken surface, causing it to flutter and billow and surge forth with vigor, as if straining to declare itself to its captivated onlooker. Although Kamar would have liked to press his yearning nose against it, he did not wish to frighten the Shahzadi. Instead he kept his desires mute, watching with breathless rapture as the two slave girls bowed their heads to lick the richly shaded pinkness surrounding this newly revealed treasure.

Alas, Kamar al-Akmar's restraint did not last for long. A strange and most disconcerting occurrence had begun to take place inside his garments. He thought that perhaps an adder (for the desert was abundantly populated with them) had slithered its sinuous way in among the linen folds, and he shimmied about to set it free. When this failed to work, he took to slapping and rubbing himself, which only served to exacerbate the problem. In frustration the Shahzada reached up underneath his garment to grab hold of the offending entity, feeling it spasm and jerk in his hand. Suddenly it spat a hot stream of venomous fluid onto his belly, extracting from him a tormented groan. Indeed, Kamar created such a disturbance that Shams al-Nahar and her female attendants leapt up in fright from the bed. "Who are you?" cried the wide-eyed Shahzadi, straightening the veil over her flushed face. "What is your business here?"

Unconcerned for their own modesty, the two slaves fetched the flustered Shahzadi's nightdress and assisted her back into it. However, it did little to cloak her nakedness. Kamar could scarcely drag his eyes away from the place that had caused him such agitation, so mesmerized was he by the silken whorls that the diaphanous linen failed to conceal. With a regal bow and as much dignity as he could muster, the Shahzada introduced himself as the son of a great and mighty sultan and proceeded to explain the unusual nature of how he had come to be in the palace of the Shahzadi. Of course Shams al-Nahar refused to believe such an impossible tale and demanded to be shown the ebony horse. Apparently, this handsome trespasser took her for a fool if he thought he could coax his way into her bed with such a fantasy. Even her two attendants could only shake their heads and titter behind their veils at hearing the lofty claim that Kamar al-Akmar had put forth.

Although this self-professed son of a sultan who had so rudely interrupted her slaves' very pleasant laving of her person readily agreed to escort the Shahzadi to the wooden horse, Shams took note of his fatigue and condescended to grant him a few moments in which to rest and refresh himself and perhaps partake of a light meal. Despite this generous offer of hospitality, Kamar dared not tally for too long in her bedchamber. The guard posted in the corridor was bound to awaken in due course, and once it had been discovered that this presumptuous foreigner had spied upon the beautiful Shahzadi during her bath, the dogs would be set on him.

Shortly before daybreak and with the discordant music of the barefooted sentinel's snores in their ears, Shams al-Nahar and her male intruder stole up to the palace rooftop. At the sight of the ebony horse with its flashing diamond eyes and jewel-encrusted accouterments, the Shahzadi leapt about in girlish delight. "Oh, do let me ride upon it!" she squealed, so excited that she dislodged the veil from her face. Only it would not be what lay behind the veil that tormented Kamar's thoughts and sent a scimitar arcing through his belly.

Swallowing hard, he pondered the eager Shahzadi's request with some deliberation. For, like his father and the wicked sage, Kamar al-Akmar, too, could strike bargains. "Your Highness, I shall be both honored and pleased to accommodate your wish. But I have a wish of my own."

"Oh, yes! Anything!" cried the Shahzadi. "Is it gold you desire? Or land? I can speak to my father—"

"It is neither gold nor land I desire."

"Well, what then?"

Kamar cleared his throat, for suddenly it felt as though the pit from a date had gotten lodged inside it. When he could finally speak, his words came out sounding rough and raw and not at all like the mellifluous tones to be expected from one of his position. "I should very much desire to sample the perfume of your rose petal."

"My *rose petal?*" echoed Shams al-Nahar in confusion. Indeed, she truly did not understand to what the owner of the ebony horse could possibly be referring. When the red-faced Shahzada indicated with his eyes the area beneath her garment to which he was alluding, the Shahzadi began to giggle. "I am certain that can be arranged," she replied with a diffident smile, raising up the gauzy hem of her nightdress.

Falling weakly to his knees, Kamar al-Akmar pressed his nose against the velvety-silk softness of Shams' proffered gift. "*Ahh*...my desert rose," sighed the enamored Shahzada. "You have been sent to me from the heavens."

Such worshipful words could not fail to ignite the Shahzadi's passions. "Take me with you!" she pleaded, driving Kamar's flushed face hard against the bisected shell-like promontory beneath her belly.

As the sun squeezed slowly out to fill the eastern horizon, Kamar al-Akmar and Shams al-Nahar
together mounted the magic horse. A quick flick of a
peg sent the couple soaring high into the early morning sky, the palace of Sana receding to an orange-toned
speck of marble beneath the beast's ebony flanks. It
would not be until the following sunrise that they
arrived in the sultanate of the Shahzada's father, for
they had stopped many times along the way to rest
and for Kamar to once again stimulate his senses with
the Shahzadi's exotic endowment.

Leaving Shams and the ebony horse behind at
his summer palace, the Shahzada traveled by foot the
remainder of the distance to the palace of his father.
Although he had not been gone from his homeland for
very long, he discovered the city and its inhabitants
greatly altered. People had taken to dressing in the
black of mourning and walked with their eyes cast
downward in sadness. Even the imperial banner atop
the palace roof had been respectfully lowered in a
manner indicating that a member of the Sultan's
family had died. As Kamar al-Akmar approached the
gates, excited shouts could be heard coming from
every corner of the palace. "The Shahzada is alive!"

Seeing the face of his son before him smiling
and beaming with health, the Sultan's tears of sorrow
turned to tears of joy. Many hugs came to be
exchanged, after which Kamar told his father of the
beautiful Shahzadi he had brought back with him.

Orders were immediately given to release the old sage from his prison cell, his evil intentions having resulted in good after all. Fully expecting to be put to death at any moment, the sorcerer was quite taken aback by his pardon, although this in no way lessened his searing hatred of the Sultan's son. On the contrary, many cruel days and nights of bloody whippings had honed and refined it; hence the happy news of the young Shahzada's return with the enchanting Shahzadi who awaited his hand in marriage did not sit well with the embittered sage, whose taste for revenge had grown ever stronger.

As celebrations were planned for the wedding of Kamar al-Akmar and Shams al-Nahar, the newly freed wizard hastened to the Shahzada's summer palace, planning to arrive in advance of the official messengers who had been dispatched by the Sultan to collect the bride. He came upon the Shahzadi sitting alongside a gaily tinkling fountain with the ebony horse, whose silken mane she combed lovingly with her slender fingers. Having departed from her own home in such haste, she had not been given an opportunity to change from her nightdress into proper street attire.

"Oh, gracious Shahzadi, allow me to kiss the ground betwixt your imperial toes," croaked the sorcerer, who could barely conceal his excitement at the sight of his enchanted horse or the alluring young woman who stroked its glossy black mane with her tiny hands. The image of those caressing fingers stirred something raw and primeval within him, and all at once the sage felt a lifetime of need welling up inside him. He knelt to press his withered brown lips against the sun-warmed earth at the Shahzadi's feet, his tongue slithering boldly and wetly between her dainty toes and eliciting from her an astonished yelp. As he sucked the flavor from her smallest toe, the sage glanced stealthily up to behold her startled face, only to have his attention waylaid by something a good deal more savory than a toe limned beneath the thin cloth of her garment. "The Sultan has sent me to bring you to the place of your wedding," explained the old wizard in a voice careening high with strain.

Shams al-Nahar arose from the stone bench encircling the fountain, pulling her toe with considerable effort out from the sage's mouth. "Then I must locate something into which I may change, for I cannot be presented to the Sultan thusly," she chuckled self-effacingly, indicating the obvious unsuitability of her attire.

"But your Highness, that is entirely unnecessary. A gown of watered silk embroidered with every precious jewel in the sultanate awaits you at the palace. Come," invited the sage with a courtly bow, mounting with unexpected difficulty the horse's elegantly outfitted back. An incommodious swelling had begun to make itself known inside the lower portion of his shabby vestments, hampering his every movement and necessitating a need for further furtiveness lest the unsuspecting Shahzadi take heed of it. "We must make haste, as it would not do to be late for the Shahzada and Shahzadi's wedding!"

Since Shams al-Nahar, indeed, did not desire to miss the day of her own wedding, she allowed the Sultan's peculiar message-bearer to assist her up onto the saddle in front of him, where he assured her she would be safe from harm. The sage knotted his long belt securely around her waist, thereby linking it to his own. With an expert twist of the peg, the ebony horse bolted high into the endless blue of the desert sky.

Although unfamiliar with the foreign landscape of her future husband, Shams knew with reasonable certainty that the palace of the great Sabur was located to the west, Kamar al-Akmar having earlier set off by foot in that direction. Therefore she grew extremely alarmed when the jackal-faced messenger piloted the magical horse toward the morning sun. "Look here, this is not the way to the Sultan's palace!" she protested. "Why do you not obey your master's orders?"

The sorcerer chuckled wickedly, displaying to the anxious Shahzadi a generous assortment of jagged yellow teeth. "I have no master!" he snorted contemptuously, cinching the belt binding them together even more tightly to emphasize his words.

"But the Sultan—"

"I, who command the secret of flight, do not require a master. As for that worthless horse thief

Kamar, I heartily advise you to forget him. I shall give you all the kisses you require and *more,* once I take you as my bride!" For in having been originally promised a bride by the Shahzada's father—who promptly reneged on the arrangement—the wizard felt entirely justified in acquiring another, especially when this other happened to be betrothed to the son of the one who had cheated him.

With so foul a proposal resounding in her ears, the Shahzadi struggled to free herself, only to discover that the sage's belt held her like a chain of iron. She tried everything in her ability to thwart the villainous wizard, her threats and entreaties having little impact. It was not so much that she possessed an actual aversion to being restrained; for in the evenings Shams would often presume upon her personal slaves to bind her wrists and ankles as she awaited their devoted ministrations. However, the unsightly visage of the old sage bore no resemblance to those of her pretty slave girls, and despite the increasingly excited shivers that shook her slight frame, the Shahzadi found herself protesting with unexpected vigor, her words seeming to encourage her abductor to commit even greater improprieties upon her person.

Laughing like a madman, the sorcerer grabbed hold of the hem of her garment and tucked it into his belt. With Shams al-Nahar's pale thighs stretched wide and clinging in trembling desperation to the horse's wooden flanks, Kamar al-Akmar's cherished rose petal became fully exposed to the elements. The cold wind lashed cruelly against it, causing it to ripple wildly about as the image of her wedding to the evil sage stung the Shahzadi's eyes and caused a corresponding burning in her loins.

By mid-afternoon, warder and prisoner approached a misty landscape of white-capped mountains and rushing blue rivers. The ebony horse finally set down in a rich green meadow. After securing a struggling Shams to its saddle with his belt, the wizard went off in search of food and drink — albeit not without first giving his captive's windblown petal a vicious tweak, which was followed by a burst of vicious laughter and a suffusion of redness to both the Shahzadi's cheeks and the object of the sage's torment. Shams al-Nahar vowed to herself that when she returned to the land of her Kamar, she would see to it that the old wizard's testicles were skewered and cooked over flame for their wedding supper.

It so happened that the ruler within whose empire the ebony horse had alighted had been out riding with his companions and had stopped to watch the amazing spectacle of the flying horse and its two equestrians, one of whom had gone scurrying off on some mission known only to him. The party of men discovered the beautiful Shahzadi bound to the finely tooled saddle of the beast with her diaphanous garment rolled up to her waist, her sole concession to modesty the gauzy veil covering the lower half of her face. She lay in helpless repose upon her back, her wrists and ankles cinched by a belt, which had been secured beneath the horse's wooden belly. Left to stare up at the darkening sky, Shams did not see the group of horsemen until they were almost upon her. However, the telltale sound of hooves tramping the earth made her tremble and writhe with a fire that grew ever hotter as the riders drew nearer.

As the riding party galloped determinedly toward her, Shams al-Nahar cried out with what sounded to the men like relief, although the breathless Shahzadi knew different. The ruler of the land had barely managed to rein his steed to a halt before her recumbent figure when Shams was already halfway through the story of her life, unable to temper her outrage as she spoke of the evildoer who had brought her to this place. "You must arrest this *shaitan* and lock him inside your securest jail!" she implored of the astonished ruler and his equally astonished companions. "For he has stolen me from what should have been the day of my wedding."

Despite the calamities this improperly posed equestrienne claimed to have suffered at the hands of the now-absent wizard, the master of this misty landscape was unable to concentrate on the torrent of words tumbling like a waterfall from her lips. For his attention had been claimed by what lay beneath the uplifted hem of the foreign Shahzadi's nightdress — as had been the attention of every man in his riding party, save for the slender, falsetto-voiced one who was summoned nightly to entertain the royal sons in their private apartments. *It must surely be more fragrant than any flower in this meadow!* mused the ruler, a powerful shiver shaking his stalwart form. In a strangled tone, he commanded his followers to locate the fiendish sorcerer and escort him to the palace dungeon. Clearly disgruntled, the men galloped off to carry out their detested orders, leaving their leader and the provocatively tethered horsewoman alone.

Without the watchful presences of others upon him, the ruler had taken to drifting with subtle stealth nearer and nearer the ebony horse and its solitary female rider, whereupon Shams al-Nahar began to writhe against the hard surface of the saddle with renewed excitement. Indeed, it appeared that her royal liberator did not act with any particular haste toward releasing her from her bonds. Although propriety demanded that she bid him to let down the hem of her garment, the Shahzadi held her tongue.

"And what might you have there to show me, my lady?" inquired the ruler, the intensity of his gaze making his point of reference unmistakable.

The Shahzadi flushed hotly, as did the object of his interest, which actually seemed to flourish with the ruler's attentions, putting forth a series of come-hither twitches—a phenomenon Shams al-Nahar had yet to experience even under the dutiful ministrations of her two slaves. Of course, she did not consider it at all appropriate to respond to such an inquiry, therefore she continued to remain silent, hoping that this seeming rescuer would accept her reticence as a sign of acquiescence.

Thusly encouraged, the ruler inclined his turbaned head toward the exaggerated junction of the Shahzadi's thighs, the discerning tip of his nose grazing the velvety tip that thrust boldly upward to meet him. His stiff black mustache tickled the shell-like surroundings, whose lustrous pink had been forced into the open by a pair of outstretched knees. As he embarked upon a leisurely nuzzle of this distinctly foreign terrain, several droplets of moisture adhered to the waxed hairs on his upper lip, and he licked them furtively away, reveling in their nectarous sweetness.

Shams could feel the twin breaths from the ruler's nostrils blowing warmly upon her, followed by their sudden reversal as they drew in the surrounding air, taking with it the fragrance of her arousal. "Please, your Majesty, I am already promised to the Sultan's son," she appealed shakily, the sensation of those stiff black hairs on his upper lip stealing away what little remained of her composure. For the ruler's nose was significantly larger than that of her dear Kamar.

Without warning, the mustachioed ruler drew forth his golden saber and sliced cleanly through the belt keeping the Shahzadi bound to the ebony horse. Rather than allowing her to go free, he seized her bodily and heaved her atop the saddle of his steed, taking care that the hem of her garment remained as before—rolled up to her waist. "And now you are promised to *me!*" he bellowed, roaring with laughter as wicked as that of the sorcerer who had stolen Shams al-Nahar from the young Shahzada. Holding her imprisoned within one powerful arm, the ruler brought his great thighs down over hers so that they were kept as deliciously parted as when he had first encountered her. Their pale inner flesh had already forgotten the luxurious memory of her slave girls' diligently laving tongues. Now they only experienced the coarse licking of the wind.

In this manner they galloped off, followed by two trusted members of the riding party who had returned to the meadow to fetch the magic horse. Approaching the fortified walls encircling the palace, the ruler shouted out orders for the household to commence wedding preparations. Indeed, the land would rapidly be abuzz with comment, a good many people having witnessed the shocking spectacle of the beautiful Shahzadi being paraded through the streets with her thighs held open and the lusty emblem of pink at their crossroads pointing the way like a defiant finger. With the eyes of hundreds of men and women burning between them, Shams al-Nahar experienced a deep thrumming in the place that had attracted so much public interest—a thrumming that reached all the way to the tips of her fingers and toes, curling them tightly into themselves. Within moments the Shahzadi would be bucking wildly about on the saddle. A tiny vermilion pearl formed on her lower lip as she bit through the flesh, the tooled red hide beneath her becoming hot and slippery with her private pleasure as her ears devoured the ruler's crude words. If only her beloved Kamar could have spoken to her like that!

Despite her present abductor's apparent gift for verbiage, it did not take long for Shams to realize just how tedious life would be to find herself wedded to this hulking tyrant upon whose horse she had ridden and in whose household his slave girls possessed the faces of boars. Therefore she devised a scheme in which to delay the taking of vows and, in the process, spare herself from being subjected to the daily, if not *hourly*, interrogation of the ruler's great hair-fringed nose. Thus it happened that the Shahzadi refused all food and drink, preferring to spend her days hurling about in a maddened fit until the ruler would at last be forced to release her. So successful was this performance that not only did he postpone the marriage ceremony, he refused to permit his dejected nostrils to graze anywhere near his stolen betrothed's fragrant attributes. Not even the household's finest slave girls could calm the feral Shahzadi. No sooner did they enter her room than she bit them, taking pleasure in the shrieks of terror she inspired. Determined not to become a topic of ridicule for his people, the ruler next summoned a succession of doctors, although he feared her condition to be beyond cure.

All the while, a grief-stricken Kamar al-Akmar had been wandering far and wide in search of his beloved Shams. Everywhere he went, he made inquiries, hoping that someone might have seen her riding the ebony horse with the old sage. Why, he dared not ponder what evils might have befallen her at the sorcerer's filthy hands. Stopping briefly to partake of food and drink at a small inn, he heard talk of the sudden and inexplicable illness of the ruler's recent betrothed—a beautiful young Shahzadi who had the petal of a rose growing out from the meeting place of her thighs. All who had been out and about on the afternoon the ruler had ridden through the streets with her had viewed it, the gentleman having gone to great pains to keep the hem of her garment raised. One might imagine that he should have desired to keep such matters a secret lest a competitor throw down his glove in challenge. But, being of a rather advanced age, the ruler wished to flaunt his good fortune by offering conspicuous evidence of his youthfulness and virility.

Hearing this strange and remarkable tale, Kamar knew at once that the demented Shahzadi was none other than Shams al-Nahar. Filled with renewed hope, he hastened to the ruler's palace and presented himself as a doctor who could cure the Shahzadi's mysterious illness. "I have repaired the broken minds of many," boasted the Shahzada, his newly sharpened saber twitching in its sheath with the desire to pierce the heart of this recent thief who had stolen his near-bride.

Overjoyed at the appearance of this specialist in madness, the ruler explained in some detail the unusual circumstances in which he had encountered the Shahzadi and the old sage, the latter of whom was at this very moment hanging from his toes in the palace dungeon. Naturally, he intentionally omitted the Shahzadi's more intimate specifics, the ruler not wanting to draw the handsome young physician's attention to those things of which he himself had been so sadly deprived. Kamar al-Akmar was next escorted to the room of the afflicted one, who, hearing the approach of footsteps, threw herself to the floor and snarled like a demon, her hands clawing at her much-tampered-with nightdress. As the disguised son of the Sultan stepped forward, the ruler took several steps back, unable to mask his fear. It appeared that his sons had been correct when they had advised him so strongly against taking a foreigner for a bride.

Kamar squatted beside this wild she-beast whom he believed to be his beloved Shams. As she continued to thrash about, her garment became even further torn and upset, when suddenly the disconsolate Shahzada spied something familiar in the place where the young woman's thighs came together. With the hovering figure of the ruler only a saber's distance away, Kamar al-Akmar placed his flushed face as close as he dared, his sick heart soaring with happiness. For not only was this tattered madwoman Shams al-Nahar, but she had been feigning her illness all along. *How extraordinarily clever of her to have devised such a plan to save herself for me,* Kamar thought with pride, confident in the knowledge that his virtuous Shams would not have allowed the ruler to so much as wash her feet. Now he, too, needed to be clever. "Your Majesty, has the Shahzadi been in contact with a wooden figure of any kind?"

"To be sure, she has!" cried the ruler, thrilled to be of assistance to the gifted young physician. If all went well, perhaps he would soon be spending his days and nights in some delightfully fragrant company. "She was found with an ebony horse."

"Then this horse must be brought here at once so that I can break the spell of evil it has cast, for its spirit has entered the Shahzadi's head."

The ruler summoned his most trusted servants, who fetched the magic horse. Kamar al-Akmar next requested to be left alone with the Shahzadi so that he might begin the difficult and dangerous process of curing her. The ruler's thundering footsteps had not even receded down the corridor before a laughing Shams al-Nahar leapt up onto the tooled red hide of the saddle, with Kamar buttressing her from behind. With a twist of a peg, the ebony horse raised its front hooves into the air and leapt out through the window, taking its two runaway riders.

Hearing the commotion, the ruler raced out into the courtyard, shaking his large fists threateningly at the sky. "Come back here, you foreign horse thief!" he bellowed. "I demand you return to me my rose-petaled bride!" A storm of arrows from the palace guards lanced the air, but not a single one managed to touch the horse's wooden flanks. By now it had soared so high that even the most courageous of hawks could not have reached it.

Kamar al-Akmar and Shams al-Nahar returned in victory to the sultanate of the great Sabur. Celebrations were held throughout the land as their wedding took place, yet no celebration would be as full of joy as the one that took place when the Shahzada came to be reunited in private with his bride. Although never to be parted from her again, Kamar quickly discovered that his newfound felicity would have to be shared with his people. For Shams required her husband to secure her daily to the saddle of the ebony horse, where she rode writhing through the streets, her cries of shameful rapture resounding over the rooftops.

Word eventually got around, and the city of the Sultan became a much-sought-after destination for visitors, who journeyed from far and wide to see the famous Shahzadi riding on her magic horse. As for the old sage, he knew an opportunity when he saw one. Having managed to escape from the foreign dungeon in which he had been imprisoned and tortured, he made his way home, where he set up shop outside his cave by selling tickets to tourists foolish enough to pay for what they could have enjoyed for free. ↦

MICHEL MICHELKLEINER'S GOOD LUCK

Undoubtedly one of the most obscure folktales in all of Europe, "Michel Michelkleiner's Good Luck" comes from the tiny country of Luxembourg. However, the tale was formally collected only in 1960. Had it not been for a decision by the Committee of Ministers of the Council of Europe to sponsor the publication of a collection of works on European folklore, Michel Michelkleiner's auspicious adventure might never have become known beyond its oral form.

When compared with the other countries of Europe, Luxembourg has not enjoyed a great deal of study of its folktales, let alone their historical foundation. Nevertheless, folktales help determine a people's unique character and outlook, and in Luxembourg one particular theme seems to crop up quite frequently — that of the poor man who turns out to be much cleverer than the rich man. Such a cleverness might come upon him in an uncontrived way; like Michel Michelkleiner, these folktale heroes are usually far too simpleminded to be calculating. Indeed, this motif of the naïve character or simpleton can be found world-wide, for he (rarely if ever does one encounter a female incarnation) symbolizes the basic genuineness and integrity of the personality. Perhaps such traits are what have made this character so popular in folktales. By pitting protagonists like Michel Michelkleiner against what is bad and having it all come to rights, these tales offer hope by demonstrating that even a simpleton can win in the end.

Despite its lack of written history, evidence can be found to indicate that "Michel Michelkleiner's Good Luck" has experienced a fair amount of diffusion. In fact, an almost identical folktale exists in Costa Rica. In "The Witches Ride," a bobo (simpleton) who beds down in a hut for the night ends up taking a wild and uncontrollable ride on a broom left behind by some witches, only to find himself plunging toward a group of robbers. Believing him to be a devil, they run off, leaving behind their booty—which is then confiscated by the broom-riding bobo, whose earlier misfortunes have now left him a very rich man.

The theme of the naïve young lad going out into the world and, after being repeatedly taken advantage of because of his guileless nature, finally encountering good fortune, can be seen in somewhat different form in Grimms' "Hans in Luck" from their *Kinder- und Hausmärchen*. Like the highwaymen in "Michel Michelkleiner's Good Luck," an endless string of opportunists strike bargains with the trusting Hans, each being analogous to thievery. For, having initially given up his lump of gold, Hans discovers himself saddled with a series of animals—none of which proves in any way useful to him. However, unlike his counterpart in Luxembourg, Hans has willingly (albeit stupidly) parted with his possessions.

My version of "Michel Michelkleiner's Good Luck" parallels the folktale from Luxembourg, except that I have continued young Michel's journey as a man of means. Alas, he seems to be no wiser for having found his fortune. Indeed, he, too, is willingly made to part with portions of it—only to be even more willingly made to part with a good deal more. ❧

Michel Michelkleiner's Good Luck

ON THE DAY MICHEL MICHELKLEINER turned the age of eighteen, he was taken aside by his father, who told his son that he had now become a man and must go out to try his luck in the world. With a bundle containing all he needed to start him on his journey slung across one shoulder, Michel bid tearful leave of his father, grateful for the confidence that had been shown in him and excited about the adventures that lay ahead.

Alas, Michel's bundle would grow to be as heavy as his heart as he walked the whole day long, the distance separating him from all he had ever known increasing with every footfall. As darkness drew close, the woeful lad realized from the rumblings inside his belly that he was hungry. He had not eaten so much as a crust of bread since sunrise. Eager to put still more miles beneath his feet, he ignored the desirous pangs in his gut and continued on his way long past the last saffron glow of the sun, until he reached a dense woodland. Most would have elected not to enter so perilous a place in total blackness, but Michel was certain that he had seen a fire burning not too far distant. And where there was fire, there must surely be friends—and perchance some nourishment for his hollow belly. "Why, they might be travelers like myself," he mused as he made his hopeful way through the fragrant pillars of pine and camphor toward the nucleus of light.

Only Michel Michelkleiner met neither trekker nor tramp nor even a caravan of motley tinkers. Indeed, those he had desired as friends turned out to be a raucous band of highwaymen, all of whom were being sought by the authorities. Each brutish fellow held a stick out toward the snapping and popping flames upon which a chunk of bloodied meat had been haphazardly skewered. The smell of grilling flesh prompted Michel to groan with hunger. Why, he would have kept company with the Devil himself if it meant that he might be given something to eat. Tipping his trusty cap, he bade the party a polite *good evening* and humbly inquired if they had anything to spare a poor traveler who had only that morning left behind the safe embrace of his family to seek his fortune in the world.

Upon seeing the young stranger, the robbers pounced on him en masse, wrenching from his slender arms his precious bundle and stripping from his travel-weary body every item of clothing he wore, including his woolen socks, which were in need of a good mending—and, after so many hours of walking, a good wash as well. Not even Michel's old felt cap was sacrosanct as it made its way onto the laughing heads of his hecklers, eventually being settled atop the cabbage-shaped specimen of the fellow who appeared to be the group's leader. Suffice it to say, a purloining of possessions would not be the worst of the lad's troubles on this eve.

Having been so rudely divested of his garments, a naked Michel Michelkleiner next found himself being passed around the cooking fire so that each of these larcenous brigands could have his illicit way with him, for the young fortune-seeker was of a highly agreeable countenance with eyes that sparkled like the blue of the sea and hair that shone like the finest gold. Indeed, the highwaymen chose to weave their calloused fingers into these glossy, sweet-smelling strands, making use of them to anchor young Michel more solidly against their stout, hairy thighs as they fitted themselves against his slight backside, seemingly determined to both take from him and give to him at the same time.

With their hot breath branding the back of Michel's tender neck with whiskey-stained scorches, the men set out to amuse themselves, spurred toward greater heights of barbarity by the woeful whimpers of their victim, who remained bowed forward at the waist with his bare knees digging holes into the cold damp earth, along with his elbows. Michel's golden hair fluttered wildly in the breeze as the robber positioned behind him performed a most extraordinary jig—or at least it seemed extraordinary to his unversed prey. It appeared to consist primarily of a repetitive thrusting of the haunches that eventually reached its ungainly conclusion with a convulsive tensing of the limbs and a guttural animal growl, intersecting with an ear-piercing squeal from Michel, who felt as if a pillar of fire had been shot through him. Several times during the course of these events a substance similar to that of clotted cream spurted forth from the lad's loins, landing on the flaming logs with a telltale hiss and leaving him weak and confused, his ensuing shudders attracting much in the way of laughter and jeers from his thieving tormentors. Dawn was barely beginning to show her shy face by the time the gang of men had finished with him, and by then Michel Michelkleiner had forgotten all about his empty belly. For he had been filled in ways he had never before imagined.

When they no longer had any use for him or were too fatigued to continue with their fleshly plunderings, the highwaymen heaved their victim into an old cask, covering it over with a lid and securing it up top with a heavy log. It would be in here that Michel remained, bruised and smarting in places he never knew could smart, as he listened to the contented snores of the marauders who had misappropriated his person until he, too, fell into a slumber. Unlike the peaceful oblivion of the ruffians surrounding the fire, Michel's sleep would be a troubled one. The unsavory business of the night had left the lad with a nagging sense of guilt. Although surely it had not been *he* who had done anything wrong?

By the time he awakened, Michel realized from the intense quality of light squeezing in through the gaps between the staves of the barrel that morning had turned to afternoon. The silence proclaimed that the highwaymen had evidently chosen to take their leave. Only the cheerful chirping of birds disturbed the stillness. Anxious to once again be on his way, Michel flung himself from side to side within his slatted prison. His slight shoulders butted painfully up against the walls confining him, the purple marks left on his flesh by the grasping fingers of his tormentors growing purpler in his struggle. The log keeping him penned inside the barrel was extremely heavy. Yet it was also round and, after a good deal of movement on his part, it rolled onto the ground with a defeated thud. Michel Michelkleiner had been freed.

The boisterous band of highwaymen was nowhere to be seen, the once-tenanted clearing now vacant of their sweating and groaning presences. Rather than relief, their young victim found himself overwhelmed by despair, especially when presented with the charred remains of the previous night's fire— a night that had been a veritable festival of male savagery. Michel stood in the middle of the dead embers, hoping to elicit from them some heat. The robbers had left him without a thread to call his own, and the chill breeze of an early autumn evening had already begun to blow. It seemed that he had no other recourse but to continue on his way where, in the course of his travels, he might happen upon a good Christian with a mind toward lending him something with which to cover his bruised and battered flesh.

Hence a shivering Michel Michelkleiner tramped on bare feet through the woodland, convinced he would reach its terminus before nightfall. Having never made the journey, he did not know that this was an unusually deep woodland, requiring those of far heartier stature than himself a full two days to traverse. The birds of darkness had taken up their posts on the cone-laden branches, and they hooted at the naked lad as he passed, reminding him of his poignant lack of success in securing for himself a chunk of fire-grilled meat. By now, so many echoes could be heard inside his belly that Michel would not have refused even the tough flesh of an owl for his supper. Yet perhaps good fortune would very soon be his, for up ahead in the dusky gloom he discerned the outlines of a tiny hut.

Having recently learned that one must not rush willy-nilly into situations unknown to him, Michel approached with caution. The hut had been constructed out of packed mud that had turned ashy-gray with age, and its thatched roof boasted the slanting remains of a smoking chimney. Although not a particularly impressive structure, it gave the appearance of being habitable in a pinch. A square opening cut into the facade glowed invitingly from the flickering flame of an oil lantern within, indicating that someone in more dire straits than this young fortune-seeker had decided to seek shelter. It was through this rough-hewn window that the identities of the hut's occupants came to be revealed.

For whom should Michel Michelkleiner see seated around a tottery old table but the very same gang of highwaymen that had robbed and then taken such brutal advantage of him? At the memory—a memory as raw and vivid as his wounds—a powerful quiver went through the lad's unclothed body, and he moaned with remembered helplessness. Despite the chill night air, his flesh grew extremely hot, as if he were burning up with a terrible fever. He even needed to reach out a hand to steady himself lest he fall to his knees. For it had been on his knees that his tormentors had placed him.

The men in the hut appeared to be in the process of dividing up their spoils. Several stacks of gold coins had been arranged on the gouged-out surface of the table, the tallest of which teetered precariously before the group's ringleader. Michel immediately recognized the silver coins his father had given him and of whose value he had been in great awe; they had been set to one side as though unworthy of being counted. The head robber wore looped around his thick neck the scarf Michel had carried in his bundle—the scarf he had been saving for the day he arrived in the city and, as a matter of convention, needed to spiff himself up. It was the same robber who not only had been the one to have broken him in, but had used him a second time as well. Michel would never forget that throaty laugh or the labored sounds of his breath, which had stunk powerfully of spirits. The sight of the man's coarse fingers allocating out the coins to their appropriate stacks inspired a tortured sigh to escape from Michel's parched lips, and he came close to giving himself away but for a sudden chorus of larcenous chortles that intervened to save him.

As these transitory inhabitants of the tiny hut continued with their unlawful pursuits, Michel Michelkleiner conceived of a plan. "I will steal in through the chimney and take these dastardly villains by surprise!" he said to himself. For in so doing, the thieving brigands might then be that much more the angrier at having had their important business interrupted, which should undoubtedly provoke them to do their worst. The mere thought of once again being so roughly manhandled by this uncouth lot of criminals was sufficient to make their erstwhile victim risk tackling the dangerously slanted rooftop to climb inside the smoking chimney. Unfortunately, Michel's bare feet could locate nothing on which to secure themselves, and he found himself sliding down through the narrowly bricked gap, the soot from many winters coloring his fair flesh black. He landed in a heap of burning logs, letting out a roar as if the gates of Hell had been opened and all its residents let loose.

The highwaymen scrambled about in terror, failing to recognize the golden-haired lad who had just the night before been the source of so much raucous revelry around the cooking fire. To them he could only be a devil, with his wild eyes and his flesh charred black from the punishing fires of Hades. The head robber was convinced that this hellish being possessed a tail and intended to sting him with it, for something long and sharp stuck out from the demon's skeletal body, the glistening red tip of which dripped with a deadly poison. Certain that they were all about to be dragged down into the underworld for their misdeeds, the men scurried off into the woodland, vowing never to rob or pillage again.

Michel Michelkleiner called out after them, but the highwaymen had run too far to hear. Crestfallen, he sat in the ringleader's chair before the table upon whose scarred surface the gold coins had been stacked with painstaking care. Perhaps if he waited long enough, the robbers might see fit to return, since surely they would wish to collect their ill-gotten pickings. To help pass the long hours of the night, the soot-covered lad counted out the shiny disks, discovering that he had a fortune at his fingertips. Although it could not make up for the absence of the villains who had manhandled him, it might be of considerable use when he reached the city.

Reclaiming his well-rummaged bundle that had been tossed carelessly into a corner, the newly prosperous Michel Michelkleiner donned what little remained of his garments—albeit not without first cleaning from his besmirched flesh the gritty black residue from the chimney. After a satisfying meal of bread and cheese left behind by the highwaymen, followed by a good night's sleep, he set off in the direction of the city, his bundle jangling with gold. In the villages and towns through which he passed along the way, he purchased new items of clothing, and by the time he arrived at his destination, he looked quite the young gentleman.

The first thing Michel did was to avail himself of a small lager in the scruffiest tavern he could locate, his engaging presence immediately attracting the unruly attention of a gang of ruffians who had been making a contest out of who among them could consume the greatest volume of spirits in the least amount of time. Bets had been placed by the establishment's equally unruly patrons, and with an impassioned quaver of voice, Michel placed a glittering gold coin in with the tarnished silver ones, stating his preference for the burly fellow who appeared to be the leader.

When the game had at last reached its conclusion and the well-attired newcomer scooped up his winnings from the table (for Michel had guessed correctly), the rowdy party led him into a dimly lit back room to celebrate with still more laughter and drink, which the blue-eyed and yellow-haired young stranger paid for and was eagerly encouraged to partake of...whereupon each man proceeded to pass around the squealing lad just as the lawless band of highwaymen had done at the cooking fire, with the burly fellow going first, and, indeed, closing up the circle by going last.

And that would be how Michel Michelkleiner came to find his good luck. ✺

PUNISHED PRIDE

Classified by folklore scholars as a seduction/humiliation tale, the punishing of prideful princesses always takes center stage in the many versions of "Punished Pride." Known from the shores of Ireland to the steppes of Russia, the tale even has echoes in Shakespeare's *Taming of the Shrew,* which clearly indicates that the theme of prideful females who must be subdued has been the fodder for storytellers both peasant and nonpeasant alike.

Collected by the Brothers Grimm in the familiar form of "König Drosselbart" (King Thrushbeard), "Punished Pride" is believed to have arisen in Central Europe during the Middle Ages, with Italy being the likeliest candidate. However, its actual roots may go beyond those of the medieval, for elements in the story can be traced to pre-Christian days in the legend of the Teutonic god Wotan, who (like the folktale king) goes about in the guise of a beggar. In fact, the German name for *Thrushbeard* closely matches in meaning that of Wotan—that is, *Horsebeard,* thereby providing evidence of a Germanic influence upon the tale's development.

As the Baroque flourished in Italy, Giambattista Basile would create his own version of the story. In "Pride Punished," the haughty princess Cinziella—for whom no suitor is ever good enough—rejects a king, who later disguises himself so that he can take employment at the palace of the princess's father. Although the first part of Basile's tale parallels "The Swineherd," the humiliation of the princess soon becomes a major theme as she finds herself greatly humbled by a pregnancy caused by a man thought to be the palace gardener. As Basile wrote, "The miserable Cinziella, agonized at what had befallen her, held it to be the punishment of Heaven for her former arrogance and pride, that she who had treated so many kings and princes as doormats should now be treated like the vilest slut." Hence the princess is forced to flee her father's kingdom with the man responsible for her condition, whereupon the disguised king inflicts upon the banished princess indignity after indignity. Only when he believes that she has finally learned her lesson does he reveal his true identity.

Although Basile would carry forth the sixteenth century's tolerance for sexual frankness in folktales into the seventeenth century, in the years following his *Pentamerone* a change in attitudes began to take place—a change exemplified by an increasing shame and embarrassment about bodily functions, specifically those related to sexual matters. By the nineteenth century, references to sex were all but gone. In "King Thrushbeard" by the Grimms, not a word can be found of the princess becoming pregnant. Instead, her lessons of humiliation derive solely from the tasks she has been made to perform, rather than from any unsanctioned sexual behavior. It would appear that the men have acted in conspiracy against her as the princess's father arranges for his daughter to take for a husband the first beggar who comes to the palace door—in this case, a common fiddler. In reality the fiddler is a rejected suitor, a king who, according to the mocking princess, has a chin that resembles a thrush's beak. She makes no secret of her contempt as she tells her suitor that he is unworthy of even cleaning her shoes—a contempt that has on occasion been expressed with slightly more erotic overtones via her suitor's apparent unworthiness to *unstrap* them. Having succeeded in winning her with his music, the royal fiddler subjects the princess to a life of poverty by sending her out to perform menial work in the palace of a king, which leads her into thievery.

The version of "Punished Pride" from which I received my inspiration flowed from the pen of the nineteenth-century writer Bozena Nemcová, who is considered one of the greatest names in Czech literature. Although her tale does not contain the sexual candor present in Basile, Nemcová was not shy in making the occasional subtle reference to passion. Indeed, her gardener/prince would find himself *burning up* with love for the princess—a burning that would be reciprocated in kind. However, no mention is made of the princess being forced into thievery or of her untimely and shameful pregnancy. Perhaps Nemcová had more sympathy for her fellow female, for it must be remembered that the other versions of "Punished Pride" were all composed by men.

Such sympathies aside, I have devised far more ingenious punishments for the prideful protagonist—punishments that, depending upon one's point of view, may not really be punishments at all. ❧

Punished Pride

YOUNG MIROSLAV POSSESSED ALL THAT a czar could ever desire...except a czarina. Within days of announcing his decision to marry, the portraits of every imperial daughter from every neighboring empire began to arrive at the palace, each sender hoping against hope that *hers* would be the portrait that the bachelor Czar chose. Although the subjects of these painted works proved most agreeable to the eye, it was the portrait of the spoiled and prideful daughter of the Kaiser that finally captured Miroslav's heart.

With the selection of a bride settled in his mind, the Czar summoned the most famous and sought-after painters in the land. He wished to commission each to paint his portrait—and the more portraits he had to pick from, the better. Attired in all his finery and with a wreath of easels surrounding him, Miroslav sat in thoughtful repose upon the throne that had once belonged to his father and to his father before him, his outward calm concealing the powerful stirrings he felt at the thought of the beautiful Krasomila, whom he hoped to entice with the gift of his portrait.

The master portraitists were most eager for their subject to decide which of their efforts he liked best, and each outdid the other in an effort to please, going to exaggerated measures to flatter the Czar in paint. Yet to the astonishment of all, Miroslav expressed a preference for the painting bearing him the least compliment, his intent being for Krasomila to find herself pleasantly surprised when she discovered her suitor to be substantially more appealing in the flesh than in paint. To further diminish the impact of his canvas image, the Czar ordered the work set into a massive gold frame studded with gems of every conceivable size and tincture. He then bade two of his finest-looking courtiers to deliver it to Krasomila, along with a request for her hand in marriage.

Miroslav waited anxiously as day after day went by without a word. When at last the messengers returned, they did not bring the answer the lovesick Czar expected to hear. Indeed, Krasomila had earned a reputation for spurning all suitors, no matter how eligible or handsome. "We were received most graciously by the Kaiser," they began with clumsy tongues, hoping this might soften the sting of what next needed to be relayed. The Czar had been known to possess a mean temper when roused, and neither desired to be made the recipient of his brutal lash. "Yet when we presented the painting to his daughter, she scarcely gave it a glance. Truth be told," they stuttered out haltingly, "she replied that the gentleman in the portrait was not fit to tie the laces of her shoes." By now the two messengers were trembling in terror. Miroslav could have ordered their heads chopped from their necks for being the unfortunate bearers of such unpleasant tidings.

"The Kaiser pleaded for us to wait," piped the older and more diplomatically experienced of the courtiers. "For it appeared that he wished to use his influence and impress upon his daughter how greatly she had erred in her judgment. Only we thought it prudent to take our leave, as we did not believe she would make a suitable czarina for His Imperial Majesty." With the words that might end their lives irretrievably spoken, the men bowed low to the floor, expecting at any moment to feel the cold blade of an ax against the prickling flesh of their necks.

"You did very well," replied Miroslav, his words resulting in a sigh of relief from the two anxious courtiers. "Perhaps I have underestimated the lady."

For nearly a fortnight Miroslav pondered the issue of the spoiled Krasomila before formulating a strategy. Delegating all matters of consequence to his trusted ministers, he embarked upon a journey that would be of some length, taking with him a few modest garments of little fashion along with a handful of coins that clinked sadly in his pockets. He refused to speak to anyone of where he was going or what he would do once there. Indeed, his business with the Kaiser's daughter was *not* finished.

One might well have wondered why a man in Miroslav's position should have bothered to pursue so callous a woman when those of finer character had made their interests known. But in his mind none could measure up to Krasomila, whose icy beauty had come to be admired in empires both distant and near. Although she could on occasion be kind and even grow tearful upon hearing of the plight of those less fortunate than herself, she actively shunned beggars for fear they might tarnish her with their dirty hands. Yet the prideful daughter of the Kaiser spent her days shunning far more than the common beggar. For numerous gentlemen of importance had put forth proposals of marriage to the haughty Krasomila, without a one being met with acceptance, let alone civility. She had requirements to which few could rise, and she made no secret of her contempt for those who failed. The man she would finally deign to wed needed to be not only highly cultured, but superior in appearance and manner as well as hailing from noble birth. Should it have been surprising that so many suitors found themselves spurned?

One afternoon as Krasomila sat in the shade of a willow tree reading her favorite prose, her father decided to seek out her company to consult her on a matter of minor consequence. "Daughter, I should very much like to solicit your good opinion on the gardener I have engaged—a most extraordinary fellow who appears to be as knowledgeable about music as he is about horticulture."

Although impressed by her father's claim, Krasomila never took anything at face value. "Just the same," she responded, "I prefer to withhold my judgment until I have met with him personally. If he is as you say, then perchance we might presume upon him to teach me to play the harp."

And so it was decided. Later that day, the new gardener presented himself to the Kaiser's daughter, his cloth cap clutched in one soil-smudged hand. He looked uncomfortably out of place in the refined surroundings of the music room, with his shabby garments and mud-stained boots, which he had made certain to brush off before entering. "Your Highness, this humble servant awaits your command," he addressed her in a husky whisper, bowing to kiss the brocaded hem of her robe. When at last he raised his head, the eyes that gazed into Krasomila's held an expression most unprecedented for one in so lowly a position. For, unbeknownst to the Kaiser's daughter, this scruffy fellow was no ordinary gardener, but Czar Miroslav himself.

Of course Krasomila failed to recognize him, having only been presented with his poor likeness in a painting—and that likeness had been attired in the grand robes suited to his high birthright. In any event, the contact had shaken her wintry composure. "Tell me, Gardener, what is your name?" she asked in a quavering voice conspicuously lacking its customary authority.

"Miroslav," replied the Czar, noting with displeasure that the name failed to inspire even a flicker of recognition upon Krasomila's face.

"Well, Miroslav, for a long time I have desired to play the harp. Are you of a mind to teach me?"

The Czar bowed again. "I shall be pleased and honored to do so."

Seeing no further necessity for his inferior presence, Krasomila dismissed the new gardener, surprised at finding herself so unsettled after their meeting. A fire raged within her body, setting her heart to burning like a flame in her chest and chasing out the breath from her lungs. It became so distressing that she was forced to seek out the sanctity of her bed, where her hands moved of their own volition beneath the woolen covers, the fingers rubbing and prodding with a desperation previously unknown to her. Krasomila passed the remainder of the afternoon in this fashion, imagining that it was Miroslav's earth-stained hands upon her, her resulting cries losing themselves beneath the heavy bedclothes. She did not show herself again until suppertime, when she was joined by her father, who promptly inquired of his unnaturally flushed daughter as to whether a suitable arrangement had been made between the gardener and herself. "His name brings to mind your thwarted suitor, Czar Miroslav. Perhaps you should have considered his proposal of marriage more carefully before acting with such haste to dismiss him," said the Kaiser in rebuke.

Nevertheless, the father's sentiments were not shared by his offspring. At the mention of her snubbed suitor, Krasomila wrinkled her nose in distaste. "Please, Father, do not speak of it again. I am certain I would have been extremely unhappy as his Czarina." And indeed, she remained wholly convinced of her words.

With the arrival of the new gardener, much would change in the Kaiser's household. Rather than spending her afternoons reading, Krasomila could be found sitting before her harp, as enthusiastic to learn as the gardener was to teach. Beneath his gentle coaxing and generous praise, the iciness of his pupil's demeanor began to thaw, becoming a much-favored topic of conversation among the maidservants. "The Kaiser's daughter is very greatly changed since taking up the harp," they would whisper conspiratorially to each other. "Before, no one could come within a footstep of her. Now she cares not a fig if that grubby Miroslav licks her hand!"

Such domestic observations held more than a smattering of truth in them, for of late the Kaiser's daughter had developed a restlessness of manner and a strangeness of temperament that did not go unnoticed by those who knew her best. Being of proud bearing, Krasomila refused to acknowledge the true reason for these symptoms. However, every morning she could be spied in the gardens, acknowledging Miroslav with a haughty nod as she loitered in the vicinity of his barrow, appearing to investigate the quality of the bulbs contained therein. Curiously enough, when it came time for her music lesson, she suddenly lost all desire for the gardener's company and dispatched one of the maidservants with an excuse for her absence, only to dispatch a second to cancel out the words of the first. It was said that Krasomila suffered considerable confusion.

One evening, as she entertained herself playing her harp and singing, Krasomila's teacher unexpectedly appeared at her side. His presence did not even allow her to reach the second refrain before her fingers ceased their graceful plucking. "Play for me," she commanded of Miroslav, her voice ragged with despair.

Taking over the instrument, the gardener selected a melody favored by his pupil. As he sang the lyric, Krasomila began to weep, overcome by her imprudent love for the handsome young man who tended the palace gardens. She hung her head in helpless surrender, a hot tear spilling onto Miroslav's expertly moving hand. Her sobs continued long after he had finished, especially when she heard the words that followed his sweet song: "This is my farewell, for I must depart on the morrow."

"But you cannot!" protested Krasomila, seizing the gardener's soil-spattered hands between hers and pressing them to her heart. "You must never leave me."

Drawn downstairs by the music, the Kaiser discovered the couple in a rather compromising and inappropriate placement, the gardener's hands having been relocated inside the swelling bodice of Krasomila's gown. Taking note of the frantic state of his daughter, he understood what had just transpired. "Is this the man you love?"

"Yes, Father. I love him with my entire heart and soul!" cried Krasomila, lavishing kiss after kiss along Miroslav's warm palm, her tongue furtively collecting the salty dampness it found there and eliciting a powerful shudder from Miroslav.

The Kaiser's face sagged with disappointment. "Are you aware that he is greatly wanting in two of the qualities set forth by you for a prospective husband?" For Miroslav the gardener neither hailed from noble birth nor possessed a noble fortune.

"It matters not to me. I should love him even if he swept out chimneys."

"Then you must marry within the hour, at which time you are to leave this land, never to return."

Despite Miroslav's protestations that he did not wish to be the cause of Krasomila's misery and loss in stature, the die had been cast and the Kaiser's will could not be swayed. A hasty taking of vows took place in the music room; it would be attended by only one witness—the harp that had brought the couple together. Stripped of her title and all her jewels and dressed in garments as ragged as those on the beggars she once shunned, Krasomila walked out of the palace gates with her new husband, banished from her father's realm...*forever*.

The newlyweds made their way on foot to the frontier of the land the Kaiser's daughter had one day been meant to rule. "We might be wise to go to the town," suggested Miroslav, indicating a miserable cluster of soot-stained structures in the equally sooty distance. "My brother lives there, and he can find a post for me."

"I, too, shall seek work until matters right themselves," Krasomila assured her husband, although she had no notion of what type of work she might be qualified for, if any.

Miroslav let for himself and his wife a shabby room from a sickly old widow whose house smelled of boiling cabbages. "I must seek out my brother," he told his apprehensive bride as they arranged their few paltry possessions inside their cheerless quarters. "If good fortune shines upon me today, he may know of a post for the both of us."

The bridegroom was absent for the entirety of the day, leaving Krasomila in the company of their landlady, whose rattling coughs came straight from the grave. Finally Miroslav returned at sundown, bringing with him a parcel containing fine linen, which he placed expectantly before his wife. "If you can sew with a perfect stitch, you shall be well recompensed."

The young bride set to work with a vengeance, determined to sew the most precise stitches anyone had ever seen. She toiled night and day, leaving the linen unattended only to prepare her husband's meals. When the pieces were completed, she delivered them to a grand house located in the center of town, placing them in the hands of a lady's maid. The maid immediately found fault with the stitches and refused to grant payment. Unused to being the recipient of such cavalier treatment, Krasomila appealed to the woman's sense of fairness, adding provocation where none was needed. For the maid possessed a most vinegary temperament, especially when dealing with the more well-favored members of her sex. Greatly humbled by the experience, the disowned daughter of the Kaiser kept the incident to herself, too embarrassed to speak of it to her husband.

Miroslav next made it known that the post of maid to a very fine lady had come available. Certain that she would make a lady's maid far superior to the disagreeable specimen to whom she had earlier handed over her sewing, Krasomila accepted, giddy with delight to leave behind the wretched room that served as the couple's home so that she could move into the lady's stately residence for a trial period. As it happened, the new maid would not be allowed to take the weight off her feet long enough to draw a breath. Krasomila performed her employer's bidding from sunup to sundown, running errands, bathing the lady and dressing her heavy black hair, lacing the lady's voluptuous curves into her fine garments—and all with a cheerful smile and an offer to do still more.

Indeed, the lady of the manor summoned this recent addition to the household at all hours, each request being more toilsome and tiresome than its predecessor. The deeds were often quite peculiar in nature, the undertaking of which left the new maid with an uncomfortable sense of wrongdoing. During the lady's bath, Krasomila would be required to spend a considerable amount of time in the laving of her demanding mistress, who disliked the coarseness of a cloth against her skin and preferred that the comely young domestic use her hands. They felt extremely soft for one employed in the lowly capacity of servant, an admission that, when offered aloud, inspired a shameful flush to stain the Kaiser's daughter's cheeks. For, like the lady to whose pampered flesh she now found herself attending, this high-blooded underling had once been accustomed to having a maid assist her with her bath.

Settling into her new routine, Krasomila spent the early hours of each evening drawing soapy circles on her mistress's back and shoulders, rinsing them away with fresh water that had been heating over the fire, only to begin the process all over again by directing her attentions to the fore. Although this might not have sounded particularly difficult in itself, the lady had been endowed with two very large conical objects that she wore proudly upon her chest, and the maid was required to employ both hands in their simultaneous laving, kneading the soft doughy sections with her palms and tweaking the stiff mahogany tips between thumb and forefinger — tips the overworked domestic was instructed to pinch with such severity that the mournful sounds soughing upward from her employer's throat could only have been those of agony.

However, it would be those unseen parts that lay far beneath the warm sudsy water that always seemed to demand the most care. Krasomila could not for the life of her fathom how such a fine lady could possibly get so dirty. She often spent upwards of an hour rubbing at the soiled areas with her fingers, reaching her hand deep into the bathwater until even the crinkles of her elbow had disappeared. No matter how thoroughly she scrubbed at the wriggly little knurl she found and the two furry puffs encasing it, her mistress refused to be satisfied. "Do not stop just yet," the lady commanded in a strangled whisper, "for I am certain that there are many more particles of dirt in need of unearthing." Hence the new maid continued to scour the region with fatigue-numbed fingertips, applying them with a palpable lack of gentleness in hopes that the infernal woman might see fit to release her from her toils. Why, not even her husband when in her father's service as gardener had been in need of so aggressive a wash!

To Krasomila's dismay, this intentional roughness only made matters worse. Within minutes her other hand had been drafted into reluctant service, the soapy middle digit of which would find itself sluicing in and out of a snug trough located at the terminus of a graceful slope of back—a trough so fiery hot it scorched the flesh of her finger. Just when the poor, forsaken daughter of the Kaiser feared her cramped hands were in danger of being permanently crippled, her mistress suffered a fit, gasping and moaning and hurling herself about in the tub, heedless to the sudsy water splashing over the rim and onto the serviceable surface of her attendant's shoes. "Yes, yes!" howled the aggrieved bather. "Oh, *yes-s-s!*"

The startled maid nearly called out for assistance, concerned that her hysterical employer might drown—and that *she* would be blamed for the mishap. Then, as suddenly as the fit had arrived, the woman returned to normal, stepping out from the tub as if these extraordinary events had never occurred. A relieved Krasomila wrapped the heat-suffused body standing before her within a fluffy white towel and proceeded to dry it off, too discreet in her duties to reflect upon the bright-red snippet jutting out from a nest of fur as she knelt to wipe the moisture trickling down the insides of her mistress's legs, most of which did not look at all like water.

It might be expected that the lady should have retired to her bed to spend the remaining hours of darkness in contented slumber, thereby allowing her hard-working domestic to get on with the normal business of laying out her garments for the morning. Instead Krasomila discovered her implacable mistress sitting up in bed, waiting impatiently for the summoned reappearance of the comely young woman in her service. "Krasomila, I fear you were very negligent in your washing," scolded the lady, throwing down her embroidered coverlet and revealing the furry creature that had only moments ago been lurking beneath the steaming bathwater.

The maid found herself shivering, for what next took place struck terror into her heart. With a hand situated upon each pampered knee, her employer extended them fully and salaciously outward, coaxing this bristling denizen of the bath even further into view. The creature appeared quite fierce as it was forced out of hiding from the safe haven between the woman's thighs, no doubt irritated at having been disturbed. A vermilion tongue of a dichotomous structure stuck rudely out from a dense coat of black fur as if in silent rebuke of this seemingly incompetent servant. Krasomila took several steps back, frightened that it might attack, as it had begun to salivate most profusely from its blood-red gash of a mouth.

The lady cleared her throat in a not-so-subtle prompting, her eyes glowing with an eerie luminosity. All at once it became clear to the weary domestic that her unappeasable mistress expected additional efforts to be expended with regard to her ablutions—as did the hirsute creature glowering at her from between the exaggerated *V* of the woman's thighs. For it, too, stood by in a state of expectancy, its flickering tongue distending farther and farther away from the furred halves of its body and bringing into exposure the dripping red maw below. As Krasomila moved to fetch a bowl to fill with warm water, her employer gripped her wrist, this minor physical contact most uncharacteristic and, indeed, most unprecedented for one in her mistress's position. "I shan't be requiring water or soap. They contain properties that have proven to be an irritant to my delicate skin."

Although she yearned very much to do so, her lowly status in the household prevented the maid from remarking that perhaps her delicately skinned mistress should not have lingered for such a long time in the bath, for, indeed, the woman's flesh always looked as puckered as a prune's after stepping from the water. But before Krasomila could inquire as to precisely what method her tiresome employer expected her to use for this washing, the answer had already reached her ears. "I believe your tongue shall suffice quite nicely," her mistress replied matter-of-factly.

With no allusion to ceremony, the lady launched her loins high into the air, drawing her knees up to her shoulders and extending them wide, propelling her furry companion completely and helplessly into the open. Left without their safe camouflage of thighs, still more of its ferret-like features had become visible. The creature appeared to observe the anxious maid from upside-down. A solitary, crinkle-edged eye as black and unfathomable as midnight peered at her from beneath its drooling mouth, blinking with such frequency and intensity that the bifurcated tongue above had taken to flickering right along with it.

Concerned for her safety — for the great hairy thing had been hissing at her ever since her first glimpse of it — the disowned daughter of the Kaiser had little choice but to comply with her mistress's wishes. Placing herself where she could best reach the spitting creature, Krasomila promptly set to work, employing her tongue as one might a cloth, albeit with far more delicacy and pliancy of touch. Perhaps if she did an especially fine job and distinguished herself from her predecessors, the creature would see fit not to harm her, and she might then be allowed to remain on in service. Although Krasomila did not comprehend this obsession with cleanliness by her employer, what did it matter as long as it put food on the table and a roof over her and her husband's heads?

At the thought of her dear Miroslav, who was probably right at this very moment also engaged in servile pursuits not entirely to his liking, the new maid applied herself to her duties with greater enthusiasm, closing her eyes to the hirsute visage before her. She swabbed and swabbed and swabbed again, traversing the same slippery terrain several times and from several different angles to ensure that her mistress could find no fault with her work. To be as thorough as possible, Krasomila smoothed back the shiny black fur with her thumbs to reach any hidden folds or fissures that might have been obscured, the creature's tongue fluttering with a companionable friendliness against her diligently licking one. In fact, she was pleasantly surprised at how tame it proved, although this in no way lessened the labors that had been foisted upon her. But no matter how exhaustively her tongue searched, not a particle of dirt was to be had. Nevertheless, the grand lady continued with her sharp harangue, ordering her frantically licking servant to clean a bit lower, then higher, and then lower again.

This eventually accounted for how Krasomila was gotten to extend her fastidious lavings to the gaping red maw that was clearly the source of so much discommode. Its sticky dribbles had been growing steadily more profuse by the moment, thus necessitating frequent and skittish forays of the domestic's tongue into the hissing mouth. By concentrating her ministrations below the location specified by her mistress as being the most heavily soiled, she hoped to put a halt to the problem before the woman took note of it and offered up yet another vitriolic scolding.

Krasomila spent a long time in the application of her duties, her neck and jaw aching with the strain of washing the hairy denizen that lived between her employer's thighs. Every time she lifted her head to smooth out the knot into which her neck had tied itself, her mistress boxed her on the ears, only to push the maid's face right back into the furry black nest with its serpentine tongue and frothing mouth and vigilant eye. More than half the night was passed in this fashion, with the lady barking out instructions and her flustered servant following them to the letter. "Clean me there!" shrieked the undulating figure on the bed, her breath coming faster and faster, her fingernails digging painfully into Krasomila's furiously moving head. "Do not cease for an instant, for I am so very, very dirty!" However, no sooner had the maid's weary tongue located the spot her mistress had specified than an entirely new one would be proposed.

The Kaiser's daughter knew full well that she was being hoodwinked by her employer, for, unlike those who had come before, she had not been born into the ignorance of domestic servitude. As tears of injustice filled her eyes, the lady of the house began to emit a series of mournful wails, followed by a violent thrashing. Her actions were very much like those she had performed in the bath, only instead of sudsy water, fluffy goose feathers went flying to the floor, having been summoned out from the pillows and coverlet by her pounding fists. Indeed, Krasomila's mistress was truly very, very dirty!

At the conclusion of her trial period as lady's maid, Krasomila returned home to her husband, weakened and defeated and having no intention of remaining in domestic service a moment longer. Upon being queried by Miroslav as to her reasons, she flushed hotly, replying that the work demanded of her had been far too difficult—as was the lady herself. Why, just because her employer had riches and possessed a grand title, she was not therefore superior to others.

Not even a week passed before Miroslav informed his wife that the Czar had chosen a bride. "The palace shall be in need of cooks to prepare food for the celebrations. Perhaps you might offer your services." Krasomila found herself in agreement. The couple could do with the money and, besides, kitchen work would surely be easier than being lady's maid to some titled virago. As for the irony of being in the employment of the Czar, so much had happened to her that his proposal of marriage had become less than a distant memory—as had the proposals of the others she had spurned.

Not surprisingly, the daughter of the Kaiser had never been inside a kitchen before, and she nearly wept when her husband deposited her in the toil-worn hands of the head cook. Without so much as a sip of water to sustain her, she was placed into service. As in her previous post, Krasomila labored so hard she scarcely knew whether the sun or the moon lighted the sky. The splendor of the arriving guests gave her much reason to bewail the lowly position to which her pride and hauteur had led, and she hung her head in shame, which was how the new kitchen maid came to collide with a grandly attired gentleman in the process of descending the stairs. "You!" he bellowed. "The laces of my shoes need tending."

The regal finery of his clothing told Krasomila that this majestic figure was none other than the Czar himself who addressed her. She dropped to her knees to perform the task, not even daring to sneak a glance at his face. Afterward as she squatted in a dim corner of the kitchen peeling her fourth bushel of potatoes, a manservant arrived to inquire as to the identity of the comely young kitchen maid who had tied the Czar's shoelaces. Raising her hand in humble identification, Krasomila discovered herself being escorted upstairs to some exquisitely furnished rooms that, with a heartfelt pang, reminded her of those she had occupied in the palace of her father. It was apparent they had been prepared for the bride. Could it be that the new kitchen maid had been drafted into personal service for the future Czarina?

Before Krasomila would be given a reason for her presence in such luxurious surroundings, a lady's maid appeared. "Select a gown and some jewels to accompany it," she invited the kitchen maid, indicating with a sweep of one leg-o'-mutton arm the magnificent garments and glittering gems that had been laid out upon a luxuriously outfitted bed. "In reward for your earlier courtesy to him, the Czar requests the pleasure of a private dance."

Krasomila could hardly believe the woman's words. She stood docilely by as she allowed the maid's expert hands to dress her, her heart pounding with excitement. It had been so long since she had worn such finery, not to mention being attended by a servant. By the time the gown had been laced and the jewels clasped into place at her ears and throat, the kitchen wench resembled the beautiful young woman she had once been. Alas, such fleeting joys did not come without the proverbial caveat attached to them. "You must not look His Imperial Majesty in the face," cautioned the lady's maid, her tone chillingly ominous. "It is considered a sign of disrespect and therefore worthy of the penalty of death. Now stand facing the wall and remember: Under no circumstances must you look upon the Czar till he bids it."

How strange it felt to be the recipient of these instructions. It had always been Krasomila or her father who granted such a permission to others and, indeed, meted out the penalty to transgressors with generous discretion. With a nervous swallow, the Kaiser's daughter took her designated place at the foot of the bed with her elegantly draped back facing outward. As she waited for the great man who desired from her the simple merriment of a dance, she studied the tapestry hanging above the bed's ornately carved headboard, her drastically diminished status making her appreciate the labor that had gone into creating so many colorful stitches. It depicted a soldier in uniform riding on horseback, his crop raised high to strike the fleeing half-clad figures of his slaves. The scene had been executed with such fleshy realism that it inspired an icy shiver to slither down Krasomila's spine. Before she could ponder her reaction to the tapestry's disquieting subject matter, she heard the door through which the lady's maid had exited creak slowly open, followed by a sumptuous swish of satin as a stately presence came to stand behind her. All at once she began to tremble, for she could feel the closeness of the Czar and smell his grassy scent—a scent that stirred something familiar within her.

Without so much as a cursory greeting, the Czar urged the tremulous kitchen maid forward until she was bending over the bed. Had Krasomila not been quick to put out both hands, she might have fallen on her face. Nevertheless, it would not be her face in which His Imperial Majesty displayed an interest. A sudden coolness gusted over Krasomila's thighs and backside when the beaded hem of her gown was flung up to her jeweled neck, exposing her to the waist. A deep, masculine sigh shook the room, sending another shiver through the young maid's stooped form. Unlike its icier predecessor, this one was made of fire.

Within moments a sharp crack fractured the static silence, leaving in its wake a stinging burn. Its recipient yelped in surprise as a swarm of leathery tails raked over the twin hills of trembling flesh the Czar had unceremoniously uncovered. Krasomila had not even recovered from their first application than a second ensued, crisscrossing the crimsoning tracks that had already been laid and creating the pattern of a draughts board. Although she wished to flee from this terrible torture, an exit would have meant turning to face her assailant — and she could not forget the portentous warning given her by the lady's maid. Hence Krasomila remained bent fully forward over the bed, staring through a salty curtain at the tapestried scene of the slaves trying to escape their fates as she relinquished herself to hers, enduring lash after lash and wondering when it would ever cease.

For apparently the dance the Czar had in mind was a dance that could only be performed solo. The Kaiser's daughter wriggled about in a frenzied waltz of pain as the punishing tails licked over her wildly shimmying backside, which had turned the shade of a setting autumn sun. A sticky substance similar to that which had earlier bedeviled her when she had been in the demanding employ of the fine lady coated the insides of her thighs, increasing with each searing crack, as did the igneous heat in the place of their convergence. When Krasomila glanced down at herself to investigate, she saw a fiery red flame extending out from her body. To her astonishment, it looked exactly like the vermilion tongue belonging to the furry creature that lurked between her former mistress's thighs. Had it somehow managed to follow her to her new post?

Before she could shoo it away, something hot and wet sprayed the kitchen maid's smarting flesh, inflicting additional distress as it insinuated itself within the raw striations that had been carved by the sizzling tails. The liquid trickled steadily downward, making its way through the quivering archway of Krasomila's thighs and toward the flickering, tongue-like flame to the fore. "You may now turn to face me," came a familiar, albeit strangled voice.

Krasomila gingerly hoisted herself up from her stooped position, only to learn that the one who had wielded the weapon that caused her such torment and, indeed, such intensity of sensation was her husband, Miroslav. "Why?" she gasped weakly, the fire between her thighs demanding further fuel from his lash.

"Because I am Czar Miroslav," he said simply, the leather tails in his hand twitching in their desire to prescribe still more of their rousing remedy for prideful young daughters of Kaisers.

At last Krasomila recognized the suitor she had so cruelly spurned. From that day forward, she remained in the palace, since it was the palace of her husband the Czar, as were these elegant rooms those of the Czarina. All concerned lived happily ever after—especially the local whip makers, whose services would be required on a weekly basis. For Miroslav wore out many a lash on his beautiful and once-prideful Czarina. ❧

A Tale of the Parrot

Acknowledged as the home of some of the oldest stories in the world, India is considered by many scholars to be the original birthplace of all folktales. Indeed, one of the oldest collections of folktales can be found in the *Jakata*, which contains fables and stories in the ancient Pali language that date back to the time of Buddha. However, there also exists a collection of lesser prominence in another ancient language — that of the Sanskrit *Sukasaptati*, or *The Seventy Tales of the Parrot*.

The folktales of India have traditionally been told by singers and tellers who traveled from place to place as well as by bardic troupes, family members, and servants. Like the French literary tales presented in the Court of Versailles, these stories eventually came to be set down in writing for the sole amusement of royalty. Despite their primary function as a form of entertainment, one could often find more lofty purposes at work, for it was standard practice in Hindu medicine for the mentally disturbed to be told tales, the contemplation of which would help overcome emotional disturbance.

"A Tale of the Parrot" is believed to be part of the much larger Sanskrit work called the *Sukasaptati*, which possibly dates back in written form to the sixth century. A sacred language, Sanskrit was used by the educated class, therefore the *Sukasaptati* would likely have been enjoyed by the highborn rather than by those of common blood. Like the stories contained in *The Arabian Nights* and *The Serendipity Tales,* those in the *Sukasaptati* were used as a form of distraction and, as such, often proved extremely erotic in nature. The Indian folktale can be characterized by its distinct sense of candor—a candor that manifested itself in matters pertaining to the sexual.

In the frame story of the *Sukasaptati,* a garrulous parrot relays a string of stories to a woman as a means of preventing her from committing adultery. (Conversely, many of the parrot's stories involve faithless women.) The theme of woman as fickle creature forever waiting to cuckold her husband is widespread in Indian literature, therefore much emphasis has been placed on the importance of a woman's chastity. Serving in the *Sukasaptati* as an instrument of this chastity, the parrot has become a popular central character in Indian folktales. In fact, speaking animals have appeared in some of the most ancient Indian texts, many dating back centuries before the birth of Christ.

The *Sukasaptati* traveled out of India, reaching the Middle East by about the fourteenth century in the form of the *Tutinameh*—a translation of the Sanskrit into Persian. Unfortunately, the *Tutinameh* does not contain all seventy tales from the *Sukasaptati,* and the plots and characters of those it does contain have been so altered that they have become unrecognizable. However, the *Tutinameh* has at least managed to retain, if not exceed, the original erotic spirit of the *Sukasaptati*—an excess I, too, have endeavored to create in my refashioning of one of the parrot's many tales. ∾

A Tale of the Parrot

A MAGNIFICENT GREEN AND GOLD PARROT had been sitting on the branch of an acacia tree for many days, observing the activities of those who passed. Annoyed that no one paid it any heed, the parrot finally decided to speak. For it had a tale to tell about the only child of an emir who received a message indicating that the great Khan who ruled the Turks desired to marry her. A dutiful daughter, she had vowed not to leave behind her widowed father, therefore she made it abundantly clear to anyone who would listen that she had no interest in the Turk, let alone his presumptuous proposal.

Within days of declining the Khan's offer of marriage, the Emir's daughter lapsed into a strange illness — an illness made all the more extraordinary by the fact that the young woman had never suffered a sick day in her life. Those of a superstitious nature entertained the belief that the rejected Khan had had a hand in it, although no evidence could be found to corroborate such meddlesome prattle. In his desperation, the Emir called out doctors from far and wide, yet none could agree on a diagnosis for the malady plaguing his daughter. Finally the wise men were summoned, their clever counsel providing the anguished father with his first real glimmer of hope. Apparently what would be required was the presence of the imperial daughter of Spain—the Infanta who had aided in the rescue of so many royal children from the clutches of an evil cult. No corner of the world existed where her name was not uttered without wonderment. If she could liberate someone from the crazed members of a cult, then surely she could help the Emir's stricken daughter.

The Emir ordered his entire fleet to set sail at once, vowing to wage war against Spain if her leader refused to relinquish to him this miracle-producing offspring. For no amount of spilled blood would have been too great in the quest to cure his daughter, who now languished by the day in her sickbed, shivering and moaning in heart-wrenching misery. There was not an eye in the emirate that did not overflow with tears for this much-adored young woman.

When the King of Spain read the message that had been dispatched to him by this faraway Emir's envoy, instead of compassion for an anguished father, he experienced a powerful rage. He, too, was willing to pick up arms rather than allow his daughter to undertake so dangerous a mission. Having already been informed by a personal spy of the distressing news that had arrived by way of a foreign emissary, the Infanta insisted upon offering her aid to this distant sister, assuring her apprehensive father that she would return swiftly and without harm. Hence she departed with the Emir's envoy, sailing across the sparkling sapphire sea to a place whose name evoked exotic images of desert caravans and black-eyed houris.

No sooner had the Spanish Infanta set foot onto the arid soil of this strange, sun-baked land than its aggrieved leader came forth to greet her with offers of tremendous riches and even his crown—if *only* she could cure his beloved daughter. Naturally, she politely declined such effusive generosity. The King of Spain's daughter had her own crown, not to mention the vast wealth of her entire country at her disposal. Indeed, her motive for coming was one of pure philanthropy.

Upon being led to the young woman who lay wasting away in her bedchamber with her once-vibrant eyes sunken to two shallow pits and her once-lush mouth a rictus of faded black, the Infanta promptly set to work, for there was no time to lose in this battle against approaching death. Smoothing back the sodden straw framing the chalk-white face against the pillow, she ordered a virtual feast to be prepared and brought up to the sickroom—a feast of food and drink sufficient to last for three days and three nights, which would be the amount of time this visitor required to effect her cure. Yet for it to be successful, she needed to be left in complete privacy, without so much as even a brief visit from the patient's devoted father. "No one must be allowed to enter this room," the members of the household were instructed by the Infanta, her tone of voice making it clear that there would be no exceptions. As per her directive, a series of iron bolts were fastened onto both the inside and outside of the bedchamber door, which the Infanta slid into place on her end, as did the anxious Emir on his.

Later that day, as the Spanish Infanta sat silently by the sickbed in the failing light of the window, it came to her notice that the servants had neglected to provide any tinder for the lighting of candles or the stoking of wood in the hearth. With winter close upon them, it was rapidly growing dark, not to mention quite cold. Loathe to spending the evening in pitch-blackness, she began to rummage about in cupboards, hoping that a few pieces of tinder might have been left over from the previous night. The King of Spain's daughter found bottles of ink for writing and sticks of charcoal for drawing, yet could not locate a single twig that could be used to induce light or warmth. Only one door still remained to be opened—and it led not to a wardrobe as expected, but to a small room. A window scarcely of a size to allow a child to pass through it beckoned the Infanta toward it. When she leaned out to look across the sand-covered landscape, she noticed an eerie light flickering in the hazy distance. Fortunately, the little window was not situated so very high up off the ground. With the ladder of rope that had been left forgotten in a corner, she should surely be able to climb down without too much risk to her person. For the increasing chill in the air made this daughter of Spain most eager to secure a source of tinder so that she and her patient would not be forced to pass the next three nights in shivery darkness.

The source of this light revealed itself to be nothing more mysterious than an ordinary cooking fire. An iron cauldron had been placed directly above it, the crackling flames licking its blackened surface like dozens of red tongues. A muscular Turk stood over this great kettle, diligently stirring the contents with a stick. Whatever kind of stew he was in the midst of preparing must have been very thick, since he required both of his hands to agitate it.

"Noble Turk, what is it you are cooking there?" inquired the Infanta, who suddenly found herself quite peckish. She had not eaten any of the fruit and cheese or broth and game delivered to the sickroom door, preferring to save it for the young woman under her care. Yes, she did, indeed, fancy a hot, tasty meal in her empty belly.

"The Khan desired the hand of the Emir's daughter in marriage," explained the sad-eyed Turk, gesturing with his dark head toward the palace. "Only she did not desire his hand in return. Therefore I must stand here and stir this pot as a bewitchment."

The Infanta patted the emissary's continually moving arm in an effort to comfort him, for it had become apparent that he was most distressed over his assignment. "You poor fellow! How tired you must be, stirring for so long."

The Turk nodded miserably, his brawny arms persisting with their steady and monotonous motions. He gripped the base of the cooking tool held out before him with such force that the brown skin covering his fingers had blanched to the white of a fish's belly. "If only someone would render me assistance!" he bemoaned.

"Then it is most providential that I have come along," relied the daughter of Spain. To provide proof of the unfailing generosity of her heart, she placed her hands with some caution upon the stirring stick (for she did not wish to pick up any splinters), thereby replacing those of the exhausted Turk. The texture of the implement felt surprisingly smooth and sleek and not in the least likely to produce injury, its surface pleasantly warm against the tactile flesh of her fingers—although this might have been a result of the poor Turk's having already held it for so prolonged a period. "Am I doing it correctly?"

"Yes, lovely Infanta," sighed the vengeful Khan's emissary, the glittering topaz of his eyes rolling upward inside their almond-shaped sockets. "But perhaps it might be more efficient if you placed your hands end to end, since they are so very, very tiny." And the Turk spoke the truth, for the hands belonging to the King of Spain's daughter failed to cover even half the surface area that he had easily enfolded with one.

Desiring only to be helpful, the Infanta did as was suggested, no longer concerned about catching splinters in her fingers. "Is this acceptable?" she asked, her hands dwarfed by what she held in them.

A garbled groan escaped from the Turk's saliva-moistened lips. Nevertheless, he managed an affirmative nod. "Squeeze while you stir," he directed, his voice a raspy whisper. "That way you shall maintain a better grip."

The Infanta tightened her slender fingers on the cumbersome instrument, which had begun to lengthen and thicken in her diminutive hands. As it turned out, the instructions given her would be of great benefit. Her grasp immediately improved, and she soon found herself wielding the stirring stick with all the culinary skill of the most favored cook in her father's kitchen.

"Now slide your hands up and down," wheezed the Turk, whose nut-brown face had turned a bright shade of henna, as did the implement clutched in the Infanta's hard-working fingers. It had absorbed so much heat from the fire-fueled kettle that her hands needed to move with ever-increasing speed just to prevent her flesh from becoming scorched. This had a profound effect upon its swarthy recipient, whose constricting throat issued a succession of alarming gurgling noises. "Faster, Infanta, faster!" came the Turk's strangled plea.

As she performed her task in accordance with the Turk's wishes, the Spanish Infanta decided to investigate the steaming contents of the black cauldron, only to learn that it contained a rich, creamy stew. Suddenly it occurred to her that she might be able to use the maliciously intended brew to benefit her ailing patient. If the Emir's daughter actually *consumed* the sorcerous stew, it could well produce the opposite effect intended, thus breaking the spell and curing her of her malady rather than being the cause for it. It certainly seemed worth a try, as the young woman's health was fast failing.

By now the Khan's emissary appeared to be breathing with considerable effort, his broad chest heaving beneath his vest with every laborious exhalation. Sweat had broken out upon his brow, the droplets gleaming against the darkly flushed flesh like beads of glass. Placing his large brown hands over the Infanta's tiny pink ones, he guided them on their journey along the ever-increasing length of the stirring instrument, moving faster and faster and inducing this surrogate cook to exert a pressure far beyond her natural strength. The Infanta's hands went skimming across the heated surface with such swiftness and absence of caution that she feared that this time she truly would receive a splinter—and that it would be driven deeply and irretrievably into the tender flesh of her palm, perchance to lie within and fester until she, too, required the healing touch of one like herself.

The Turk's spittle-flecked lips had taken to flapping open and closed like that of a sea bird desperate for a meal. He seemed to be trying to say something, although the words that came out sounded hopelessly foreign to their listener. Despite having been schooled in the tongues of various lands, the Spanish Infanta found this particular form of parlance as alien and complex as if the aggrieved speaker had simply invented it on the spot. She strained her ears to decipher the gurgling syntax, only to have them abruptly assaulted by a primitive cry. The Turk's body froze, his stilled hands crushing hers against the flint-like hardness she had been battling to contain in her fingers. For it had apparently taken on a will of its own, thrusting deeper and deeper into the fire-blackened cauldron until the simmering broth had reached the level of the iron brim, whereupon it went splashing out onto the flames below, nearly dousing them.

Fully expecting the battered flesh of her palms to be chafed and flayed and, indeed, blistered beyond repair, the King of Spain's daughter gingerly unlocked her cramped hands, finding instead a healthy flush of red upon their sticky cushions. She pressed at various points with a tentative fingertip, meeting not the slightest soreness. The exhausted Turk had fallen shuddering to the sandy earth, his hands continuing to clutch what he had used to agitate the stew. For some inexplicable reason, it had greatly diminished in size. To see it now, the Infanta could not imagine how so insignificant a tool had ever been successful in preparing the hearty brew that was cooking inside the iron pot. A drinking vessel of tarnished pewter lay on the sand alongside the panting form of the Khan's emissary, and she borrowed it to collect what she could of the overflowing broth. Although she would not have minded sampling some herself, there could be no time for delay. The Emir had placed his only child's life in her hands — and she dared not fail in her task.

The Spanish Infanta hastened back to the little window and up the ladder of rope, taking care not to spill a single drop of the precious panacea she had stolen from the Turk. Upon reaching the sickbed, she propped up its frail occupant with one arm, holding the pewter cup to the cracked lips she located with the other. The pungent steam that arose from it seemed to activate the young woman's nostrils, for they twitched and flared with hunger. A skeletal hand crept shakily out from beneath the woolen blanket to grasp the life-giving vessel, pressing it more forcefully against the shriveled hole located in the center of the pillow. And in an instant the entirety of the cup's contents had vanished down the patient's wasted gullet.

Encouraged by her success, the Infanta searched her ward's bedchamber for a more sizable container. A chamber pot had been placed discreetly beneath the bed; fortunately it had recently been emptied and scrubbed clean by a servant. With this in hand, she once again sought out the Khan's emissary, whom she found just as before—lying lifelessly upon the sand, his trusty cooking accomplice having by this time dwindled to the size of a twig. As the Infanta strode purposefully toward him, his topaz eyes flickered in recognition...and perhaps something more, for the shrunken stirrer of sorcerous stews managed to produce a few forlorn twitches. Ignoring the Turk and his feeble attempts to once again solicit the aid of her hands, the daughter of the Spanish King used the pewter cup to fill the chamber pot with still more of the creamy brew, emptying out the entire contents of the cauldron in the process. Although it required extra time and effort for her to mount the ladder of rope, this dedicated healer of the sick managed to reach her patient with hardly any spillage.

In the morning, when the Emir's daughter awakened, she was given a second cup of the curative stew, followed by another at lunchtime and yet another at supper. By the third day the young woman's condition was markedly improved. Her face and figure had filled agreeably out, their cavernous hollows only a horrible memory in the concerned eyes of her father. The rosy bloom had returned to her cheeks and lips in full force, and after one final cup the adored daughter of the Emir was up and about as if she had never taken to her bed. Upon witnessing this remarkable transformation, the Emir offered the miracle-producing Infanta all that his desert emirate could provide, and more. Nothing else mattered to him but to have his only child back, happy and healthy. As before, the Infanta declined his generous offer and bid her leave, wishing them both well.

Rather than keeping her promise to return home to her own father, the daughter of the King of Spain returned to the source of the flickering light—and to the Khan's dutiful and topaz-eyed emissary, who had once again taken up the indomitable task of stirring the now-empty cauldron. And it was fortunate for him that she did, for the great pot most assuredly needed filling. ❧

Little Red Riding Hood

Possibly the most analyzed fairy tale in existence, "Little Red Riding Hood" has long been fraught with controversy over its purported sexual meaning. Many experts suggest that the story of the pretty red-hooded girl is but a thinly disguised parable of rape. Yet if one looks back at the tale's more cannibalistic ancestors, it will easily be discovered that this interpretation results more from the cultural notions of sex roles in post-Renaissance Europe than the historical reality.

Having experienced a long oral tradition in Asia, "Little Red Riding Hood" takes its roots from the folktale "Grandaunt Tiger," in which an old woman who consumes human flesh disguises herself as an elderly relative to lure a pair of sisters into her bed the better to eat them. On being offered her sibling's finger, the surviving sister outwits the old woman by claiming a need to relieve herself, thereby making her escape. Widely found in China, Japan, and Korea, "Grandaunt Tiger" likely gave birth to the European oral tale believed to have evolved into the "Little

Red Riding Hood" we know today. In "The Story of Grandmother," a werewolf disguised as a girl's grandmother fools his young victim into cannibalizing her elderly relative, only to coerce her into a ritualistic disrobing—whereupon the girl joins the werewolf in bed. The story ends much the same way as its Chinese counterpart, with the expressed need for urination/defecation, followed by the escape.

Despite its Asian origins, elements in "Little Red Riding Hood" can be traced to tales of antiquity. In the Greek myth of Kronos, the Titan swallows his children, one of whom has been replaced with a stone (a motif featured in the versions by the Brothers Grimm). The use of trickery to deceive the innocent can be seen in a fable by Aesop, where a wolf disguises its voice like that of a mother goat to fool her young. Other elements adding to the tale's development appeared in medieval days, such as in the Latin story "Fecunda Ratis," in which a girl wearing a red cap is found in the company of wolves. Even the distinctive repartee occurring between the wolf disguised as grandmother and the girl has its historical counterpart in the Nordic fable "Elder Edda," where it is explained why Thrym's would-be bride Freyja (the thunder god Thor in disguise) possesses such unladylike physical characteristics.

In Europe, "Little Red Riding Hood" began in the oral tradition during the late Middle Ages in France, northern Italy, and the Tyrol, giving rise to a series of warning tales for children. Indeed, hunger had driven people to commit terrible acts, and the prevalence of superstitious tales circulating in France during early Christianity and the Middle Ages resulted in an epidemic of trials against men accused of being werewolves (and women accused of being witches)—with the accused werewolves routinely charged with devouring children. Yet these so-called werewolves may have existed in primitive cultures as well, which could make "Little Red Riding Hood" far older than initially believed. Puberty and religious initiations practiced by ancient tribal peoples often consisted of sending an initiate into the forest to learn the secrets of nature by reverting to animal ways, only to return reborn to the community. Those who failed might out of hunger resort to cannibalism—and were thus considered werewolves.

With the decline of the witch-hunts in post-seventeenth-century Europe, werewolves lost their significance, which might explain why Charles Perrault changed the figure of a werewolf to that of a common wolf. In "Le Petit Chaperon Rouge," Perrault omits many elements from the oral tale, regarding them as too shocking and improper for his courtly audience. No mention is made of tasting the flesh and blood of grandmother, let alone a desire to urinate or defecate. Nevertheless, Perrault had no qualms about the girl undressing and joining the wolf in bed. A man of his time, he changed the nature of his protagonist to suit prevailing gender roles. Whereas in the folktale the girl is brave and shrewd, by the time of "Le Petit Chaperon Rouge" she has become gullible, vain, and helpless — and, as such, brings her fate on herself for dallying with the wolf.

Perrault's popular version inspired a massive circulation in print, resulting in the tale's reabsorption back into the oral tradition — which later led to "Rotkäppchen" (Little Red Cap) by the Grimms. The brothers likely got their story from a lady-in-waiting raised in the French tradition and already familiar with "Le Petit Chaperon Rouge," only to be doubly influenced by Perrault by means of Ludwig Tieck, who based his verse play *Leben und Tod des kleinen Rotkäppchens* on the French literary tale. Yet while Perrault mostly intended his tale as a form of amusement for adults, the Grimms aspired to a more didactic tone, hence they revised the tale for children, eliminating any erotic undertones — and, in the process, stressing the evils of unsanctioned conduct. For the girl's freedom from restraint as she frolics through the forest enjoying nature (and perhaps her own budding sexuality) was not a thing to be encouraged in the nineteenth century. The only allusion to any prior sexual content seems to be in a later version of "Rotkäppchen," in which the rescuing huntsman calls the wolf an "old sinner" — an expression used to represent one who seduces, particularly young girls.

Having already followed in the footsteps of the Grimms by taking inspiration from their standard version of "Little Red Riding Hood," I find that I have apparently done so again. Only rather than stopping with the wolf, I have extended the lecherous qualities of the Grimms' "old sinner" to those of a less furry nature. ❧

Little Red Riding Hood

THERE WAS ONCE A YOUNG LASS WHO owned a hood of the reddest and plushest velvet. She wore it upon her pretty head at every opportunity, for it had become her most treasured possession. Mind you, this was no ordinary shop-bought hood, but a special one presented to her as a gift by her grandmother, who had toiled many long hours stitching it with failing eyes and quivering fingers. Indeed, its delighted recipient could rarely be seen going anywhere without it. The hood suited to perfection her fair coloring and bright eyes, the intense shade of red kindling their innocent blue into two twinkling sapphire stars. With such a distinctive fashion trademark, this much-favored granddaughter came to be known as *Little Red Riding Hood*.

Or, to those with whom she was on more intimate terms: *Red*.

Now it so happened that Red adored her elderly relative, therefore she made no protest when called upon by her mother to deliver some teacakes and a pot of strawberry jam to the old woman, who had been feeling poorly and could not leave her sickbed. "Now, set out before the sun grows too hot," came the maternal warning. "And mind not to stray from the path, as thou might suffer a mischief." Of course the dutiful daughter promised to do just as her mother said, although she could not for the life of her imagine what sort of mischief could possibly befall her upon such a fine spring morn. However, the mother knew her offspring far better than her mildly creased brow indicated; residing in a village, it usually proved difficult to keep one's activities a secret.

Grandmother lived in a tiny, shingled cottage set in the middle of a vast woodland, a fair distance from the bustling village of her granddaughter. Armed with her precious gifts, which would be certain to add cheer to the convalescing woman's day, Little Red Riding Hood sallied happily forth on her journey. The distance and the isolation did not for a moment concern her. She liked taking solitary strolls along the periphery of the wood, although she had never ventured out this far all on her own. Yet it seemed like such a grand day to be strolling among the invigorating scents of pine and rain-soaked earth that any dangers awaiting her would surely be minimal. Besides, Red had heard that the wood contained handsome young huntsmen and thought it might be of benefit to ascertain the truth of this claim, since those of the local variety were already familiar to her. Many a time did she go skipping by the village tavern in hopes of meeting one of its rugged patrons, her red-hooded presence in the vicinity inspiring considerable gossip, which undoubtedly accounted for this sudden dispatch to Grandmother's. Indeed, Red had become very well known in huntsmen's circles.

Just as she would likewise become well known in other circles.... Despite the fact that she had no legitimate business in the vicinity, Red frequently made a point of passing a busy construction site located down by the docks on the east end of the village—a place notorious for its unsavory activities and equally unsavory characters, several of whom appeared to have been hired as laborers. These men worked outdoors in the open, balancing precariously upon planks of wood as they slathered mortar onto bricks and joined them together to form sections of wall. Beads of sweat glistened like diamonds on their sun-bronzed flesh. They had stripped down to their dungarees in the heat of their labors, exposing their naked chests and backs to onlookers. The pretty, red-hooded presence of Little Red Riding Hood was most inconsistent with these rough and grubby surroundings, to say nothing of attracting the kind of attention on which her mother would likely have frowned. For each time she approached the brick-strewn rubble of the construction site, the workers called down to her in greeting: "Oy, Red—show us yer hood!" Whereupon they grabbed hold of the bulges at the front of their sweat-stained dungarees, shaking them about as they blew her a noisy kiss. In response, the beneficiary of this friendly salutation twirled merrily about, leaving her sweaty admirers with the memory of a forbidden flash of skirts…and what had lain beneath.

As the hooded lass made her carefree way along the woodland path toward Grandmother's cottage, the wind of a departing wintertime set the hem of her garments aflutter. Giggling good-naturedly, she smoothed her skirts back down to rest flatly and neatly against her hips, only to be forced to repeat the process again and again with each successive gust until she ultimately abandoned her efforts. For who was there to take heed? Red quite enjoyed the stimulating sensation of winter's cold breath swirling about the bare flesh of her thighs and nether regions. To derive the maximum benefit possible, she hitched up her dirndl skirt and ruffled pinafore to better appreciate what the season had to offer, fully aware that by doing so she was providing the casual observer with amusements of an altogether different nature. Indeed, Little Red Riding Hood took tremendous delight in displaying what others may have regarded as shameful.

Beneath her cherished hood, Red's face glowed with all the luminosity of a full moon, her eyes a sparkling set of perfectly matched gemstones against the surrounding mantle of red velvet. Several wisps of springy yellow curls escaped to frame her face. Rather than tucking them back up underneath the hood as modesty would have advised, she allowed them to have their freedom. How wonderful it felt to suddenly be unburdened by the opinions of others! Creatures both great and small emerged to watch this blithe damsel as she passed, hanging precariously from the branches of trees or scuttering up from holes dug into the winter-encrusted earth. Perhaps it was to be expected that this spirited bearer of gifts should come to the attention of the local wolf, who made it his vocation to be conversant with the business of the wood.

Having never before made the creature's acquaintance, Red had no knowledge of the wickedness of his character and his cunning lupine ways. Therefore, when he stepped boldly out from behind the frosted trunk of a fir, she experienced neither fear nor distrust. "Good day, my pretty one," the wolf greeted, his grin framing sharp yellow teeth whose greatest desire was to sample the supple young flesh he had seen parading with such insouciance through the shadowy woodland.

"And good day unto thee, kind sir," answered Little Red Riding Hood with an amiable nod. She had always been told by her mother to demonstrate the utmost in politeness in her dealings with others, even if those others might only be strangers. Of late, though, her mother had been given much cause to regret such counsel — if the village gossips were to be believed. Since Red had no reason to be wary of this pitifully unprepossessing creature whose intentions seemed merely to while away a few dull moments of the morning engaging in carefree banter, she acted in the manner most natural to her.

"And where art thou off to on so fine a day?" inquired the wolf, his sanguineous eyes gleaming with an unwholesomeness far beyond the worst imaginings of the mother of his chitchat partner.

"I am going to visit my gran, who is feeling poorly and hath not the strength to leave her bed."

"Indeed…" mused this hirsute busybody of the woodland, his broad grin never once wavering. A trickle of saliva had begun to make an escape from his darkly furred mouth, and a carmine tongue darted forth to collect it before it could cause offense. "And where might she live, thine old granny?"

"In a cottage ringed by hazel bushes and situated beneath three large oak trees. It is the only dwelling in the whole wood." Red stated this with pride, as if the old woman's isolation were a thing of status.

The wolf nodded thoughtfully, scarcely able to contain his mounting excitement. "Pray, may one be so presumptuous as to inquire what treasures thou hast got hidden there?" For the hooded lass appeared to be in the process of transporting a receptacle of some sort. With any luck, it might contain something tasty to eat. The poor wolf was growing quite weary of a diet of small animals and the occasional bit of gristle procured from a woodland neighbor's leftovers.

Deliberately misinterpreting the object of the inquisitive creature's interest — for she could never resist an opportunity to flaunt herself — Red raised up the hems of her skirts and pinafore, revealing to a vigilant pair of eyes a little cherry. It had been the source of great pleasure as she went skipping along the earthen pathway with her garments aflutter, just as it had been when she twirled about for the bricklayers at the construction site, each of whom had been most effusive in his praise. It boasted a hood of the same shade of red as the one she wore upon her head, and as the gift-bearing granddaughter stood indulgently before the wolf, a gust of wind inspired this velvety sheath to flutter festively in the breeze. All at once the sinewy legs of the beast threatened to give way beneath his weight. This must be the hooded lass of whom he had heard all the huntsmen speak. And she had just revealed to him a treat for which his discontented palate had been desperately longing.

A fruit of unparalleled glossiness sprouted forth from a downy vale, its plump contours bursting with a succulent sweetness that caused its beholder to sway in drunken delirium. This lone harvest had reached the perfect pinnacle of ripeness, all but demanding to be plucked and, indeed, consumed. *This pretty maiden shall provide me with a very choice morsel,* mused the creature with an impassioned shudder. *Yet perchance if I am clever, I might also manage to secure a somewhat less tender bill of fare to help remove the edge from my appetite.* For in having just set his lupine sights upon Grandmother, the greedy beast planned to save the juicy tidbit before him for dessert. "My, what a nice little hood thou hast there," remarked its furry admirer in a strangled tone, the unwavering direction of his stare clearly indicative of which hood he meant. "Wherever did its charming owner manage to acquire it?"

"Forsooth, I cannot say. For it has always been there whenever I look beneath my skirts."

Aye, it shall not be there for long! the wolf snickered inwardly, an image of the blue-eyed damsel staring up her skirts and discovering a vacancy in this once-fertile dell giving him even more to chortle about.

Red coughed as if trying to free something from her throat, her patience with the beast wearing dangerously thin. "Sir, hast thou perchance spied any young huntsmen about?" she interrogated, hoping this unprepossessing creature might actually be of some use to her. After all, she had better things to do than pass the time holding up her skirts for silly wolves. She needed to make the obligatory visit to Grandmother, then get on with the *real* business of the day.

"*Huntsmen?* Nay, there are no huntsmen in this wood," lied the wolf, in whose best interest it was to avoid such bloodthirsty individuals in the first place. Putting forth a courtly bow, he accompanied Little Red Riding Hood through the wood, pointing out all the colorful flowers that had turned their faces toward the slanted rays of the sun. "Perhaps thine old granny might like a nosegay," he suggested, his motive being to delay the granddaughter's arrival at the old woman's cottage, which would grant him the running start he required.

Red gazed all around her, the melodic singing of birds and the busy buzzing of bees seeming to encourage her in this pursuit. Why, a cheerful bunch of blooms sounded the very cure for her ailing relation. Perhaps she might even locate a blossom whose narcoleptic petals could be brewed into a tea, thereby sending the old woman to sleep, at which time her gift-bearing granddaughter could make her escape. For indeed, Red had no wish to listen to laments of aching joints and failing eyes when there might be handsome young huntsmen about.

With this in mind, the dutiful daughter disobeyed her mother's strict instructions, leaving behind the wolf and the earthen pathway so that she could set about collecting the most perfect and beauteous of blossoms. With each stem she pulled from the earth, yet another floral specimen of greater beauty sprang up within her line of vision, drawing her deeper and deeper into the wood and farther and farther away from the path that would have taken her to Grandmother. To keep her skirts and pinafore from getting soiled, Red tucked them up out of the way, which would also prove advantageous in the event a huntsman might be passing, since she did not entirely believe the wolf's protestations to the contrary.

Meanwhile, the crafty creature dispatched himself with lightning swiftness to the tiny, shingled cottage surrounded by its hedge of hazel bushes and sheltered beneath three large oaks. Indeed,

Grandmother's residence was impossible to miss. Aside from being the only dwelling for leagues around, the eaves of the cottage had been strung with lanterns that blazed both day and night, serving as beacons for those who passed. As the wolf knocked with false familiarity upon the front door, he wondered what kind of foolish old woman bothered with outdoor lighting in the middle of a sunny day, especially in such a low-crime area.

"Who goes there?" came a creaky voice from inside.

The wolf cleared his throat in readiness to reply, only to be interrupted before he could do so.

"Art thou a huntsman?" The voice sounded slightly stronger the second time, the note of hope in it unmistakable. It was followed by a clamorous clattering and clanging, as if the occupant of the cottage was in the midst of preparing for an unexpected visitor.

The wolf shook his furry head in amusement, for it appeared that the old woman possessed the same aspirations as her lively granddaughter. Of course he had no way of knowing that Grandmother had in her youth worked in a bawdy house on the south bank of the village docks — an establishment heavily frequented by huntsmen. It was in these very surroundings that the fertile seed of some nameless huntsman had caused her to beget Little Red Riding Hood's mother, a fact that probably accounted for the latter's concerned vigilance for her red-hooded daughter.

"'Tis I, Little Red Riding Hood," answered the wolf in the lilting soprano of the young lass he had met in the wood. "I have brought some nice teacakes and a pot of tasty strawberry jam."

The clamor inside the cottage abruptly ceased, only to be replaced by a deep sigh. "Alas, I am far too ill to greet thee properly. Pray, lift up on the latch and come hither," instructed Grandmother from her sickbed of pink satin, a ragged cough setting her ancient bones to rattling within their cage of withered flesh. Before she could haul herself up into a sitting position, a monstrous figure of fur loomed over her. Fortunately a pair of clouded eyes saved the ailing woman from the horror that would within moments befall her.

The wolf soon made himself comfortable upon the slippery, satin-covered mattress, adjusting the unfamiliar garments of his most recent repast on his oversized limbs. He placed Grandmother's floppy nightcap atop his large head, taking care to tuck his ears beneath it. Because of their pointy nature, they sprang right back out again, and any further attempts to camouflage them were subsequently abandoned. Thusly settled, the sly creature pulled closed the bed curtains, sealing off both himself and the bed in a cozy cocoon of chiffon.

Unable to locate any blossoms whose petals might send Grandmother into an expeditious slumber, Little Red Riding Hood made her way back to the foot-path leading to the cottage, resigned to an afternoon of listening to the old woman croak out a detailed description of each malady. Upon arriving, she discovered the front door standing wide open and the interior of the tiny cottage silent save for the sound of heavy breathing. "Hello!" she called cheerfully, receiving no response. Perhaps Grandmother was sleeping and had not heard her young visitor arrive, in which case Red could leave behind her gifts and beat a hasty retreat.

Placing her burdens upon the bedside table alongside the cup used to hold the old woman's teeth, Little Red Riding Hood carefully drew back the wispy curtains enclosing the bed so as not to disturb her relative. Rather than snoring peacefully, Grandmother lay in a slothful sprawl against the pink-satin sheets with her garments all askew, a salacious expression distorting her bristled face. Never had the granddaughter seen the old woman in such a state, and she wondered if her elderly relation might have taken to ingesting some of the strange mushrooms one often stumbled upon in the wood. "Why, Grandmother, what big ears thou hast!" Red cried in astonishment, for they stuck up most uncharacteristically.

"All the better to hear thee with," came the cackling reply, the bloodshot eyes beneath the nightcap widening as the red-hooded visitor moved closer.

"Why, Grandmother, what big eyes thou hast!"

"All the better to see thee with," the wolf replied with a suggestive wink, his ungrandmotherly paws fluttering in a flurry of palsy at his sides.

"Why, Grandmother, what big hands thou hast!"

"All the better to hug thee with," croaked the disheveled figure in the bed, reaching out with false affection toward Little Red Riding Hood, the pink-satin duvet working its way downward toward this sly impostor's furry haunches. A furious thumping had begun against his partially sated belly, its point of origin growing larger and larger at the thought of what lay beneath the pretty granddaughter's skirts.

"Why, Grandmother, what a portly member thou hast!" squealed Red. For the great hairy thing writhing and wriggling before her bore scant resemblance to the sleek specimens belonging to the handsome young huntsmen from the village. She wondered whether this might be characteristic of those who lived in the wood — in which case she would henceforward confine her activities to the village!

The wolf thrust his lap lewdly upward. "All the better to fuck thee with," he growled, his tongue darting in and out of his salivating maw.

Such unseemly language and gestures were not at all what Red expected from a sickly old woman. In fact, up until this moment they had only been directed toward her by the sweaty bricklayers down at the docks. However, she soon realized that there was something else very much out of the ordinary about her aged relative. "Why, Grandmother, what a big mouth thou hast!"

Now *this* was what the cunning beast had been waiting for. He sprang forth from Grandmother's satin-covered sickbed, hurling Little Red Riding Hood to the floor and swallowing in all its flavorful and hooded entirety the savory morsel that had been the cause of so much pleasant rumination on this fine day. To his delight, it had grown even riper since morning, and his carmine tongue fed greedily upon the sweet juices flowing abundantly out from beneath where it sprouted. How wise he had been to save this delicacy for dessert!

Once the wolf's hunger had finally been appeased, he returned to Grandmother's bed for a much-needed rest, his satisfied snores shaking the cottage walls and dislodging several shingles from the roof. He would sleep so soundly that he failed to hear the approaching footsteps of a huntsman.

Attracted by the blaze of lanterns and alarmed by the discordant noises coming from within, this concerned citizen decided to check on the cottage's elderly occupant. He knew that the woman lived alone and was of a very advanced age. He also knew she had a granddaughter, for he had heard many stories in the village tavern about the young damsel's famous red hoods, one of which she did not wear upon her head. Intending to get into the old woman's good graces, the huntsman brushed the woodland detritus from his garments and straightened his feather-tipped cap before making his approach. Only whom should he discover snoring contentedly in Grandmother's bed and wearing

Grandmother's clothing but the crafty wolf he had tirelessly pursued for far too many days? "Ah-*ha!*" cried the huntsman in victory. "I have found thee, infernal rascal!"

As he cocked his gun in readiness to fire off a shot, it suddenly occurred to the huntsman that this plague of fleas and fur might have eaten the feeble old thing in whose pink-satin bed it had taken up residence. So, setting down the weapon, he reached into his sheath for his knife and before the snoring beast realized what was happening, the huntsman proceeded to carve a line down the wolf's meal-swollen belly. A bright flash of red appeared within the incision, and as he continued to draw the blade steadily downward, the huntsman saw what looked to be a hood of red velvet. Before he could reflect more fully upon an explanation for its presence, out leapt the nimble figure of a pretty lass.

"Oh, kind sir, I thank thee with all my heart!" cried Little Red Riding Hood. "For it was black as pitch in there and smelled unspeakably!"

"I am pleased to have been of assistance," bowed the huntsman, tipping his feathered cap in respect. The eyes of the little damsel who had occupied the wolf's fattened belly reminded him of stars in a winter night's sky, so brilliantly and with such clarity did they shine. With faltering fingers, he reached out to touch the pale softness of her cheek, surprised that so innocently intended a gesture should leave him quaking like when he was a young lad on his first visit to the bawdy house down by the village docks.

Red stepped out of the steaming viscera of her prison, using the hems of her skirts and pinafore to dry the grateful tears from her eyes. She spent several long moments doing so, peering stealthily through the weave of the cloth to gauge the huntsman's reaction. In the event his eyesight was not up to usual huntsmen standards, she raised up one foot and set it atop the fallen wolf, bringing further into the light what even a blind man could not have failed to miss.

All at once this helpful passerby spied what had been the focus of the wolf's desperate hunger. A cherry of mouth-watering proportions burst forth from a modest garden, sporting a hood even brighter and redder than the one atop the wearer's head. It had been draped quite jauntily, leaving much of the pulpy flesh beneath exposed to view and effecting considerable consternation in the mind and body of its beholder, who at this moment felt very much like a wolf himself. This must be the lass of whom he had heard his fellow huntsmen speak.

Before the huntsman could pluck the fruit out from the downy vale and sink his yearning teeth into its delicate barrier of skin, a garbled squawking from within the depths of the wolf's knife-rent belly stayed his hand. Unless he was mistaken, it sounded like the cries of an old woman. Although he would have preferred to ignore them, they stubbornly refused to be ignored. On the contrary, the cries gained in both intensity and pitch, becoming a monotonous series of *Help me*'s that grew ever more impatient and irate as he dawdled. *Dash the feeble old witch!* the huntsman grumbled inwardly, praying for the incessant wails to cease before the doubly hooded lass had taken heed of them and let her skirts back down. At the moment this Good Samaritan had far more pressing matters deserving of his attention than undertaking another rescue. The saliva of desire pooled in his mouth, making him giddy as a drunkard. How could he draw another breath without at least a little nibble upon the glossy riches flaunting themselves beneath a heart-stopping flash of skirts?

"Art thou a huntsman?" came a muffled voice, which was followed by the sight of arthritic fingers as Grandmother clawed at the bloodied sides of the wound the huntsman's knife had created. Indeed, she struggled with a spryness long unknown to her, for she recognized the feathered cap of a huntsman when she saw one. Apparently all that money from her old-age pension that had gone toward the cost and mainte-nance of the lanterns had finally paid itself back.

Ergo the huntsman found himself obliged to reach inside the wolf's fetid belly to save its remaining occupant. With the same blade that had freed its two unwitting victims, he promptly skinned the beast, cer-tain that its pelt would look quite elegant upon the floor before his hearth, to say nothing of providing comfort for whoever might wish to lie beside the fire. As he departed the cottage with a hearty wave, he thought that perhaps one day the old woman's granddaughter might choose to pay a call to offer her thanks, at which time the huntsman planned to seize the opportunity to sample what had ultimately cost the wolf his life.

Grandmother was at last allowed to enjoy the teacakes and strawberry jam Little Red Riding Hood had brought from home, pausing between bites to inquire with unprecedented vigor as to the whereabouts of the handsome young huntsman who had been their rescuer. As for Red, she had begun to regret that the old woman had not been left inside the wolf's stinking belly. Of course, had she known about the wolf's pelt being slated for use as a rug, she might not have been so keen to pursue a relationship with the huntsman. Although Red harbored no great fondness for wolves, she disapproved most heartily of animal fur's being employed as a form of decoration.

After many sunrises had passed, another wolf with a wicked gleam in his sanguinary eye accosted Little Red Riding Hood on her way to Grandmother's. Ignoring his friendly *good day*, she kept straight to the footpath, striding resolutely onward with her skirts dancing high about her thighs. Aside from being very much on her guard against lupine lechers, she knew that the hunting season was now in full swing. Reaching Grandmother's cottage unmolested, Red rapped soundly upon the door, knowing that the old woman's hearing was fast failing.

"Art thou a huntsman?" came a raspy, albeit hopeful voice from inside.

"'Tis I, Little Red Riding Hood," the red-hooded caller replied in exasperation.

Grandmother could not hide her crestfallen expression at seeing the nubile young figure of her granddaughter breezing through the door. For she was also well aware that the hunting season had begun and did not think it at all unreasonable that a weary huntsman might seek out her tiny abode for a brief repast or possibly even a bed for the night. In anticipation of such an occurrence, the old woman had appealed to her granddaughter several times to bring with her a bottle of French scent on the occasion of her next visit, only to be deluged with yet another delivery of stale teacakes and sour jam. It would seem that the lass believed her mind to be as feeble as her body!

As grandmother and granddaughter sat in the parlor drinking their tea and eating their teacakes, Red relayed what had just transpired with the wolf. Not wanting to take any chances, the two conspired to draw the bolt across the door, refusing to open it to this opportunistic creature who—like his less auspicious predecessor—proclaimed himself to be Little Red Riding Hood with some teacakes and jam for Grandmother.

Possessing a highly persistent nature that would ultimately be the cause of his downfall, the wolf refused to be put off by his cold reception. Had he been wiser, he might have declared himself to be a huntsman, thereby guaranteeing the door being thrown open in welcome. Instead, this furry trespasser prowled around the hazel bushes, eventually clambering up onto the shingled roof of the cottage to wait out the remains of the day. Darkness was close upon them, and the old woman's granddaughter would soon be making her way home, granting the sly beast his opportunity to strike. He had overheard many tantalizing tales about the succulent, rosy delicacy beneath the charming damsel's skirts, the huntsman who had recently murdered his lupine colleague being most loose-lipped when in the company of his fellow killers.

Grandmother guessed the wolf's clever scheme from the scuttering-about taking place above her and her granddaughter's heads. It sounded like the sneaky beast was plotting to slip down through the chimney, whereupon they would both be done for. Wishing to spare her granddaughter such a fate, the elder pushed the younger out the door. That was when Little Red Riding Hood saw the wolf placing one of his furry feet inside the chimney. Obviously she could not leave her poor old gran behind to face certain death, so she did the only thing she could think of. She sprang out into full view of the beast, calling up to him a succession of nasty jeers and dancing fearlessly about with her skirts held high in taunting merriment. While she was at it, perhaps she might also catch the attention of a passing huntsman, in which case her efforts would be doubly rewarded.

The wolf peered eagerly down over the lantern-lighted eaves of the roof, leaning farther and farther out in an attempt to glimpse the famous hood of which the chatty huntsman had spoken with such lip-smacking relish. The previous night's rain had left the mossy shingles quite slippery, and suddenly he felt himself lose his footing. The wolf went tumbling to the ground, landing upon his head and dying instantly.

Grandmother cooked him up for that evening's supper, convinced that the smell of fresh wolf stew would bring a huntsman to her door. Being a strict vegetarian, Red declined to stay — much to the relief of her grandmother, who could do without the competition. After helping the old woman put a fresh set of pink-satin sheets upon the bed, Little Red Riding Hood went skipping merrily home through the woodland, hoping to meet a huntsman or two along the way with a mind to pluck her hooded cherry. ❧

THE TRAVELING COMPANION

"The Traveling Companion" has been attributed to many tellers of tales and appears in many variants worldwide. Classified as a riddle tale, it features as its most popular character the riddle princess, who either poses a riddle or solves it. A number of these tales got their start in India, making their way into Persia, North Africa, and Europe. Yet it would be in Scandinavia that this tale was creatively reworked into what is likely the most widely known riddle tale of all time.

Considered more a writer than a collector of fairy tales, Hans Christian Andersen based his version of "The Traveling Companion" on the Danish folktale "The Dead Man's Help." Although the theme of upward social mobility has always been prevalent in folktales, for Andersen it seems to have held particular importance. A social outsider with a slavish admiration for royalty (for he was the humble son of a peasant cobbler), Andersen was attracted to stories that contained protagonists of lesser standing who sought the attentions of a beautiful princess.

By reaching for the unattainable, his characters likewise reflected his own life.

Because of the late conversion of the populace to Christianity, the countries of Scandinavia developed more independently than those in the rest of Europe. This resulted in a more authentic form of folklore, with the Scandinavian folktales evolving primarily from ancient mythologies and the influence of the landscape rather than from external influences. Of course, exceptions can always be found. Although Andersen patterned his story on a folktale from his native land, the adventures of his two traveling companions closely parallel a tale from Brittany. Perhaps the most significant element in this variant is the presence of the magic potion a soldier uses to help a young nobleman who wishes to put forth a riddle to a princess—a magic potion featured quite prominently in Andersen. Had it not been for its existence, Poor Johannes might never have been successful in winning the princess. This use of alchemy can also be seen in the animation of the puppets, indicating a possible connection to primitive cultures, whose folklore was filled with elements relating to the magical and metamorphic.

Like its Danish counterpart, Grimms' traveling duo in "Das Rätsel" (The riddle) set off on an adventure, which leads to the proverbial princess, who offers the challenge that she would accept as husband any man who proposes to her a riddle she cannot solve. In the manner of Andersen's princess, the German one relied on methods not entirely ethical in her desire to solve the riddle, taking the bold action of sitting alongside the traveler as he lay asleep in bed in hopes that he might divulge the answer—an act the puritanical Grimms and their editors somehow appeared to have missed as inappropriate.

However, not much else would be missed. Like those who worked on the *Kinder- und Hausmärchen,* many editors and translators of Andersen's tales came from the Victorian age, therefore any indicators of passion or eroticism failed to make it into print. Even a kiss on the mouth would be modified into a kiss on the cheek. Such pristine examples of physical emotion can be seen in a number of fairy tales that have made their way through the Victorian age (and past the Victorian editor). Be that as it may, neither Andersen nor his editors displayed any objection to physical violence, as for example Poor Johannes's traveling companion makes ample use of the switch against the riddle-posing princess, even going so far as to draw blood.

This punitive whipping with birches can be traced to the old peasant tradition of the "wedding bath." A purification ritual designed to cleanse the bride of harmful influences (such as the princess's contact with the troll), the process consists of the bride being whipped until all evils have been purged from her, whereupon she is bathed with milk. Indeed, it appears that this practice may have been widespread enough to have made its way into folk literature—and hence into "The Traveling Companion."

In keeping with the spirit of Andersen, I, too, have made generous use of certain punitive measures, for, like the Danish princess, the one in my version protests unconvincingly (if at all) against their frequency. ❧

The Traveling Companion

POOR JOHANNES WAS A GOOD SON. Therefore he saw to it that his father was placed respectfully beneath the rich green earth when Death arrived to claim him. With little remaining to keep him behind but memories and the freshly turned soil of his father's grave, the bereaved son decided to seek his fortune far from the safe environs of home and all that he had ever known in his young life. As the sun cast its golden rays upon the breeze-swept leaves in the churchyard, Johannes bid his father a final farewell, certain they would meet again in the afterlife.

The next morning, the orphan packed a small parcel containing everything he owned in the world. After hiding his modest patrimony within his belt, he embarked upon his adventure. Since Poor Johannes had never been away from the village of his father, he allowed himself to be guided by the experienced flutters of doves' wings. The faces of the flowers in the fields smiled their encouragement as he passed, straining their slender necks to receive the kiss of the sun against their petaled cheeks. As darkness fell, Johannes was obliged to make for himself a bed in a haystack. Yet not even this untoward accommodation could diminish his good cheer, for above him he had the moonlit sky and beside him the sweet fragrance of wild roses and below him the comforting rush-and-tumble of the river.

The insistent tolling of bells finally roused Poor Johannes from his peaceful slumber. It was Sunday morning, and the farmers and their families could be seen wearing their best garments as they walked toward a tiny chapel in the misty distance. The orphan joined the procession, intending to offer a prayer for his father. As he approached the gate, he suddenly noticed a beggar loitering outside the churchyard. Despite the fellow's destitute appearance and out-stretched palms, none of the parishioners paid him any mind. Without a moment's thought for his own difficulties, Johannes bestowed upon the bedraggled specimen all the silver coins he had in his belt — indeed, nearly half of his paternal legacy — and then quickly rejoined the others as they entered the chapel. Exhilarated by his selfless act of charity, Johannes remained oblivious to the snickers of the beggar, who flagged down a passing hackney coach and jumped inside, followed by a pair of heavily painted women who had been waiting hopefully on the corner.

Later that afternoon a frightful storm erupted, and the fatherless young traveler decided to seek shel-ter before its black wrath engulfed him completely. Arriving at another little chapel, he went inside to wait out the night in an available pew. However, he was awakened shortly after midnight by a heated argument, the subject of which concerned a dead man in a coffin. Unable to bear the sound of voices raised in anger, Poor Johannes intervened at once, only to learn that the coffin's occupant had cheated the quarrelers out of money owed to them by dying before the debt could be paid. As a result, the men wished to cast the deceased out into the rain and chop up his coffin for firewood. Having been a good son to his own father, Johannes could not permit such a sacrilege to be committed upon the father of another, so he made an offer of money to pay off the debt—the entire remainder of his inheritance—the agreement being that the debtees leave the debtor in peace. Chuckling at this outsider's soft-headedness, the men agreed, snatching the precious gold coins from Johannes's outstretched palm and leaving him in the company of the dead, who had already been left in the coffin far longer than advisable.

Once the storm had seen fit to blow off toward the distant foothills, Poor Johannes set off once again without waiting for the arrival of morning, relieved to be leaving behind the gamy remains of the chapel's lifeless parishioner. A silvery moon lighted his way, showing the orphan that he was not alone. Naked elves frolicked to all sides of him, undisturbed by his presence in their wooded glen. They danced around him in carefree circles, which caused the young wanderer's spirits to rise and his step to bounce. Indeed, he did not even take offense when they used their tiny elfin nozzles to spray him with their special elves' milk, for they said it brought prosperity—and prosperity was exactly what Poor Johannes needed. As the moon began to relinquish its post to the sun, the wee creatures scurried back inside the flower blossoms in which they lived, and Poor Johannes emerged from the shadowy glen into the full bright yellow of morning. Before he could adjust his eyes to the light, a voice greeted him heartily, inquiring of his destination.

"I am but a poor orphan out to seek my fortune in the world," answered Johannes, the stark contrast between his previous actions and his stated objective apparently lost on him.

"Aye, I am of a like enterprise. Shall we keep company together?"

Poor Johannes eagerly agreed, pleased to have found a companion upon his lonesome journey. The two immediately became fast friends, although it would soon become evident that this congenial stranger was very much the wiser of the pair. He had traveled the world many times over and knew intimately of its capricious nature. In fact, there seemed to be no subject unknown to him.

As the sun lifted itself high above their heads, the travelers settled their weary limbs beneath the shade of a tree to partake of a meal, which had been thoughtfully brought forth from the stranger's knapsack. At the same time, an old woman could be seen hobbling up the grassy slope toward them, the weighty burden of wood upon her back causing her to become more stooped than she already was. She came to a groaning halt before the two lunchers and leaned unsteadily upon her walking stick, the logs shifting threateningly along the hump of her spine.

"Good day," replied Poor Johannes, tipping his hat respectfully as his father had taught him.

The old woman nodded warily, suspicious that this fresh-faced young laddie and his older and more polished accomplice might be of a mind to steal her handbag, which dangled precariously from one of the logs. While she stood there perusing them with eyes that had long ago lost their focus, a fly stopped to rest upon the tip of her nose. Reaching up to shoo it away, she lost her hold on her walking stick and collapsed in a spindly heap at their feet. From the grievous manner in which she shrieked, the two travelers realized that the old woman had broken her leg.

Johannes proposed they carry her home, for she would perish if left to her own devices. However, his worldly-wise friend appeared to have something different in mind. He rummaged around inside the worn burlap of his knapsack until his hand emerged with a jar, which he declared to be a special salve capable of curing any malady—including that of a broken leg. Scooping up a portion of the ointment in his fingers, Johannes's traveling companion proceeded to rub it high up beneath the broken-limbed woman's skirts. Almost immediately she began to writhe and moan. The leg that had lain broken and useless stretched slowly out and away from its healthier twin, twitching and jiggling with renewed life. The jar's benevolent custodian continued with his ministrations, no doubt determined that the cure should be complete. By now the old woman's legs were kicking like those of an excited colt, her withered thighs flung wide as she endured her restorative treatment from this stranger. With a cry like that of crackling parchment, she sprang up from the ground and sprinted off down the hill, leaving a trail of logs in her wake.

With their bellies full and a good deed done, the two travelers continued on their way, moving toward a range of dark mountains whose tall peaks snagged the passing clouds. Although they looked fairly near, it would require the entirety of a day to reach the dense black forest that marked the entry point to the great metropolis located at the far side of the range. Ever mindful of the dwindling daylight and the resultant drop in temperature, Poor Johannes and his companion decided to avail themselves of a modest inn they found along the way. A puppetmaster was in the process of setting up a little theater inside the taproom, and everyone had gathered around to watch, including the inn's new arrivals. Unfortunately, the burly butcher from the village and his slobbering bulldog chose to settle themselves directly before the miniature stage, thus procuring for themselves the best seats in the house and blocking a good many views, including that of Poor Johannes, who contented himself with half a view rather than complain.

The play got under way, its central characters being those of a king and queen. Other dolls had been positioned at points to the right and left, playing the roles of courtiers and ladies-in-waiting. As the queen arose from her throne and glided crossways over the miniature stage, the bulldog suddenly let loose with an angry barking, only to bound forward and, hence, away from the reach of its master. Seizing the delicate figure of the queen within its powerful jaws, the animal gnashed its sharp teeth together, cracking the puppet at the neck. Satisfied with the carnage, the dog trotted proudly back to the butcher, whereupon the two made a hasty exit—although not before alerting the innkeeper that the boyish presence of Poor Johannes would provide payment for the chalk marks that had accrued upon the slate beside the butcher's name.

The show having reached its premature conclusion, the audience dispersed, leaving the inconsolable puppetmaster on his own with his broken queen. With great tenderness, he fitted her serenely smiling head back atop the jagged remains of neck, not daring to blink for fear it might roll off again. At that moment the stranger who accompanied Poor Johannes stepped forward, promising that all would be put to rights. As

the puppet man looked doubtfully on, the worldly
traveler removed from his knapsack the very same jar
of ointment that had cured the old wood-collector's
broken leg. Yet rather than concentrating the mysterious unguent's application upon the doll's headless
neck, he rubbed it high up beneath its skirts in the
same location he had the old woman.

Like magic, the puppet-queen came to life. Her
disseevered head knitted itself back onto the splintered
shards of her neck, leaving behind not a mark to indicate it had ever been separated. Fully restored to its
rightful place, the doll's tiara-crowned head rolled
recklessly about as she kicked her wooden legs and
pumped her wooden arms—and all without the
slightest pull upon her strings. The puppetmaster was
absolutely delighted, for no longer did he need to
orchestrate the movements of the queen doll at all; she
could move about entirely on her own and, indeed,
with a will of her own.

Later, after everyone at the inn had retired for
the night, a lamentable sighing could be heard in the
taproom. It carried on for so long that it roused the
sleepers from their beds. Concerned that the bulldog
might have returned, the puppet man sought out his
little theater, since it was here whence the sighing
seemed to originate. Yet what he discovered would
have made him question the rightness of his mind had
not the two travelers also borne witness. Scattered
every which way across the stage were the puppets,

their wooden limbs intertwined like a heap of kindling. The king and his courtiers along with the queen's ladies-in-waiting had been reduced to a jumble of confusion. It was *they* who sighed so piteously, their glass eyes staring entreatingly at those who had come to investigate. For like their queen, they, too, wished to be rubbed with the magical ointment.

At the sight of such terrible anguish upon the prettily painted faces of his wooden friends, the puppet man could only stand there weeping and promising to give the stranger with the knapsack his entire takings for the month if he would anoint his cherished dolls with the miracle-producing salve. But the prospect of money did not interest Poor Johannes's traveling companion, who instead proposed to the puppet troupe's tearful orchestrater that he relinquish his sword, which glittered sharply at his side. By now the plaintive wailings of the king and his subordinates had grown so grievous that the puppetmaster would have been willing to pay *any* price to put an end to it. Hence a bargain was struck and the jar of ointment brought forth.

No sooner did the traveler unbutton the dolls' breeches and lift their skirts to apply the embrocation than a celebration erupted. After much flapping of arms and kicking of legs, the male puppets hopped up onto their wooden feet to dance with the flesh-and-blood ladies who had gathered in the taproom, the female puppets taking a turn with the flesh-and-blood gentlemen. In all the excitement, Johannes's worldly friend had not been given an opportunity to refasten the courtiers' breeches, thus their pink appurtenances normally kept concealed bounced wildly and discourteously about, severely stiffened by their curative rubbing. The ladies-in-waiting danced with their human partners, demonstrating equal if not greater abandon, their skirts swirling higher and higher up their wooden thighs and revealing smaller and daintier versions of this appurtenance. As for the puppet king, his majestic representation rose out from his braided breeches, only to be attended by the rouged mouth of a comely barmaid, as would the queen's rosier counterpart. It proved to be a merry eve for all.

The next morning, Poor Johannes and his traveling companion resumed their journey. Together they ascended through fragrant stands of pine and juniper until they could ascend no more. To the far side of the summit, a new world lay before them, offering mile after mile of exciting adventures to the two trekkers. A city with many towers of crystal shimmered in the distance, and from its center arose the turrets of a magnificent castle. It was in this direction that the travelers would go, although not without stopping once again for rest and refreshment.

As with most inns, the proprietor was of a mind to bend the ears of strangers, which is how it came to pass that Johannes and his friend learned that the monarch whose castle they had espied from afar had a daughter—a young woman with a most blood-thirsty reputation. Through her calculated wickedness, many men had lost their lives, for, whether prince or pauper, Princess Hannibella—for so she was called—invited all and sundry to woo her. If the prospective suitor could provide the answers to three riddles the Princess put forth, she would condescend to marry him. If he guessed wrong, she promised to dispatch the failed candidate to the executioner's ax, if not perform the deed herself.

The monarch had long ago removed himself from his daughter's personal affairs, therefore he could do little to halt this slaughter of innocent men. Despite having been warned beforehand of their possible fate, none shied away from the challenge of the three riddles that might win the bloodstained hand of Princess Hannibella. However, all who made an attempt had failed, and over the years many heads had been collected by the murderous Princess, several of which still retained the scream of death upon their shrunken lips. As the innkeeper relayed with undisguised relish this gruesome tale to his audience, Johannes found himself bristling in affronted anger. Did the fellow take him for a fool? For such an outrageous yarn could not possibly be true.

The innkeeper was interrupted by an exaggerated roar of adulation coming from outside the walls of the inn. The two travelers followed the other patrons into the road, curious to learn the reason for the clamor. An open-topped carriage of hammered gold rolled slowly past the swelling crowd, the team of horses drawing it as black and sinister as the river Styx. Seated high upon a velvet banquette was the daughter of the monarch, who acknowledged her subjects with a menacing wave. The overhead sun turned the rubies in Princess Hannibella's crown into fiery sparks, their reflections making it look as if her hair had been formed from the flames of Hell. The mantle cloaking her fine figure had been sewn from the flesh of her victims and remained open in the front, exposing the steel breastplate she wore as protection when she went out in public. Hanging from one slender wrist was a small pouch made from the scrotum of her most recent suitor — the innkeeper's brother-in-law. It was rumored to contain her cache of riddles.

The commotion drew Poor Johannes to the dusty edge of the road, where he felt his heart softening to jelly inside his chest. Surely this breathtaking creature could not be the bloodthirsty Princess of whom the garrulous innkeeper had spoken. "I, too, shall endeavor to answer Princess Hannibella's riddles," he vowed. "For I am desperately in love!" Of course everyone tried to dissuade him, including his older and wiser companion, who genuinely feared for the innocent orphan's life. Alas, Johannes's smitten ears chose to deafen themselves to these well-intentioned warnings. Making himself as presentable as his humble parcel of possessions would allow, he set eagerly off for the city of crystal towers and the castle at its center, heedless of the town crier's pronouncement of "Princess Hannibella strikes again!"

Known for his equitable nature, the monarch received the young traveler most cordially. But when he realized that upon his doorstep had arrived a new aspirant for his daughter's murderous hand, he commenced to weep in a most unregal manner. Indeed, here was yet another head to be added to his offspring's grisly collection. To think how many lives might have been spared if only he had never agreed to adopt her!

The monarch begged Poor Johannes to reconsider, even going so far as to escort him into the private gardens of Hannibella in hopes that this might dampen the orphan's youthful spirits. For suspended from the branch of every tree was the head of a former admirer, many of whom had been handsome princes from neighboring kingdoms. Flowers and vines sprouted haphazardly from the graying skulls of those that had been dangling for some time in the garden, twisting and twining sinuously outward from the vacant sockets—sockets that once held eyes that had gazed in adoration upon Princess Hannibella. "Do you not see what will become of you?" bemoaned the monarch, who strongly suspected that his adopted daughter had not been entirely ethical in her dealings.

However, Poor Johannes had a plan.

Upon being informed that she had a gentleman caller, Hannibella came out into the courtyard, whereupon the fatherless son knelt to the ground in a respectful bow, his love for her now greater than ever—especially when she presented her foot to receive a kiss from his worshipful lips. The Princess entertained her guest in the drawing room, where he was plied with sweetmeats and petit fours before being presented with the challenge of his first riddle, the answer to which Hannibella claimed to have written down on a slip of paper beforehand. Although as hopelessly in love as one of only so vernal an age could be, Johannes knew his limitations when it came to matters of the intellect. Therefore he had taken the precaution of borrowing from his traveling companion's burlap knapsack the jar of magic ointment.

By the time Hannibella had put forth her first riddle, Poor Johannes had already scooped up a generous portion of the salve in his fingers and, when her attention momentarily lay elsewhere, slipped them high beneath her skirts, rubbing in the approximate vicinity he believed his worldly friend had done with the old woman and the troupe of wooden puppets. To his surprise, his fingertips alighted upon something warm and wiggly that stood straight up like the fin of a fish. It seemed to grow warmer and more voluminous with his ministrations, turning increasingly pliable as he worked. The fin-like object felt quite pleasing to the touch, and Johannes found himself rubbing it with substantially more vigor than he had witnessed being demonstrated by the keeper of the miracle-producing unguent.

As expected, Princess Hannibella kicked her legs recklessly about and flapped her arms like those of a crazed bird, prompting a sigh of relief from Poor Johannes. Why, in her state *any* answer he proposed would be the right one! It was then arranged for the resourceful orphan to return the following morning, at which time he would submit his final answer and learn whether he might be allowed to keep his head for another day — or at least until the time came to solve the Princess's second riddle. For neither prince nor pauper had as yet managed to draw a breath beyond the first.

Now it just so happened that Poor Johannes's traveling companion was very concerned about the fate of his young friend. Not wishing to place faith in the fickle hands of Providence, the worldly-wise traveler decided to take matters into his own capable hands. Wishing to do good where it could best be done, he departed shortly after supper for the castle, determined to intervene before Johannes was obliged to take permanent leave of his foolish head. To make certain he would not be followed, he had plied the lovesick orphan with enough drink to keep him in blissful slumber until the arrival of daybreak.

It was an unseasonably warm night, and the traveler had no difficulty in locating an open window, in fact, several open windows, one of which belonged to Hannibella herself, for he saw her restless figure hovering before it. He waited for the great clock in the city center to chime midnight, at which time he planned to enter her bedchamber and exert whatever influence he could on the Princess. But before the bell managed to alert him of the hour, the room's lethal occupant had already departed through the window.

Johannes's traveling companion blended himself into the shadows, waiting until Hannibella had gotten clear of him, only to set off after her in stealthy pursuit. He did not need to keep too closely on her heels, as the white cape she wore billowed around her like a ship's sail against a sea of indigo sky. For nearly an hour they walked toward the mountains, together yet separate, until at last they could go no farther — whereupon the Princess strode purposefully up to a boulder set into the mountainside and rapped against its adamantine surface as one might a door. All at once a terrible rumbling could be heard. When it sounded as if the earth itself would open up to swallow them both, the boulder swung inward, the hermetically sealed interior of the mountain releasing a puff of fetid breath into the air.

Just beyond this blackly gaping mouth lay a deep cavern. Its corrugated walls glistened wetly in the moonlight, the moisture forming tiny blue icicles. Having already come this far, the traveler decided to follow Princess Hannibella into the stygian bowels of the mountain. An unwholesome smell irritated his nostrils, worsening with each footfall. He stifled a sneeze, puzzled that the bothersome effluvium seemed to have no effect upon his quarry's highborn nostrils. Its origin would soon become known, for at the end of the cavern awaited a troll. A swarm of fat flies buzzed happily about his stunted person, drawn to what had so thoroughly repelled his clandestine observer. Hannibella placed her foot forward, allowing the unsightly creature's withered purple lips to kiss it. Poor Johannes's traveling companion pressed close to the jagged wall, resolved to learn the reason for the Princess's visit and praying he would not be discovered in the process.

"I am in need of a second riddle," declared Hannibella. "For I have a new suitor who appears quite resourceful and may have already guessed the first."

The troll nodded sagely, his stench growing stronger within the airless confines of the cavern until the traveler found himself choking on it. "This new suitor...does he come to thee generously equipped?"

"Oh, Poppa, what does it matter, since I only wish to kill him anyway?"

"In that case, thou must choose something so simple it would never occur to him," advised the troll in a voice as thick and rattling as rancid curd. "Then the Princess shall gain for herself another handsome head for her fine collection. And prithee, Daughter dearest, do not forget to bring me his manhood so that

I may fry it up in butter with some fava beans and wash it down with a nice Chianti."

The traveler's head ached from all he had seen and heard, the noxious interchange leaving him greatly confused as to why the daughter of the monarch should have addressed the troll as if *he* were her father. Returning unobserved with her to the castle, he again stationed himself outside Hannibella's open window until enough time had passed for her to get into bed for what little remained of the night. Hearing the silence for which he had been waiting, Johannes's traveling companion entered the Princess's bedchamber to find her exactly as expected—sound asleep in her bed. She appeared to possess not a care in the world as she lay upon the embroidered coverlet, her breathing steady and without the inflections indicative of a troubled sleep. The first thing he noticed were her feet, the elegantly arched soles of which glowed pinkly and innocently in the moonlight. The finely woven lawn of her nightdress had ridden up to her waist, exposing a pair of graceful thighs and the corresponding hills above. Trembling with indignation and perhaps something more, he drew back his arm in heartfelt readiness as he intended to seek redress for the obliquity intended Poor Johannes.

Indeed, the peacefully slumbering form positioned with such indecorous abandon upon the bed ignited a raging conflagration within its beholder's soul, hence the worldly-wise traveler wielded his hand with enthusiasm, spurred onward by the milky mounds before him and the fiery red splotches his actions imprinted upon them. The prone recipient cried out with every resounding smack of his palm, her legs kicking every which way, her arms flailing uselessly at her sides. It might even be believed that she welcomed them, for she raised herself up to meet each strike, falling back down again with a sated sigh.

Poor Johannes's traveling companion slept soundly that night, as did Princess Hannibella, who dreamed she had melted into a warm puddle. That morning as Johannes shook off his drink-enhanced slumber, his friend greeted him with unusual tenderness, for, thanks to him, the lovesick orphan would live to see the dawning of another day. After enjoying a tasty meal of sausage, eggs, and black bread served courtesy of the innkeeper's wife, it came time for the Princess's latest suitor to depart for the castle. The itinerant stranger saw his trusting ward off at the door, confident that his less-than-tender ministrations of the wee hours should have persuaded the Princess to exercise far more liberality when weighing the answer to her first riddle.

Johannes found himself being ushered into the grand salon, where a team of judges awaited him, along with the teary-eyed monarch himself, who, in anticipation of the unsuspecting orphan's fate, sniveled through many a kerchief. The moment Hannibella entered the room, this petitioner for her hand felt his heart soaring with love. The Princess's cheeks had taken on a fine rosy glow—a glow similar to that which heated the cheeks she now struggled to sit upon. She extended her foot for its reverential kiss, her manner all sweetness and benevolence. Yet for Poor Johannes this was to be no mere social call.

As the monarch wept into his kerchief and the judges mopped their sopping brows, Johannes took a fortifying breath. Ascertaining that he had gained the Princess's full attention, he placed a fingertip against his right earlobe and wiggled it about in suggestion of his earlier ministrations with the salve upon the little fin he had located beneath her skirts. Hannibella's eyes widened in acknowledgment, and she bit the pink plump of her lower lip in remembered ecstasy, the slip of paper containing the riddle's solution tucked inside her perspiring palm dropping to the carpet in a wet ball. Only then did Poor Johannes put forth his answer.

The Princess (who had gone quite red in the face) nodded helplessly at the judges, whereupon the monarch burst into cheers of joy. For the sparing of a life, however momentary, was a thing to celebrate. Johannes next received a command to join Hannibella in the drawing room so that he might be presented with her second riddle. Once again he had taken the precaution of bringing along his traveling companion's jar of magic ointment, and once again the words had barely left Princess Hannibella's lips before he had his fingers high up in her skirts rubbing the now-familiar fin they met there. It grew bigger than ever beneath his fingertips, and the fatherless orphan soon found himself working the whole of his arm up to the shoulder joint.

That evening the worldly stranger did not need to ply his young friend with spirits, for the day's exertions had sent Poor Johannes to bed very early, and his exhausted snores could be heard all the way to the inn's front door. The traveler sallied forth to the city with greater haste than ever, determined to reach the Princess before she sought out the venomous troll for a more foolproof conundrum to have ready as insurance in the event her latest attempt to stump her suitor also met with failure. Since it was to be her second riddle for which the fatherless orphan would be risking his silly head, Johannes's traveling companion thought it might be of benefit to put into practice *two* hands instead of just the one.

Hannibella had taken to her bed for a much-needed respite after her encounter with her suitor, only to discover that there would be no respite as her midnight caller brought his palms savagely down upon the symmetrical swells of her nether cheeks in a steady *one-two* motion, refusing to let up until the strength had ebbed from his arms. Fortunately, the clock in the city center quickly rejuvenated him, and the traveler matched each strike of the midnight hour with a strike of his own, the twin mounds of milky flesh launching themselves high into the air, flushing redder and redder with every persuasive blow. It would not be until the predawn hours that the resonant smack of palm against flesh had finally been silenced. Indeed, Princess Hannibella's feet would do much kicking about on this night.

The following morning, with a carefree bounce in his step that left heads shaking in disbelief, Poor Johannes set off on the road to the castle, where he was once more ushered into the grand salon to hear his fate. Having been briefed by his worldly friend beforehand, he offered up an answer of ridiculous obviousness—albeit not without first securing the Princess's attention by twiddling the lobe of his ear with a readily available fingertip. Hannibella's sharp intake of breath sliced through the stillness of the room like a scream. A crumpled slip of paper rolled from her hand onto the floor. Had those present bothered to unfold it, they would have discovered it to be blank. Twice thwarted in her acquisition of a new head for her garden, she nodded in flushed affirmation toward the anxious team of judges, thereby gaining for Johannes another reprieve.

The sight of the orphan's brazen finger manipulating the dangling lobe of flesh had caused the Princess to grow quite faint, and she bade Poor Johannes to lead her to a settee so that she might rest. It was from here that she posed her third and final riddle, her palm-tenderized nether regions too ill-humored to allow her to even sit up properly. How could it be that she was suddenly helpless to thwart the young man who sought her hand? Finding herself without the foul counsel of her blood-father the troll, Hannibella did the best she could, calling upon the resources of her own mind. "What is it I am thinking of at this moment?" she inquired languidly, not entirely certain of the answer herself, but comforted by its conveniently transitory nature.

However, Johannes's salve-anointed fingers were already journeying high beneath her skirts, rubbing and kneading the voluminous fin they had come to know so well—a fin so fiery hot that it singed his enterprising fingertips. Princess Hannibella's legs were flung every which way upon the settee, offering no resistance and, in fact, making her suitor's ministrations all the easier to perform. It was not long before her arms flapped like broken wings at her sides and her feet kicked the air. Despite his success, Johannes refused to desist from his labors for a moment. If his response to her third and final riddle was deemed correct, not only would he live to see another day, he would also receive the Princess's hand in marriage. With so much at stake, he massaged more and more of the magical ointment beneath her skirts, not stopping until he had emptied out the jar.

Just before midnight, Poor Johannes's traveling companion paid a final call to the Princess's bedchamber, knowing that the morning would determine

whether his young friend should live or die. Although
a storm appeared to be brewing in the east, he was not
the sort to allow a few raindrops to deter him. He discovered Hannibella cloaked only in nature's garb as
she lay face down upon her bed, so depleted of
strength she could not even summon a maid to assist
her into a nightdress. These circumstances would suit
the traveler well. Rubbing his hands together to warm
them for the task ahead, he raised them high into the
air, hesitating briefly and with unexpected relish
before bringing them down against the twin hills
before him, the sharp crack of thunder creating an
alliance with the sharp crack his palms made upon
contact. A flash of blue-white lightning illuminated
his target, revealing a veritable chaos of reddening
splotches and inspiring their wrathful administrator
to add several more in a stormy crescendo of blows.

Hannibella gasped for breath, pushing herself
up from the embroidered coverlet so that she might
meet these cruel kisses, their stinging burn reactivat-
ing the burn induced by her suitor's earlier
application of ointment. The pink bottoms of her feet
flew about in maddened circles, and her fists pummeled the pillows until she eventually lost
consciousness, only to be revived by still more prim-
ing from her intruder's able palms. For Johannes's
peripatetic companion had no intention of allowing
the Princess's writhing body a reprieve until he was
certain he had earned one for his friend.

That sunrise before Poor Johannes departed for the castle for the very last time, the owner of the jar of magic ointment presented the orphan with explicit instructions that he should clap his hands sharply together when the moment came to provide an answer to Princess Hannibella's third riddle. Indeed, the palms of his own were cracked and peeling, indicating they had been given good usage. Not understanding the significance of this piece of advice, yet not wishing to appear ungrateful, Johannes nodded his humble thanks, suddenly experiencing a terrible sense of guilt over having borrowed without permission the special salve—the empty jar of which was still contained in the pocket of his coat. Perhaps, if all went well with the Princess, he might make amends to his itinerant friend by having his future father-in-law offer him a knighthood, particularly since the traveler had already managed to procure his own fine sword.

As Poor Johannes approached the castle, he noticed a delivery coach double-parked outside with two men unloading a coffin. Before he could inquire as to who in the monarch's household had passed away, he was escorted into the grand salon, where the tearful monarch sat hunched forward in misery upon his throne, his unregal trembles visible to all. The covey of judges chewed their quills in dreaded expectation, their stern faces creased with more worry than usual. The deliverymen Johannes had seen earlier arrived and just as swiftly departed, having placed the empty coffin discreetly in a corner. After several strained minutes, Princess Hannibella made her entrance, her face the white of chalk, her eyes ringed by dark circles. With considerable effort, she lowered herself onto the settee, wincing when contact had been made. "Pray, persistent Sir, what have I been thinking of since you last came before me?" she inquired of Poor Johannes, her voice so enfeebled that all had to strain to hear it.

As the judges and the monarch looked in hopeful eagerness toward him, rather than answering with words, Johannes brought his palms sharply together as instructed by his worldly friend. For additional insurance, he also tweaked both earlobes between thumb and forefinger until they had turned bright red with blood. At the sight, Hannibella fainted dead away — although not without first flapping and flailing her arms and legs in the frenzied manner so familiar to the one whose actions had incited it. This time, the Princess's hand was conspicuously empty of any slips of paper.

The chorus of *hurrahs!* from the grand salon could be heard as far away as the inn, where, in an upstairs room, Johannes's traveling companion smiled with heartfelt pleasure, taking pride in the role he had played — a role that would allow the fatherless orphan to keep his head. With the wedding celebration at the castle already underway, he sallied forth toward new adventures, the burlap of his knapsack slightly lighter upon his shoulder with the absence of his jar of ointment.

It never occurred to the Princess's victorious suitor that without the oleaginous contents of the jar and the traveler's secret midnight spankings, the marital bliss he had hoped to enjoy with his new wife would be severely limited. Indeed, Hannibella found herself greatly disappointed with the quality of her husband's insipid fumblings beneath her skirts, to say nothing of his lack of imagination regarding the appropriate application of the palm. What Johannes did not seem to realize was that he had won the Princess under false pretenses.

Sadly, all that effort put forth by his well-meaning traveling companion would come to naught, since in the end Hannibella beheaded Poor Johannes anyway. ❧

THE TURNIP

Tales that contain as their main protagonists a pair of brothers have always featured prominently in folk literature and narrative. Although tales of brothers can be found in nearly every European country, their earliest written form has been discovered in the papyruses and steles of ancient Egypt. Since folktales are generally considered to have arisen from the wishful thinking of the poor and the unsuccessful, perhaps it should not be surprising that one of the most commonly occurring themes is that of the poor and virtuous brother happening on sudden riches, thus allowing him to gain parity with his wealthy, but less virtuous, brother.

A widely known example of the rich brother/poor brother tale is "The Turnip" by the Brothers Grimm. Unlike many of the stories they collected over their lifetimes, the Grimms' "Die Rübe" may genuinely stem from the true German folktale tradition—one characteristic of which is the concept of a man of little or no means achieving equal footing with his financial betters by rising in social class as a result of his industriousness. Given the prevailing social order of the day, one often sees this emphasis being placed on an individual's industriousness, an industriousness that in turn was tied to the agrarian pursuits of the peasantry. For the basic structure of most folktales appears to stem from the social situation of the agrarian lower classes.

Although "The Turnip" clearly corresponds to the German tradition, the Grimms rarely provided the names or dates of their sources, therefore the origins of many of their tales have been difficult to trace. No doubt the reason for this lack of disclosure relates to the fact that the majority (if not all) of their sources were family members and friends of literate middle-class backgrounds rather than the peasant narrators from whom the brothers claimed to have collected their tales. Furthermore, since the Grimms apparently saw fit to destroy the manuscripts that had been used for the first edition of their *Kinder- und Hausmärchen*, it has proven impossible to confirm that the original source material for the text of their stories received accurate treatment. It is believed, however, that substantial discrepancies do exist, and that these discrepancies flourished with each subsequent edition of the *Kinder- und Hausmärchen* as the Grimms continued to stylistically revise and edit their tales up until the seventh and final edition. Hence we may never know the true origins of tales like "The Turnip," let alone know whether such tales are, in fact, German.

As one of the few fairy tales containing no female characters, "The Turnip" demonstrates that the feminine presence is not always necessary to make a successful story. The feminine presence is surely not needed in *my* version...or at least, not needed by the bachelor king. ❧

The Turnip

I N DAYS OF YORE WHEN GREAT WARS WERE
fought in exotic lands over exotic bounties, there
was never a shortage of men willing to take up
the lance and shield. Those of a clever nature pros-
pered from their situations, leaving others of simpler
character to perish. During one of these conflicts, there
were two brothers who happened to serve honorably
as soldiers in the same bloody battle. Upon the final
laying down of armaments, one emerged a rich man,
the other poor. To free himself from the weighty
shackles of poverty, the less fortunate of this fraternal
pair decided to take up the plow, for the agrarian life
seemed a logical way to feed himself, not to mention
profit from the feeding of others. The fellow managed
to purchase a small piece of land, which he sowed
throughout with turnip seed. It so happened that
turnips had become very popular in the kingdom and
were served at the King's supper table every night.
Therefore, the decision in favor of the turnip would be
an easy one.

Farming was hard and, indeed, hungry work,
and the aspiring farmer liked to chew a few of the
seeds as he hoed and sowed, since many an hour

remained before he could sit down to partake of his own supper. Despite the many hardships he endured, the impoverished brother believed that all his long hours of sweat and toil would one day prove worthwhile. And his dedication to the soil served him well. As the seed took hold, turnip leaves began to display themselves in abundance along his modest parcel, their thick roots burrowing happily downward into the dark rich earth. Only the farmer would have far more success than he had originally bargained for. There was one turnip in particular that grew and grew until it looked as if it would never stop growing. Although this should have provoked great joy in the poorer of the two brothers, it instead provoked great dismay. For this most vigorous of vegetables did not sprout from the ground as had its leafy companions, but from the farmer himself.

Indeed, it surged aggressively forth from beneath the pale paunch of his belly, its stout base surrounded by a dense cluster of leaves that shaded the equally pale flesh of his thighs. The turnip would become so heavy that this devoted tiller of the soil eventually found it difficult to walk, let alone hoe his plantings or climb a ladder or perform any of the normal tasks of daily life. Each time he sat down for a meal, it bumped the underside of the table, upsetting the weathered rectangle of pine along with everything that had been placed upon it. It got so that the farmer had to slide his chair so far back that he could barely reach his plate. Soon the wearing of trousers became an impossibility. He would be forced to either cut away the buttoned flaps at the front or go about trouserless, the latter option proving most distressing whenever a chill wind blew.

Perhaps the poor brother should not have eaten so many turnip seeds. For what other reason could there have been for this curious phenomenon? The root that sprang out from his overburdened groin eventually grew to be so enormous and cumbersome that, to simply move about on his land, the farmer had to place it atop a cart, which would then be drawn by two strong oxen. Even a trip into the village necessitated a harnessing of the beasts, a fact that probably explained his ever-increasing reluctance to undertake the short journey. The aggrieved fellow did not enjoy being a public spectacle and enduring the titters of tot and parent alike. Yet as the days passed and the size of his leafy burden increased, he began to wonder whether such a seeming misfortune could possibly be turned into an advantage. Although the farmer could likely sell the vegetable at market for a tidy sum, the prospect of making a gift of it to the King held more appeal, for His Majesty's fondness for turnips was well known. Why, there could be no telling the rewards he might reap from so reverential a gesture!

So it was that early one morning the turnip farmer harnessed up the pair of exhausted oxen. After carefully situating his weighty impediment inside the wooden confines of the wobbly cart, they set creakily off for the palace. Doubtful as to whether he would even be granted an audience with the King—for indeed, he was only a humble man of the soil—he traveled with greater haste than might have been advisable under the circumstances, overturning the cart and its clumsy cargo several times along the way, to say nothing of causing considerable anxiety to the two oxen. To the farmer's surprise and delight, the King agreed to receive him immediately, having been informed by his courtiers of the unusual nature of the call. Because the cart and its grunting beasts could not be allowed inside the palace, two of the brawniest courtiers were dispatched to assist the caller with his encumbrance.

"Many wondrous things have these eyes of ours borne witness to, but never such a monster as this!" squealed the King when the farmer and his turnip were presented to him. "How did this miracle come to pass?"

The farmer bowed his head reverently, not daring to meet the monarch's astonished eyes—which gleamed with a brightness rather in excess of the occasion. "It is as much a miracle to His Majesty as it is to me," he said deferentially in response.

With a nod, the King indicated for his nervous subject to carry on and the farmer took a deep breath in readiness to put forth his offer. "Unlike my elder brother, I am a poor soldier who has naught but a tiny plot of land upon which to make my meager living. Therefore I would be most honored if His Majesty would accept this turnip as a token of my humble obeisance."

"Indeed," replied the King, his moist, beef-colored lips quirking up in one corner. "Might we be allowed to touch it?"

"By all means!" effused the farmer, both flattered and embarrassed at the same time. "It is His Majesty's to do with as he wishes."

The King reached forward a be-ringed hand and traced with his fingertips the purple-tinged waxiness of the turnip's surface, shuddering violently as he did so. Beads of moisture had broken out upon his brow, and he mopped them irritably away with the monogrammed kerchief he kept tucked beneath the cuff of his doublet. "This is truly a most lusty specimen," he croaked, clearly overcome by a powerful emotion. The farmer flushed with pride and glanced modestly away toward the royal courtiers, all of whom stood silently by wearing knowing smirks upon their normally impassive faces. Suddenly the King grabbed hold of the proffered turnip, his great hands dwarfed by its massive bulk. He began to squeeze it all along its length, as if testing for quality. "We shall be most pleased to accept this fine gift as a token of your loyalty."

"His Majesty honors me," wept the grateful pauper, his breath inexplicably quickening at the touch of the King's fingers. At that moment he would have bent to kiss the monarch's feet in appreciation had not the impediment surging out from beneath his belly prevented him from doing so.

Arising from his throne, the King tapped the kneeling man's head with his staff. "Thou shalt be impoverished no more." And with that, he ordered his courtiers to arrange for his turnip-bearing subject to be moved into the palace posthaste.

The lowly farmer was given the fine suite of rooms adjoining the King's private apartments, since His Majesty had as yet no queen to inhabit them. As if such luxuries were not reward enough, he also had bestowed upon him large sums of gold as well as the most fertile of green pastures to do with as he pleased. However, the farmer no longer had any need for the tilling of soil or the sowing of seeds. Instead he sat back and watched as his fortune grew and grew in startling conjunction with the growth of the turnip attached to his body, until he discovered that he could no longer leave the sumptuous confines of his quarters. Many a time did he respectfully propose to the King that the turnip be removed, for, upon his initial offering of it, this had been the farmer's intent. He even used a gold coin to bribe one of the servants to bring him a knife from the palace kitchens so that he might get an advance start on what was certain to be an arduous task. Surely His Majesty should have preferred to have the great root at his full disposal, particularly since his interest in it seemed to center more on the corporeal than the culinary.

Indeed, the King's unnatural fixation with the turnip had begun to prove most embarrassing to the simple farmer, who was not at all accustomed to being in the intimate company of such important personages, to say nothing of being party to such curious pastimes as those His Majesty had devised. For whether morning, noon, or evening, the portly monarch insisted upon saddling his doughy posterior atop the turnip, where he commenced to canter up and down, accelerating his movements to a wild gallop, his shouts of "Go, horsy, go!" reverberating all through the palace and broadening the smirks of the royal courtiers. The poor farmer's scrawny thighs would nearly be pummeled flat beneath the weight of the King, so forcefully and with such enthusiasm did the gleeful sovereign hurl himself down upon his turnip-bearing subject. It would not be until the King had trumpeted his last "Ye-hah!" that he finally leapt off, only to amble unsteadily away from the florid-faced former soldier without so much as even a cursory nod of thanks.

The farmer's sudden and undesired position as court stallion further served to convince him that the moment had long since passed for him to remove the cumbersome growth from his body, for what had originally been intended as a gift had now become a curse. Yet no matter how tactfully he put forth the helpful suggestion that the turnip be harvested, His Majesty refused to hear of it. In fact, he went quite red in the face at the mere mention of any type of excision being performed, until the farmer, who dared not risk further offense, was forced to drop the matter.

News of the poor farmer who had been taken in by the King traveled far and wide, and the prosperous soldier eventually came to hear of his brother's good fortune, which by this time greatly outrivaled his own. He wondered how the gift of a simple root could stimulate such royal generosity. Why, if his pauper of a brother had been able to gain so much with so little, imagine what a wiser and wealthier man like he himself could do! Therefore he, too, set off for the palace, bringing along with him the shiniest of gold pieces and the swiftest and blackest of steeds with which to impress His Majesty, for he had heard that the mighty monarch had become quite the equestrian.

Although the King accepted these gifts with typical good grace, he replied that he had no item of great value or rarity to offer his generous subject in return. "*Nothing?*" choked the brother, certain he was being made an ass of.

Now this set His Majesty to thinking. "Hmm...perhaps there might be *one* small thing." The courtiers were then instructed to show the caller into an adjacent room.

As he waited for his reward, the soldier realized that he occupied the King's bedchamber. Never had he expected to receive such an honor. Indeed, his riches were trifling compared to the stately opulence he saw all around him. Oriental carpets of varying shapes and shades crisscrossed one another upon the gleaming wood of the floor, each more intricately woven than the next. Tapestries of extraordinary richness and beauty hung from the silk-upholstered walls, relaying tales of bloody battles fought by previous realms. A damask-covered settee fashioned from maple and inlaid with mother-of-pearl had been advantageously situated before a hearth within whose marble borders a fire popped and crackled with merriment, suffusing the soldier with a comforting warmth. Yet most spectacular of all was the place where His Majesty rested his head each night. For directly beneath a soberly executed painting of the mighty King himself was a large four-poster bed, its elaborately carved teakwood encrusted throughout with opals that reflected iridescent rainbows against a coverlet of red velvet.

And there upon this plush red counterpane lay the soldier's brother, naked and bleary-eyed with exhaustion, the enormous growth below his belly weighing him to one side. The heavy damask draperies at the window had been drawn back to welcome in the fine spring morning, and streaks of incoming sunlight cast the turnip in stark relief, showing the enormity of its size and the greasy yellow slickness coating its waxen flesh. A porcelain bowl of lard had been conveniently placed upon the bedside table; it was nearly empty.

Upon seeing the familiar face of his brother, the farmer tried to raise his hand up from the bed in greeting, but even this small effort was too taxing. The opportunistic soldier fled the palace in horror, leaving behind his gold and his horse—and leaving behind, his brother who, upon the death of the King some years hence, would find himself possessing more wealth and commanding more courtiers than he could possibly have use for. Nevertheless, no amount of wealth could free him from the burden he was forced to carry day after day, until at last he was allowed to experience the blissful release of death. ❧

THE
SLEEPING
BEAUTY

"The Sleeping Beauty" can be found in various incarnations worldwide, making it almost as popular as "Cinderella." Although the names most linked to the story of the sleeping princess are Charles Perrault and the Brothers Grimm, the tale can be traced to medieval days, with its most essential elements possibly reaching back in history to tribal societies.

Like "Rapunzel," "The Sleeping Beauty" is considered a puberty tale, with the young princess also finding herself confined at the age of puberty — a confinement that in primitive cultures would often be imposed on a young girl at the onset of menstruation. Yet instead of having an awareness of her surroundings like her golden-haired counterpart in the tower did, the princess in "The Sleeping Beauty" undergoes a long sleep cast on her by mystical means — an element that may offer further proof of the tale's primeval origins, for the practice of sleep magic filled the folktales of tribal societies.

Undoubtedly the most major and, indeed, erotic fore-bear to "The Sleeping Beauty" can be found in Basile's "Sun, Moon, and Talia." Rather than the proper prince of later versions, an adulterous king comes upon the sleeping and virginal Talia. Unable to resist her, "...he felt his blood course hotly through his veins in contemplation of so many charms; and he lifted her in his arms, and carried her to a bed, whereon he gathered the first fruits of love...." Having been in a state of sleep, Talia knows nothing of what has transpired. This unawareness of the sex act likely stems from the influence of Christianity, prompting Basile to bestow on the sleeping female an immaculate conception of sorts, for Talia's ravishment results in the birth of twins whom she calls *Sun* and *Moon*. She finally awakens when one of her infants mistakenly suckles her finger, drawing out the fiber from the spindle on which she had pricked her finger. Returning for another pleasurable dalliance, the king comes upon Talia with their children. When his wife (an ogre) discovers the reason for his absences, she plots to gain possession of the twins so that she can have them cooked and inadvertently fed to her philandering husband.

However, long before Basile put ink onto paper, "The Sleeping Beauty" existed in the story of "Brynhild" from the *Volsunga Saga*. According to this Old Norse myth, Brynhild falls into an enchanted sleep after being pricked by a thorn, thus preserving her youth and beauty for the man brave enough to make his way through the flames surrounding the castle in which she lies asleep. Despite these parallels to "The Sleeping Beauty" structure, one can locate an even more obvious precursor to Basile in "Histoire de Troylus et de Zellandine" from the fourteenth-century French prose novel *Perceforest*. Here a prince takes unbridled sexual advantage of the sleeping princess Zellandine, on whom a curse has been laid and levied out by means of a distaff of flax. Having satisfied his desires, the prince abandons her, whereupon Zellandine later awakens to find herself with child.

Indeed, these copious references to the spinning of flax may have far greater significance to "The Sleeping Beauty" and its historical counterparts than its popular use as a vehicle for the levying of curses. In primitive societies, spinning was considered a sacred female initiation act. It became common practice in some countries for women to expose themselves to the flax and ask it to grow as high as their genitals, for in so doing, the flax would supposedly grow better. Hence spinning came to represent the essence of female life, with all its fertility and sexual implications. It may be that the princess's inadequacy at spinning was meant to signify her lack of sexual development—a deficiency that would be long gone by the time of her awakening.

As the French literary tale came into vogue, Charles Perrault would put forth his own version of the princess's story in "La Belle au Bois Dormant" (The sleeping beauty in the wood). Only this time the protagonist appears somewhat more animated than her predecessors, for "the princess awakened and looked at him [the prince] with fonder eyes than is really proper at first meeting…." Like her folktale ancestors, she, too, gives birth to two children, albeit with far more cognizance of how this phenomenon came about. Of course Perrault would have been all too aware of the inappropriateness of telling a story at the court of Versailles about a married king who sexually ravishes a sleeping maiden, only to leave her pregnant and alone. Instead he continues his story in Basile-like form, in which, on learning of her son's marriage, the prince's mother (an ogre) seeks out her grandchildren to eat them and afterward make a meal of her daughter-in-law.

No doubt the best-known and best-loved version of "The Sleeping Beauty" tale has to be "Dornröschen" (Brier Rose) by the Brothers Grimm. It is here that the princess finds herself charmingly awakened by the famous kiss. Absent of the cannibalistic characters from earlier versions, the brothers departed from their predecessors in other ways as well, excising the sexual content in the story. Yet let it not be said that "Dornröschen" has been rendered barren of the erotic, for the beauty of the princess so stirs the prince that he is inspired to kiss her—a kiss that up until the Grimms had not made an appearance. Perhaps this kiss might be representative of a young woman's sexual awakening, just as I have chosen to make it in my version in a conspicuously more complex form. ❧

270

THE SLEEPING BEAUTY

I N A CASTLE FRINGED BY A MEANDERING river of blue, there resided a King and Queen who spent their days with only the members of their court for company. It would be an arrangement that was not a result of their own choosing, for the couple yearned more than anything to have a child to brighten their empty eyes and fill the interminable hours of the passing years. Yet with each change of the season, no such child was forthcoming, and a cloud of sadness settled permanently over the castle and its occupants.

Word of the royal couple's barren status quickly spread, and an endless succession of wily opportunists came forth to offer their aid. There were those who hailed the reproductive properties of snake oil and others who swore by onion suppositories. Indeed, the poor Queen was nearly at her wit's end — as was her husband, who did not much care for the odor of onions wafting from his wife's womanly parts.

On one unusually warm winter's morn, the Queen went down to bathe in the river that burbled past the castle. Afterward, while she sat drying herself in the sun, a frog of the brightest and most iridescent green hopped up onto the stony bank beside her. Her initial impulse was to shoo the slimy little creature away lest it be of a mind to wipe its muddy feet upon her queenly flesh. Moreover, its raucous croaking had begun to annoy her, as did the stink of spirits on its amphibious breath. But what transpired next would stay the Queen's hand as the nonsensical sounds emanating from the frog's ballooning throat abruptly took on the form of words. "Despair no longer, my good Queen," croaked the web-footed interloper. "Before the year is through, a daughter shall spring forth from thine imperial loins."

"Pray, tell me what I must do to make this so!" the Queen implored, ready to embark upon any means necessary to increase her fertility. Although repeatedly chastised by her husband for being gullible, she found that it made perfect sense that if the frog possessed the ability of speech, it was just as probable it possessed other preternatural abilities as well.

"A night with Her Highness is all I ask," the frog stated with a telltale burp, its watery eyes bulging in appreciation of the rosy flesh left exposed both above and below the fluffy towel with which the royal bather attempted to cover her modesty.

This was not the answer the Queen had been hoping to hear. So far, she had washed in the blood of pregnant women, eaten afterbirths for breakfast, stood upon her head after performing her marital duty, and endured onions stuffed within her person. Granted, she might have been desperate for a child, nevertheless, she *did* have her limits. The mere thought of this slimy green creature huffing and puffing on top of her set her flesh to crawling. Bad enough to have to endure it from her husband, the King. "I think not, frog."

The frog shrugged its shiny shoulders, apparently nonplussed by the Queen's reaction. Over the years it had grown accustomed to these rebuffs, therefore it always made certain to have a backup plan in place. "I ask then for a simple reward. A mere pittance." And perhaps it *was* a pittance, for the frog requested that the royal household supply it with a lifetime's supply of spirits. According to the amphibian grapevine, the castle cellars were stocked full of fine port and brandies and even several kegs of ale, which should surely see the frog into its golden years. Seeing no alternative, the Queen agreed to the creature's terms, whereupon the frog disappeared with a gaseous splash into the sparkling blue river as quickly and unexpectedly as it had first appeared.

Being of a practical nature, the King refused to give credence to such a prophecy. As a result, it took quite a bit of convincing for him to relinquish the precious contents of his cellar to a frog, who, rather than coming in person, had dispatched a team of amphibious cohorts to the rear door of the castle to collect this special honorarium. His Highness watched solemnly as the bottles and kegs from his cellar vanished downriver upon a caravan of lily pads. Expecting nothing in return, the King himself was astonished when the frog's prophecy actually came to pass. For nine months later his wife gave birth to a baby girl so beautiful he wept with joy each time he looked upon her perfect, pink form.

To wish the infant well in her new life, the proud father ordered a feast to outrival all feasts, inviting friends and relations from near and far, along with the local wise women, whose presences were considered an absolute *must* upon such occasions. As one might have imagined, the guest list grew and grew until no more guests could be accommodated. Because the household had remaining to it only twelve place settings for what should have been thirteen wise women, this meant that one would need to be left out. In the single-mindedness of his joy, the King failed to anticipate that something so ostensibly minor would be interpreted as a major snub.

The festivities were celebrated with great lavishness, with food and drink aplenty and laughter and good cheer all around. When it came time for the wise women to present the child with their gifts, the first gave virtue, the second beauty, the third wealth, the fourth grace — and on it went until the infant girl had been given everything her parents could have wished for her. As the twelfth wise woman stepped up to the royal crib to offer her gift, a disturbance arose as the uninvited thirteenth elbowed her way inside the grand hall. She felt most vengeful on this day, having taken considerable offense at the absence of her name from the King and Queen's guest list. As number thirteen, she had experienced a lifetime of being the odd one out. Even at home, when her twelve colleagues paired off each night to their respective bedchambers to bill and coo beneath the bedcovers, she would be left on her own to entertain herself...and without so much as the comfort of a bed to do it in. Ergo this latest exclusion was the last straw.

Forgoing the respectful bow demanded of all those who came before the royal couple, the thirteenth wise woman marched directly up to the happily gurgling infant and put forth her gift, saying, "In her fifteenth year of life, the King and Queen's daughter shall prick her finger on a spindle and die." Whereupon she spun about on her heel and departed, leaving the guests gasping and clutching their throats in horror. Indeed, she was quite pleased with herself, having no fondness for the royals, let alone their pampered progeny.

The wise woman who had been interrupted hastened forward in a panic. Although she could not cancel out the curse that had just been wished upon the child, she might be able to alleviate some of its sting. It was also a matter of pride, since she had no affection for the thirteenth member of her group and would not have liked for the woman to get the last word. The twelve had grown weary of number thirteen's endless rantings and ravings about abolishing the monarchy and creating a state in which the producers possessed both political power and the means of producing and distributing goods. Why, if such a system actually came into being, where would that leave wise women like herself?

Touching the infant's forehead, the twelfth wise woman offered what she hoped would be a remedy. "The King and Queen's daughter shall *not* die, but shall fall into a deep sleep to last one and ninety-nine years." Not given to take the pronouncement of any wise woman lightly, the child's father issued a proclamation commanding that all spindles in the kingdom be destroyed forthwith, convinced that by doing so, he had outsmarted the vicious gate-crasher.

As the little Princess grew older, each gift that had been given her by the wise women befell her. She would be beautiful and kind, clever and virtuous, musical of voice and light of step. Yet as each of the twelve gifts came to pass, it was inevitable that so, too, should the thirteenth.

During their daughter's fifteenth year of life, the King and Queen found themselves called away on urgent court business. This would be the Princess's first occasion to be alone without the watchful eye of a parent upon her, and, having an enterprising nature, she planned to take full advantage of the situation. The custodial eye of her father had become stifling over the years, and it frustrated her that she had been prevented from participating in activities her young peers so freely enjoyed. Why, other princesses her age were already keeping company with handsome suitors, whereas she was still keeping company with dolls! Although her first thought was to invite a prince or two to the castle, the servants had been ordered not to let anyone pass through the gates, especially young men with a special gleam in their eye.

With no other form of amusement available, the bored Princess embarked upon an investigation of the majestic structure that had been her home since the moment of her birth and from which she was never allowed to leave. She entered every chamber and parlor and opened every door, as well as every lid and drawer. Not even the den of a dormouse could be kept from her. The Princess's explorations eventually led her to a crumbling old garret in a part of the castle that had long ago fallen into disuse. She ascended the narrow stone steps winding around the tower, each dusty footfall bringing her closer and closer to an arched door located at the top. The rusted iron of a key had already been set into the lock, inviting her inquiring fingers to give it a turn. And this she did, dispensing an expert clockwise flick. The door creaked open upon antiquated hinges, revealing a room of diminutive proportions. Inside, the hooded figure of a man dressed from head to toe in black sat before a distaff.

"I bid thee greetings!" hailed the Princess. "May one inquire as to the nature of thy labors? For it appears most interesting."

"I am spinning flax," replied the man without looking up.

Stepping closer the better to examine the apparatus, the Princess noted that the spindle had been placed conveniently in the spinner's lap. It was long and sturdily constructed, the topmost portion containing a tiny hole through which the finished threads came out. The man operated the device by moving his hands up and down in a brisk, steady motion. Since her arrival, he appeared to be applying himself to the task with greater vigor than before. Fascinated — for she had never observed anyone spinning — the Princess grabbed hold of the rapidly bobbing spindle and attempted to spin a thread herself. Yet no sooner had she touched it than she experienced a strange fluttering in her belly that made her go quite woozy. Within moments she collapsed onto a straw pallet that had been set beneath the soot-covered window, falling into the deep sleep foretold by the twelfth wise woman, who had apparently been successful in counteracting her colleague's lethal spell.

For rather than pricking her finger on a spindle and dying, the young Princess had fallen asleep by touching a prick.

Upon the King and Queen's return and their discovery of the events that had transpired in their absence, the wise woman who had spared their only child's life by altering her predecessor's spell was immediately summoned. Powerless to rouse the sleeping Princess, wise woman number twelve did the next-best thing. Ergo the very same state befell the parents as well — as it would the whole rest of the court, along with horse and hound alike. Even the flies spiraling about the kitchen became affixed to the walls in a buzzless slumber. The fire in the hearth gave one last sickly sputter as the pheasant roasting upon the spit stopped turning. The red-faced cook fell asleep over a mound of chopped parsley, his ravishment of the scullery maid not yet having reached its blissful conclusion. Beyond the thick stone walls of the castle the wind stopped blowing and the river ceased to flow, freezing into a gelatinous ribbon of blue. Not a leaf stirred in a tree. The twelfth wise woman had placed everyone and everything into a deep sleep so that when the Princess awakened in one hundred years' time, she would not find herself in a house of death.

Yet even in slumber the King's fervent protectiveness of his daughter continued unabated, for he had earlier arranged with the wise woman further warranties against harm's coming to the young Princess. A protective hedge of thorns began to encircle the castle, growing higher and thicker until every stone and turret vanished behind it. Not even the royal banner waving from the castle roof could be glimpsed. Indeed, the King would sleep a peaceful sleep, secure in the knowledge that no man could possibly succeed in getting through the deadly hedge — and thus getting to his precious daughter.

Over the years, amazing tales came to be heard in the surrounding countryside about a beautiful Princess who could not be awakened, such accounts inspiring many a passing prince with an ear tuned to the local chatter to fight his way through the hedge of thorns. Alas, such herculean efforts were generally to no avail. The moment anyone put a foot through the hedge, the prickly brambles came together, intertwining and interlacing around the struggling figure and holding it fast. Generations of promising young potentates suffered a miserable end in this lethal enclosure, which only made the story of the sleeping Princess travel farther and encourage still more adventurous sons of kings to meet the challenge of this thorny barricade.

As for the occasional few who managed to defy death by reaching the little garret room where the famous Princess lay in slumber, their successes went unreported and their fates remained a mystery. At the intrusion, the Princess would come briefly awake — for she had always been a troubled sleeper — only to discover her visitor seated at the distaff spinning flax. Indeed, she would be amazed at the variety of spindles to be had. Some were long, some short, some fat, some thin — yet each needed to be worked with a vigorous and relentless pumping of hands. Wishing to master the art of spinning, the accursed Princess seized hold of the bobbing spindle so that she might spin a thread herself...whereupon she fell back into a deep sleep all over again.

A number of births and deaths occurred before a prince from a very poor kingdom happened by. While stopping off at a tavern for a tankard of ale, he overheard an old peasant talking of the hedge of thorns and the castle, behind whose walls of stone a princess — or so it was said — had lain in sleep for nigh on a hundred years. The peasant had been told many stories by his grandfather about the sons of kings who had forfeited their lives battling to get through the deadly copse in their desire to locate the Princess, as well as stories of those who had disappeared in the process, their fleshly remains likely having been picked over by the castle's hungry ravens. "Perhaps I shall succeed in reaching the Princess, for I am not afraid," announced the visiting Prince, downing the last of his ale with youthful bravado.

Naturally, the old peasant sought hard to dissuade this naïve newcomer, who knew naught of the terrible dangers awaiting him at the castle. But no amount of pleading from the peasant or the other patrons had any impact upon the Prince, who hoped to achieve fame and fortune by becoming what he believed would be the first man alive to cast his eyes upon the legendary Princess's sleeping form. The descriptions of the daughter of the King and Queen had greatly piqued his interest, therefore he was most keen to be the one to finally awaken her. Undoubtedly her parents would be so grateful they would make him their son-in-law — a situation that should please his father, who made no secret of the fact that he regarded his son as little better than a ne'er-do-well more interested in chasing butterflies than accruing wealth for the kingdom.

All the while, the one hundred years' sleep the twelfth wise woman had conferred by amending the evil thirteenth's sentence of death was reaching an end. As the Prince approached the castle, rather than the cruel hedge of thorns he had been led to expect, he was greeted by a colorful myriad of blossoms. Like the thighs of a waiting lover, they parted willingly at his approach, granting him permission to pass through to the other side unharmed. Finding himself inside the hushed courtyard, he made his way toward a side entrance to the castle without the slightest mishap. It was all so easy that he could not understand what all the fuss was about, and he wondered how it could be that so many before him had failed in their attempts to reach the Princess.

The entrance the Prince had selected led him to the kitchen, where he came upon the stout figure of the cook, who had fallen forward with his head resting against the chopping table, the pile of parsley before him having dried to a dusty green powder. Beside him a scullery maid remained bent over with her skirts hiked up to her waist, her fingers clutching the feathers from the crumbling bones of a guinea fowl she had been in the midst of plucking. Continuing on into the grand hall of the castle, the

Prince next encountered the members of the court, along with the majestic presences of the King and Queen themselves, who slumped sidewise in dreamless dormancy upon their thrones, their chins crushed against their chests from the weight of their crowns. At their feet lay the royal hounds, their sleek forms curled into tight balls. Indeed, it certainly appeared that he had come to the right household.

After undertaking an exhaustive and fruitless search of the castle proper, the Prince next moved in what he believed to be the direction of the turret he had observed from outside, a process of elimination indicating that it would be here that the sleeping Princess could be located. His heart pounded with a sickening force as he climbed the winding steps, his footfalls muffled by the thick coat of dust blanketing the worn stone. The silence in the castle was so profound that the sound of his breath rang out like the clanging of church bells. The door of the little garret stood part of the way open, as it had for the past one hundred years, and the first thing the Prince saw was the abandoned distaff. Behind it upon a straw pallet lay the figure of a young woman. Her pale limbs were sprawled every which way as an incoming ray of sunlight from a small window illuminated her motionless form. He knew instantly that she had to be the daughter of the King and Queen.

Tresses of burnished copper formed a frame for the perfect ivory oval of the Princess's face, spilling across the sun-faded brocade of the pillow supporting her head. The delicate blue-tinged lids of her eyes remained tightly closed against the intruding shaft of light, making it appear as if she had just lain down for a nap. The scattering of dainty freckles adorning the bridge of her nose overflowed onto her cheeks, although they would not reach as far as her lips, the pale pink of which reminded the Prince of a blush not yet come to fruition, prompting an invisible glaive to pierce his heart and the region directly below his belly. A gown of a diaphanous silk draped the young Princess's sleeping form in elegant folds, the lustrous threads clinging to her curves so precisely that one might have thought a team of silkworms had spun the garment expressly for her. Two gentle hillocks rose outward from her torso, the serene rise and fall of her respiration causing the tender pink nibs at their peaks to etch graceful swirls into the garment.

With great care, the Prince lowered his weight onto the straw-filled pallet. Although awakening the Princess had been his original intent, he now desired for her sweet slumber to continue without interruption. Pinching the finely sewn hem of her gown between trembling fingertips, he slid it slowly and deliberately upward, his knuckles grazing the soft warm flesh his bold actions uncovered. It would not be a particularly lengthy journey, the garment having only been cut to knee length. It had likely been intended for use as a nightdress and was, as such, not a suitable item of attire to be worn in the company of others, especially young sons of financially strapped kings who rarely had the funds to enjoy the pleasantries of female companionship.

A pair of gracefully rounded thighs came into view, their pale ivory as smooth and polished as an Oriental carving. Concerned that she might awaken and discover him in a position of compromise — for he suspected that his furtive movements might be deemed inappropriate and possibly deserving of an affronted slap to the cheek — the Prince kept an attentive eye on the steady up-and-down movements of the Princess's chest, which had quickened ever so perceptively since his arrival. The translucent hem continued its steady ascent, offering to the incoming sunlight and the Prince's eager eyes the entirety of the sleeping figure's thighs as well as the discreet *V* located at their crest. All at once he cried out in delight as the pearly silk of the gown uncovered a little pink butterfly.

A pair of gossamer wings began to slowly unfold, as if readying themselves for flight. However, no such enterprise would be forthcoming, for it appeared that the fragile creature was being held back by two fuzz-covered pods, which had closed fast around its struggling body. Perhaps it had alighted upon this predatory plant and, like the many ill-fated sons of kings who had endeavored to break through the prickly hedge of thorns outside the castle, found itself hopelessly and helplessly trapped. Not wanting to cause damage to the delicate wings, the Prince placed his thumbs against the sericeous surfaces of each pod and pried them gently away from each other. To his surprise, they yielded quite easily, revealing an interior as smooth and pink as their faltering victim and unmarred by even a hint of fuzz. Once the Prince had gotten them separated as far as they could go, he noticed yet another reason for the creature's plight. Indeed, no wonder it could not fly, since the means that should have propelled it had been weighed down with moisture.

Like a worshipper in prayer, the Prince bowed his head in readiness to flick away with his tongue the beads of dew that had collected upon the fluttering instruments his thumbs held exposed. Although it might have been more efficient, he dared not risk using the sleeve of his doublet for fear of causing damage. Applying the benevolent tip of his tongue with caution, he dabbed it along the surface of each dew-speckled wing, accelerating his efforts by allowing it to slither up and down and from side to side, even attending to the sinewy niche whence the two gleaming appendages branched away from one another. Confident that they had been sufficiently dried, the Prince lifted his face from the divided pods, their downy fuzz tickling the moistened tip of his nose. To his astonishment, still more droplets had managed to form. Despite his lack of success, he did not feel at all presumed upon at having to expend additional effort. Granted, the Prince might have spent more time on his labors than necessary—a fact that would be made apparent once the butterfly began to struggle in earnest beneath his fiercely licking tongue.

The sleeping female figure lying upon the pallet trembled and twitched, her eyes swimming frantically from right to left beneath their sealed lids, the muscles of her throat constricting in silent entreaty. Slender fingers reached blindly out to claw the mattress, tearing out clusters of ancient straw. With a rapturous cry, the daughter of the King and Queen awakened. Her belly hurled itself upward, her hands coming down to grasp the back of the Prince's head and pressing his dew-bespattered face against the source of the heavenly sensation taking place in her loins. The Prince shouted out a warning, which became hopelessly muffled by the pods. When the Princess finally loosed her grip, he permitted himself to open his eyes, fully expecting to be met with Death. Instead, the tenuous wings beneath him stretched themselves wide, showing their relieved observer all the vibrancy of their true nature. Only this time there were more drops of dew upon them than ever before!

The Princess smiled drowsily up at her visitor, and their lips came together in a tender kiss, his own tasting of a sweetness she could not identify, but very much desired to savor. "Have you come here to spin flax?" she asked dreamily, for she could see that the

Prince's spindle was already standing straight up from his lap and had been spewing out threads by the bushel-full.

In the grand hall of the castle, the King and Queen arose from their lengthy slumber, as did the rest of the court, who glanced at each other in hazy confusion, as did the hounds, who wagged their tails and leapt about like fools. In the kitchen the flies resumed their hungry buzzing, for the wood in the hearth had once again sparked into flame and the pheasant upon the spit began to turn. The cook gaped in bewilderment at the fine green dust he had been chopping. Regaining his wits, he set about the business of locating some fresh sprigs of parsley and happily resumed his ravishment of the scullery maid, who lethargically plucked the last of the feathers from the withered remains of a guinea fowl.

Naturally, a good deal had changed in one hundred years, since not all who had risked the deadly hedge of thorns in hopes of awakening the sleeping Princess were entirely unsuccessful in their endeavors. Over time the household had gained many new occupants—men of every age, shape, and temperament. Some walked more slowly than others and were even quite stooped as they hobbled along upon walking sticks, leaving behind them a potent trail of flatus that set the royal hounds to howling. The King and Queen discovered that they had amassed a sizable collection of prospective sons-in-law over the years, many of whom were considerably older than themselves.

With her father's reluctant blessing, the Princess came to be joined together in marriage to the Prince, who by virtue of youth had been deemed the most suitable of the candidates. Indeed, from the moment he had placed his spindle in his lap and commenced to spin flax, the Princess's interest would be irrevocably piqued, for his was the most impressive of all the spindles she had seen. With a fine spindle such as this, perhaps she might finally master the art of spinning. Therefore she insisted upon taking over the task from her new husband, only to fall right back into yet another deep sleep, the duration of which no one could predict.

For rather than pricking her finger on a spindle and dying as originally foretold, the Princess would continue to fall asleep by touching a prick. ❧

THE TWELVE MONTHS

The theme of reward and punishment can be seen in the folktales of many lands. One particular offshoot of this theme that has been put into standard usage is that of the kind girl and the unkind girl. As patriarchal beliefs and attitudes found a stronghold in Europe, it was only a natural progression for such beliefs and attitudes to find a stronghold in European folk literature as well. As a result, the kind and respectful girl and her rude and ungracious counterpart soon became prevalent in tales like "The Twelve Months."

It appears that the story of the twelve months and the two female characters who encounter them most likely originated in Mediterranean Europe. It is here that the tale appears to be the most typical and, as such, shares the same essential elements. However, many of these elements may have entered the tale from the savage cultures of prehistoric times. The twelve month-men and their miraculous ability to control the weather bears an obvious correlation to the legendary magicians and holy men of the past who were believed to possess the ability to suspend the laws of nature—a tradition that goes back to the shamans and professional magicians of primitive tribes in

Europe and Asia. The element of the club employed by the twelve brothers in "The Twelve Months" may also be related to this function via its application as a charm to bring on a change in weather. Talismanic charms were often used by primitive cultures and would continue to be used by peasant and aboriginal communities up until modern times.

As one of the earliest recognizable versions of "The Twelve Months," Giambattista Basile's tale "The Months" tells a rich man/poor man story of two brothers, Gianni and Lisi. Lisi (the poor brother) finds himself aided by the twelve months, whom he encounters in a tavern. Hence the adversarial relationship between the two protagonists was one based on economics rather than temperament or, indeed, sexual rivalry. Nevertheless, sex roles and attitudes would undergo great change since Basile's collection *Il Pentamerone*, so it should not be at all surprising that the two male siblings in his tale evolved into two siblings of the female variety—and, in the process, developed the exaggerated characteristics that the patriarchal society of nineteenth-century Europe imposed on them.

Perhaps no better example of this can be seen than in the version of "The Twelve Months" collected by the Brothers Grimm. In "The Three Little Men in the Wood" (also known as "Saint Joseph in the Wood"), a girl sent by her stepmother and stepsister into the forest on a series of impossible errands receives assistance from three men, whom she repays by performing chores and sharing with them her meager meal of bread. Seeing that the girl has accomplished the tasks allocated her, the stepsister insists on paying a visit to the three men—although, unlike her kinder sibling, she treats them with callous disregard, refusing to perform any of the chores requested of her. The stepmother next sends the girl to rinse yarn in a frozen river, where a king happens by and marries her. Hearing of the girl's incredible good fortune, both stepmother and stepsister ingratiate themselves at the king's palace, disposing of the new queen so that the stepsister can take her place. But the deed is soon discovered, whereupon mother and daughter are disposed of, with the queen returning to her rightful place. No doubt the Grimms found the punishment of the unkind sister to have particular appeal—just as the reward granted to the kind (and therefore *obedient* sister) would likewise have appeal. For, by their actions, the sisters served as stellar examples of what *was* and was *not* considered appropriate behavior for females.

Known as "the Slovak Grimm," nineteenth-century writer Pavol Dobsinsky composed his own equally patriarchal version of "The Twelve Months," a version conspicuously lacking the royal marriage and its subsequent production of an heir that his German contemporaries, the Grimms, included in their tale. It is the story of his Maruska from which I received my inspiration. For it only goes to prove that kindness (be it from man or woman) most definitely has its rewards. ❧

The Twelve Months

I N A RUSTING OLD TRAILER SET ALONG THE edge of a snowy moorland, there lived a woman and her two daughters. As the eldest and (in accordance with tradition) the first in line for a husband, Holena was the fruit of her mother's womb and, indeed, was very much like her in appearance and temperament. As for the junior of the siblings, Maruska was merely a stepdaughter and thus of little consequence. In fact, the mother could hardly bear to cast her eyes upon the latter, whose prettiness so outrivaled her own flesh and blood that even the sound of the girl's voice brought her pain. Had it not been for the conditions of her late husband's will, the woman would have sent her to a workhouse a long time ago.

Because of the absence of mirrors in the household, Maruska did not realize she was pretty — and it did not behoove the members of her family to tell her so. In her mind, she and her sister were the same, which only made all the more baffling the cross expression that fixed itself upon her stepmother's face each time the woman looked at her, or the bitter venom spat from her stepmother's tongue with her every word. Therefore Maruska did everything she could to please her displeased parent. She did the cooking and cleaning and washing and ironing; she mended and sewed and raked and hoed; she even looked after the scrawny goat that provided milk and cream for the tiny household and, if it ever gained some fat around its middle, might have provided the meat for a few stews. (Suspecting this, the goat rarely ate a morsel.) Meanwhile, Holena whiled away the hours dressing up in garments she never had occasion to wear and gossiping with anyone who had been unfortunate enough to have come to the trailer's front door.

As Maruska grew more pleasing with the passing of years, her stepsister grew less so, thereby necessitating much fawning over by the occupants of the little trailer. Concerned for her blood-child's well-being and marital prospects, the mother decided that it might be wise to get her nubile stepdaughter out of the house and, hence, away from the line of sight of any young man who might come courting, fearing it would be the lovely and sweet-natured Maruska with whom they would fall in love, not her precious Holena. So mother and daughter began to plot out a course of strategy on how best to rid themselves of this female thorn in their sides. *Permanently.*

One day, in the bleakness of a harsh January winter, Holena suddenly experienced the unprecedented urge to smell violets. "Sister, dear," she trilled with false affection, "go and fetch me some violets."

"*Violets?*" cried Maruska in disbelief. "Wherever shall I find violets growing in the snow?"

"You worthless good-for-nothing! How dare you speak to me in that manner!" screeched Holena, her unprepossessing face purpling with rage. "If you do not bring me what I ask for, I shall beat you till you are black and blue—and then I shall beat you some more!" To reinforce her daughter's words, the mother thrust the girl out into the bitter winter's morning, slamming the trailer's rickety screen door against her.

Shivering with the cold, Maruska stumbled through the unwelcoming moorland, knowing she dare not return until she had performed the impossible task demanded of her. The entire world had turned to white. All she could see for miles around was snow, with the leaden gray sky above threatening to spill still more of the icy stuff onto her uncloaked head. She had barely managed to trudge a short distance before her footsteps got covered over with an all-new layer of snow, obscuring the trail she had left and making her fear she had lost her way.

Just when she thought she would have to turn back to face her stepsister's wrath, Maruska glimpsed a reddish-yellow light in the endless landscape of white. Its friendly flickerings drew her toward it, leading her to the crest of a craggy hill—where she discovered a blazing campfire. A dozen rocks of varying heights had been positioned around it, and upon each one sat the stoic figure of a man. Three of them, all in a row, looked very old, possessing long white beards that reached nearly to their toes. The next three beside them looked slightly younger, and the next younger still, until Maruska's gaze finally came to rest upon the remaining three, who were by far the youngest and most agreeable to the eye, their smooth, handsome faces untenanted by whisker or wrinkle.

Unbeknownst to Maruska, the occupants of this cozy circle were the twelve months. With the arrival of each new month in the year's cycle, the men changed places, each moving over one space to an adjacent rock—and so on and so on as the months followed the course of a year. This being winter, January held court upon the tallest of the rocks, his hair and beard as fluffy and white as the snow covering the ground, making it difficult to determine where the fleece on his face ended and the earth itself began. In one gnarled hand he held a club, which rested at his side.

The sight of the twelve months gave Maruska a start. She was not accustomed to the company of gentlemen, especially so many at one time. The family's trailer rarely received guests of either gender, and on those infrequent occasions when a man *did* come to call with some lard or a slab of bacon to sell, she found herself locked inside her room for the duration of the visit. Even a toothless peddler might be considered marriageable material, and her stepmother did not wish to forfeit any opportunity to make a match for Holena. As the winter wind bit cruelly through the inadequate protection of Maruska's nightdress—for she had not been given time to don her coat and wore only the thin gown in which she had slept—the fire offered so much heat that she forgot her apprehension. "Please, kind sirs," she stammered, "may I be allowed to warm myself by your fire?"

Taking note of her pitiful state, January indicated for this waif-like figure to move toward the flames. "And what might a little thing like yourself be doing wandering about the moor in this foul weather?" he inquired. Indeed, a considerable amount of time had passed since he had enjoyed the company of anyone other than his eleven brothers.

"I am searching for violets," answered Maruska, only to realize how completely ridiculous such a prospect must have sounded.

"*Violets?* Surely you must have noticed that we are waist deep in winter snow."

"Yes, but if I dare to return home without them, my stepsister says she will beat me till I am black and blue!"

"I see..." mused January, his knotty fingers combing thoughtfully through the long white tendrils of his beard.

"*Beat* you?" cried another brother from several rocks down, his youthfully unlined eyes suddenly bright and feverish.

"There may be something I can do to assist you," offered January, directing an impatient glare toward the month who had interrupted. "Yet before I do, perhaps you will be so good as to prune this for me?" With a telltale dip of his fluffy-haired chin, he indicated his lap out from which the gnarled branch of a tree grew lopsidedly upward. "For my old joints pain me too greatly to perform the task myself."

"I would be pleased to assist you. But as you can see," Maruska held out her palms in dismay, "I have no implements with which to do so." Now for certain she would be made to return to the trailer and receive the terrible beating Holena had promised.

"Perhaps you might consider using your teeth," came the elderly brother's helpful suggestion.

With the details settled, Maruska knelt between this most senior of the twelve brothers' knees and set to work, only to find that it demanded far more effort than she had anticipated. The dense nest of white in January's lap offered her the most difficulty, although the pruning of the branch itself would not be too arduous a process — especially after she had mastered the technique of absorbing it into her mouth. Unfortunately, old January had much to complain about with regard to the sharpness of her teeth.

Nevertheless, such complaints did not deter the others. For the instant Maruska stood up to brush away the debris January had left upon her nightdress, yet another brother felt compelled to call upon her. "Prune *me!*" demanded February, pointing frantically toward his lap whence a similar limb surged resolutely forth, speckled and distorted with age and the ice of too many winters.

"I am in need of a pruning as well!" piped March with even more boisterousness.

"A pruning would be most beneficial," concurred April with a mischievous grin.

And on it went around the circle, with each of the months clamoring for Maruska's horticultural services. Twelve specimens of varying shapes and textures came to be offered to the violet-seeking girl, whose teeth would be rattling in her gums by the time she finished. The older months in particular seemed in need of the most care and attention, whereas their younger siblings sloughed off their deciduous residue quickly and with little necessity for additional attention. A gasping and wheezing December had not even gotten halfway through his own turn when January arose from his rock. "Brother March, come and take my place," he instructed, passing over his club.

Settling himself upon the tall rock vacated by his elder brother, March waved the conferred club over the fire. The flames rose higher and higher, growing so hot that the surrounding snow melted almost completely away. The exposed earth had sprouted tiny buds, forming a patchwork of green. Winter had turned to early spring and violets pushed upward from the craggy ground. "Make haste!" cried March, his voice unnaturally high with the strain of his deed.

Maruska plucked flower after flower from the viridian patches beneath her feet until she had amassed a collection of violets worthy of the most finicky and disagreeable of stepsisters. After thanking each of her new friends with an affectionate kiss to the cheek, she hurried happily home, nearly colliding head-on with a gypsy tinker who had made the mistake of calling in at the trailer to offer his knife-sharpening services.

Already annoyed at having yet another potential husband slip through her fingers, Holena was even more put out upon seeing Maruska and her lavish offerings. A scowl of dismay took root upon the faces of both daughter and mother as a beaming Maruska came prancing through the front door, the sweet perfume of violets overwhelming the cramped rooms of the trailer within seconds of her arrival. "Wherever did you manage to find them?" choked Holena, rubbing the fragrant petals between thumb and forefinger as if suspecting they might be fake.

"On the top of the moor. There are hundreds of them!" cried Maruska, her joy at having been able to bring pleasure to her family streaming from her eyes.

Alas, such a joy would be all too fleeting. The very next morning Maruska was once again summoned by her stepsister, who, along with the mother, refused to be thwarted in their goal of ridding the household of this unwanted sibling. "Maruska, I do believe I fancy some strawberries. And I fancy them *now*."

"But, dearest sister, wherever shall I find strawberries growing in all this snow?"

"You worthless good-for-nothing! You dare to answer me back?" roared Holena, her homely features distorted with hatred. "If you refuse to do as I ask, I shall beat you to a pulp—and, indeed, take great pleasure from doing so." The stepmother grabbed hold of an astounded Maruska by the scruff of the neck and hurled her outside into the freezing cold, the trailer's screen door clanging cruelly shut behind her.

Without even a dressing gown to warm her, Maruska roamed the moors for hours, the thin nightdress cloaking her shivering form clinging to her like a sodden skin. She thought of the old wood stove at home and the figures of her mother and sister in a cozy huddle before it with their third hot toddy of the day. The sky chose that moment to open up its gates, spilling still more of its snowy burdens onto this lone wanderer. Surely she would perish out here in the cold and wet, for there were no strawberries to be had, and yet she dared not return to the trailer without some. Just when all hope seemed lost, she saw a reddish-yellow light at the top of a craggy hill—in fact, the very same light that had drawn her to it the day before.

Maruska followed the familiar pathway up the snowy slope on two frozen sticks of leg, praying she would locate the warmth she sought before Death stole her away. She found the twelve months seated in their usual circle before the campfire, with January continuing to occupy the tallest of the rocks. "Kind brothers, may I be allowed to share some of this heat with you?" she asked respectfully.

January beckoned for the quaking figure to move closer, only to recognize the charming seeker of violets who had stopped by the previous day. "And what brings you here again, pretty one? You should be at home and in bed, since the bed is what you are attired for!" he chuckled good-naturedly, winking meaningfully at his brothers. As if to confirm his words, a pair of tiny nibs the color of port thrust through the thin bodice of Maruska's snow-saturated garment, hitting home to the brothers just how long it had been since they had last been in the company of a female.

"I am looking for strawberries," explained Maruska, suddenly feeling very silly standing about in a wet nightdress expressing so absurd a venture.

"*Strawberries?*" January reiterated in disbelief. "But strawberries do not grow beneath the snow."

Maruska nodded in defeat. "Nevertheless, my stepsister wishes for me to pick some strawberries, and if I do not, I shall be punished most severely. I beg you, kind January, to direct me to the nearest patch lest my poor bottom be tanned by the leather of a strap." And indeed, Maruska was not overstating the fact, for Holena owned a whole assortment of leather straps, which she kept conditioned with a special oil to guard against the cold. She kept them inside her hope chest along with a gas mask and a black silk negligee that had yet to see wear.

The brothers took to mumbling among themselves, especially the younger of the twelve. For these springtime months possessed a more randy disposition than their elders who, by virtue of age, had gained more experience in the world and had thereby learned to better temper their masculine desires. A whisper began at one brother's ear, making its way around the campfire until it reached the last brother's ear. All nodded in silent agreement, their eyes riveted to the two points visible through the strawberry-seeker's sopping garment. The month Maruska presumed to be April because of his youth and uncompromised handsomeness seized her hand in his strong fingers, asking, "And what will you give us in return if we decide to aid you in this quest of yours?"

Maruska stared humbly down at her slippered feet, which had become wet through from her long trek in the snow. It shamed her that she had so little to offer when her new friends had already given her so much. Why, she could not even extend to the brothers an invitation for supper, since the family's trailer was far too small to accommodate so many guests at one time. "I do not know what I can possibly offer, for I am without wealth or possession. However, I place myself entirely at your disposal."

This would be all the jaunty month of spring needed to hear. Maruska next found herself straddling his lap, her legs draped awkwardly to both sides of the rock upon which he was seated. Something rigid burrowed into her tender place, making it wet and sticky and even a little sore. The hem of her nightdress had been turned into a collar for her neck as April's smooth hands squeezed the exposed knolls rising outward from her chest, his fingertips tweaking the port-colored prongs that crowned them until they tingled with heat. As he bounced enthusiastically up and down upon his rock, Maruska bounced right along with him, oblivious to the commotion her presence created and likewise oblivious to the indecorousness of her pose, for the other months commanded an unobstructed view of yet another port-colored prong that had earlier been hidden by her nightdress. Occasionally the brother whose lap she occupied would roll it about with a fingertip, evoking many a wriggle and giggle from its genial proprietor. Never had Maruska imagined that sitting upon a lap could be so enjoyable.

Maruska made her way from season to season, leaving each month to lean back against his rock for a much-needed rest. After a time, the branches that she had so scrupulously tended only the day before lay wilted and defeated in the laps of all twelve brothers, oozing with a sticky sap. Had it not been for the corresponding presence of sap at her tender place, Maruska would never have believed any of it possible!

"What did you say you were looking for?" queried a breathless January, who wondered how many more of such visits he could possibly survive.

Maruska tidied her rumpled nightdress. "Strawberries, kind sir."

"Ah, yes...*strawberries*. Brother June, I beseech you to take my rock."

June, who still had considerable energy remaining and many notions of how to make use of it with their pretty guest, grudgingly exchanged places with his elder. Accepting the club, he waved it over the fire until the snow surrounding them melted away, leaving not a trace of frost in its wake. The song of birds filled the air, along with the fragrance of strawberries. From north to south and east to west, it was summer.

Conscious of June's tenuous hold over the elements, Maruska moved quickly, gathering the little fruits in the hem of her nightdress until it could hold no more. Waving her thanks to the twelve months and sending a kiss through the air for June, she set off with her tasty treasures, her heart filled with happiness at the thought of how pleased her stepsister and stepmother would be. As she made her way across the once-again-wintry moorland, a warm liquid trickled down the insides of her thighs, only to freeze when it reached her knees, puckering the skin and making it awkward to walk. No sooner did the first sticky trail crystallize than another went cascading over it. Yet Maruska paid this bothersome phenomenon little heed, secure in the knowledge that she would soon be safely at home basking in the warmth of the stove and the praise of her family.

Seeing the crop of fresh strawberries tucked into the hem of her stepsister's garment, Holena's equine jaw dropped to the floor. Maruska had barely gotten a snow-caked toe in the door before their sweet aroma permeated the little trailer, overpowering the strong scent of leather coming from Holena's room. "Wherever did you find them?" screeched the older girl in horrified disbelief. Although she very much desired to savor their delicious flavor upon her tongue, the desire to be rid of this detested family member was significantly greater.

"On the top of the moor, dearest sister. They are so plentiful that my slippers are stained with their juices!" To prove the truth of her words, Maruska upended a foot to proudly display its pinkened sole.

Snatching up the strawberries, Holena and her mother consumed the fruits until their well-fed bellies could accept no more, not even deigning to offer a single one to the hungry waif who had brought them.

The next morning as Maruska prepared a pie from the last remaining strawberries, Holena unexpectedly appeared. The elder sister rarely darkened the kitchen with her presence. Like her mother, she preferred to leave any form of domestic labor to her younger sibling. "Sister, I do believe I have a craving for red apples."

"*Red apples?*" gulped Maruska, her mixing spoon clattering to the floor.

"Go and fetch me some this instant!"

"But wherever shall I find apples in the wintertime?"

"You dare to answer me back? Perhaps your lazy bottom might like to be introduced to a leather strap, aye, little sister?" snarled Holena, her eyes gleaming with sadistic malice. Indeed, she was most keen to try out her newest strap, which had arrived just that morning by special delivery. Unhappily, when she had shown it to the delivery boy in hopes of enticing him inside the trailer, he had taken off down the moor in a sprinter's run.

"No, Sister," answered Maruska in a frightened whisper.

"Then do not show your ungrateful face again until you have brought me some apples. And do not presume to bring green ones, as I shall accept only the shiniest and reddest of reds."

Once again Maruska found herself being hurled out the trailer door and into the bitter cold by her stepmother. Clad only in her nightdress stained with the pink of strawberries, she stumbled across the harsh moorland, her slippered feet sinking deeper and deeper into the snow. Yet rather than wandering aimlessly about as she had done in the past, Maruska made directly for the welcoming light on the hill, where a blazing campfire awaited her — as did the twelve kindly brothers.

Seeing the bedraggled figure staggering through the snow toward them, January's fluffy white eyebrows shot up in surprise. Had not the girl already gotten her fill of both his and his brothers' company? "Now what might you be doing out in weather like this?" he inquired.

"I am looking for red apples," croaked Maruska, whose voice had frozen inside her throat.

"Surely you realize that apples do not grow in the wintertime."

"Yes, but my stepsister sent me to collect some, and if I fail, my bottom shall receive a terrible beating with a leather strap!"

"A leather strap, you say?" repeated January, his words strangely garbled.

Maruska nodded miserably, feeling the phantom sting of leather against her tender flesh. If she returned to her family empty-handed, Holena would see to it that she could not sit down until the arrival of spring — or even summer.

"And where might this strap be applied?" asked October in a high-pitched squawk.

"On my bottom," mumbled Maruska, hanging her head in disgrace. "Oh, can you not help me, dear brothers?"

She was answered by twelve nervous clearings of throats, followed by a good deal of fidgeting about upon their rocks by the brothers. At last January broke the tense silence, for he appeared to be the only one who still had any command over his vocal cords. "Perhaps it might be helpful if you show us the precise location in which your stepsister plans to beat you so that we can gain a clearer understanding of the situation."

"Yes, show us!" piped the younger months, suddenly finding their voices.

Maruska pulled up the back of her nightdress, bringing into exposure a pair of gentle rises that together formed the shape of a heart. "I think I am beginning to get the picture," January replied thoughtfully. As the girl moved to let down her hem, he stopped her. "No! Leave it thusly so that we may contemplate your fate and decide how best to alter it."

By this time the throat clearing had turned to a low rumble as the brothers discussed the situation, apparently reaching a swift and unanimous decision. January bade the anxious apple-seeker to approach. Unlike the occasion with the strawberries, he preferred to exert the seniority of his position rather than placing matters in the hands (and in the lap) of a subordinate. "We are all of a mind to assist you. But for us to be successful, you must be willing to do your share as well."

Maruska exhaled with relief, grateful to have found such caring friends so willing to help her—and to help with little thought toward any personal gain to themselves. "I shall do whatever work is needed. I can cook and clean and darn and weave; pray, tell me what it is you require!"

The twelve months chuckled in unison, causing Maruska to blush pinker than the strawberries she had fetched for her sister. Could it be that the brothers considered her guilty of braggadocio? Yet she had put forth no claims to which she could not live up. Just as she was about to set them to rights on the subject, January interrupted. "I do not believe any of those tasks will be necessary," he proclaimed. "For all we require is your charming company."

"Yes, your company!" cheered July, who tumbled off his rock, so great was his enthusiasm.

"Come, sit upon my lap to warm yourself," invited the senior brother, flinging his long white beard out of the way. A gnarled branch with a fluffy copse of curls at the base sprang into full view — as did those of the other months as they, too, pushed their beards to one side. Those who did not wear a beard or whose beards had not yet attained such spectacular lengths merely needed to alter the drape of their garments to accommodate the growths in their laps. The months of spring possessed the straightest and, indeed, the most *upstanding* specimens; therefore these youngsters sat proudly upon their rocks, basking in the envious glances of their elders, who looked back with bittersweet fondness to days when similarly endowed.

As Maruska lowered herself onto January's lap, she groaned with the strain. Never had she experienced such terrible difficulty in the simple act of sitting.

Sensing her troubles, January fitted his hands to her waist, guiding her slowly and steadily downward. Little by little the crooked limb disappeared until all that remained was a thicket of snowy white, which tickled Maruska like dozens of tiny fingers, summoning from her an impish giggle. Perhaps, she mused, January had planted his misshapen old bough inside her bottom so that it might be given an opportunity to grow as long and straight as the smoother-barked versions of his younger brothers. For what other reason could there be for its presence in so peculiar a locale?

Maruska next discovered herself impaled upon February's lap as he, too, endeavored to entrench himself as deeply as had his brother. This sowing and reaping continued with each of the months, although it would be the youngest of the twelve who caused the most problem. Indeed, Maruska could not fathom why such mighty limbs should even be in need of cultivation. (It so happened that the following morning when she awakened in her bed, Maruska fully expected to find a tree growing out from her bottom. Instead, the sole evidence of the previous day's energetic tillings was a sticky puddle of sap on the sheet beneath her—a puddle she dutifully gathered up with a spoon. Just imagine what a treat it should be for her family to enjoy some on their griddlecakes at breakfast!)

As Maruska pried herself off December's dwindling lap with a distinctive *thwock,* January suddenly remembered why she had come to their hilltop encampment in the first place. "Brother October," he called, "come and take my place."

Accepting the club offered him by his senior brother, October waved it over the fire. The flames leapt higher and higher, their increasing heat melting the snow. A brisk wind blew in from the north, turning the moors a deep orange. Autumn had arrived, bringing with it an apple tree that dangled two shiny red apples. "Hurry!" urged October, his voice cracking with the exertion of holding off the encroaching winter.

With a kiss to all and both apples tucked safely inside the hem of her nightdress, Maruska hastened through the newly falling snow toward home, where her stepsister and stepmother waited — indeed, waited with the smug certainty that this time their undesired relative would *not* be returning. Holena had already drawn up blueprints to convert the cramped room Maruska slept in into a torture chamber. However, a familiar pounding on the trailer door set their hearts to sinking in their chests. "But how? Where?" croaked mother and daughter in astounded accord when they saw the shiny red bounties the ecstatic girl carried within her garment.

"They were on top of the moor. Is it not wonderful?" Maruska cried excitedly, waiting for the praise that was surely her due.

"Why did you bring back only two?" barked Holena, who scraped at the skin of the apples with a fingernail to determine if its vibrant color had been painted on.

"It is all the tree had to offer."

"You selfish good-for-nothing! You must have eaten the other apples. Perhaps I shall go myself and collect some more."

"Yes," urged the mother. "Do that, daughter dear. For it is clear that this ungrateful wretch has stolen them from our hungry mouths."

Donning her warmest fleece coat and cloaking her head with her warmest fleece hood, Holena went stomping off through the snow, annoyed at having to leave behind the cozy warmth of the little trailer. Despite her younger sibling's frequent forays into the moorland, it would not be an easy journey to make, and she grew tired very quickly. Just when she decided to turn back, she noticed a reddish-yellow glow at the crest of a craggy hill. With the tangy taste of the apple still fresh upon her tongue, Holena clomped irritably upward toward its source. This must be the place of which her miserable stepsister had spoken...although she could see nothing even remotely resembling an apple tree. There was, however, a fire, and Holena fully intended to make use of it.

Gathered in a circle around this fire were twelve men at various stages of life, some quite young, some quite elderly. Strange that her detested relative should have made no mention of their presences!—particularly when there were so few men of *any* age about, other than that dreadful gap-toothed peddler with whom her mother kept trying to fix her up. Without asking for permission, Holena stepped boldly up to the crackling flames, only to seat herself comfortably before it. She even went so far as to remove her fleece-lined boots so that her large, flat feet could be more efficiently warmed.

"And what brings you out today?" inquired January, for it was hardly a day to be taking a stroll on the moor. In fact, it had almost come time for him to pass his club to his brother February.

"Mind your own fucking business, Gramps!" snapped Holena, sticking her middle finger up in the air for emphasis. Pulling off her thick woolen socks, she set about massaging her benumbed toes, which resembled a sequence of paddles of varying sizes.

A scowl fixed itself above January's curly white beard. Because of his advanced age and the respect it commanded, he was not accustomed to being addressed in this fashion. Nor had he liked the look of that middle finger. From the manner in which this disagreeable Miss covered herself up, one might have thought she had something offensive to hide—as perhaps she did, if her toes were any indication. Suitably provoked, January waved his club high over his head until the somber sky above vanished behind clouds the color of smoke. The fire sputtered, dying out as a fierce wind blew through the small encampment, stealing away the last of the warming flames. Leaden balls of snow rained down from the darkened heavens, and within moments a thick blanket of the stuff covered the moor and everything upon it.

Including Holena.

Meanwhile, back at the trailer, the mother looked apprehensively out the window at the bleak landscape whose craggy contours were now completely hidden from view. Darkness would shortly be upon them, and still her blood-daughter had not returned from her visit to the apple tree. Finally she could wait no more. Dressing in her warmest fleece coat and donning her warmest fleece hood, she set off to follow the route Holena had taken, calling out the girl's name to the barren moor.

Day after day Maruska waited at home for the return of her stepsister and stepmother. Yet neither would be seen again until the spring thaw, when a passing bear desperate with the hunger of an overly long winter took an interest in the pair and made of them a most disappointing meal. With the loss of her family, the trailer now belonged to Maruska, as did everything both inside and outside of it, including the scrawny goat and the patch of scrubby land surrounding it. She lived there for a time by herself. Then one sunny morning a handsome young man came up to the screen door seeking directions. Rather than continuing on his way, he chose to remain behind with the trailer's pretty owner, who had taken an instant fancy to him. Indeed, he possessed a branch very much like the one handsome young April had had growing out from his lap—a branch of unswerving straightness whose supple bark oozed with a sap so sweet that Maruska could enjoy it on griddlecakes for breakfast, lunch, and supper.

Had she been more observant of the weather, Maruska might have realized that springtime had passed unusually swiftly this year—in fact, so swiftly that winter seemed to have gone directly into summer. For the young man she so willingly sheltered was none other than the month of April himself. ❧

About the Author

Mitzi Szereto writes and edits across the genres. Her titles include *Wicked: Sexy Tales of Legendary Lovers* (Cleis), the *Erotic Travel Tales* anthologies (Cleis), *Getting Even: Revenge Stories* (Serpent's Tail), *The New Black Lace Book of Women's Sexual Fantasies* (Random House), and *Dying For It: Tales of Sex and Death* (Running Press). She's the pioneer of the erotic writing workshop in the UK and Europe, and lives in London.

Her blog "Errant Ramblings: Mitzi Szereto's Weblog" is located at mitziszereto.com/blog. The creator and presenter of Mitzi TV, Mitzi can be seen on her own Web TV channel at mitziszereto.com/tv.